The
Sweet Taste
of
Muscadines

The
Sweet Taste
of
Muscadines

A Novel

Pamela Terry

BALLANTINE BOOKS

NEW YORK

Published in the United States by Ballantine Books, an imprint of Random House, a division of Penguin Random House LLC, New York.

BALLANTINE and the HOUSE colophon are registered trademarks of Penguin Random House LLC.

Library of Congress Cataloging-in-Publication Data
Names: Terry, Pamela, 1956- author.
Title: The sweet taste of muscadines: a novel / Pamela Terry.
Description: First edition. | New York: Ballantine Books, [2021]
Identifiers: LCCN 2020007056 (print) | LCCN 2020007057 (ebook) |
ISBN 9780593158456 (hardcover; acid-free paper) | ISBN 9780593158463 (ebook)
Classification: LCC PS3620.E7726 S94 2021 (print) | LCC PS3620.E7726 (ebook) |
DDC 813/.6—dc23
LC record available at https://lccn.loc.gov/2020007056
LC ebook record available at https://lccn.loc.gov/2020007057

Printed in the United States of America on acid-free paper

randomhousebooks.com

2 4 6 8 9 7 5 3 1

FIRST EDITION

Book design by Caroline Cunningham

Frontispiece: Vineyard-grape on trellis: iStock/Maria-Hunter; title page, part title, and chapter opener ornament: Vineyard scroll ornament: iStock/ggodby

For Andrew, Jim, and Steve

And for Pat, always

After dark vapors have oppress'd our plains
For a long dreary season, comes a day
Born of the gentle South, and clears away
From the sick heavens all unseemly stains.

—JOHN KEATS

Life is a mystery
Everyone must stand alone
I hear you call my name
And it feels like home.

—MADONNA

The
Sweet Taste
of
Muscadines

PROLOGUE

The first time Mama died, I ran off to hide in the muscadine arbor. She'd been coming around the corner of the swimming pool with a tray of iced tea in her hands when Abigail stuck her leg out and tripped her. I don't think Abby really gave it much thought before she did it; it was just an impulse, like a sneeze, over before she even knew what happened. Mama should've just fallen into the pool. She would have been mad, and Abby would have been in for it, but that's about all. Might even have turned out to be a funny story to tell company. But no, Mama split her head open on the concrete before she fell into the water, sinking like a stone to the bottom while we all just sat there staring. Red blood floated up like Easter-egg dye. The world counted to three, and then everybody started screaming. I think it was Uncle Audie who fished her out, but I was running flat out by then. They told me later she'd died, just like I thought. She wasn't breathing at all for a minute or more, until Aunt Jo pushed everybody out of the way and started pounding on her chest like you do on a round steak, and Mama woke up spitting out mouthfuls of chlorinated water. But by that time I was deep in the middle of the muscadine arbor, hidden by the vines, getting used to the idea that my mother was dead.

When my brother, Henry, finally found me, the afternoon sun was turning pink behind the pine trees and I had pretty much written a brand-new narrative for my future. I could almost see myself, handling Mama's funeral with a dignity far beyond my years, moving serenely through the crowd of grieving relations in an unwrinkled black dress. Then the letter would arrive. The letter telling us the army was sending Daddy straight home from the war because they'd never allow Henry, Abigail, and me to be left all alone now that Mama was gone.

Of course it didn't work out that way. Mama was only dead for about as long as it takes to fry an egg, but three weeks later when a bullet found Daddy's left temple on that road in the jungle, he was dead for good. The principal came to get me from English class just as Miss Hester was telling us the meaning of the adjective "capricious." It became a word I would forever associate with God.

I dreamed about the muscadine arbor last night. It must have been August, because the lime-green leaves were so thick the summer sun couldn't find a way in. I sat in the middle of the arbor, cross-legged in the shade, like I used to when I was little, with my bare toes dug down deep in the brown velvet dirt. What I didn't see was Mama lying there beside me, facedown with her legs stuck out the end of the arbor, her fuzzy blue slippers all gummy with pollen and dew, dead for the second and very last time. But that's exactly where Abigail said she was when Abby found her this morning at dawn.

PART ONE

ONE

As a child I was afraid of tornadoes. Actually, "afraid" is a puny word to describe how I felt when an unusual stillness would thread the air of a late-spring afternoon, weaving a blanket of quiet that silenced birdsong and suspended the breeze. The skies over Wesleyan would darken to horror green, and the wind would awaken with the soul of a dervish, causing the pines and poplars to wring themselves into fraying, flailing knots. Though meant for good, the sound of the tornado siren was as welcome as a scream. As the witchy webs of lace curtains reached out for me in the wind, I would run through the house in blind panic, grabbing up my diaries and favorite photos, all the books I could carry, all the while herding a grumbling Henry before me like a wayward sheep. Into our dark rabbit hole of a cellar I would vanish like Alice to wait it out, nervous and shaking, while in my mind's eye I could clearly see the swirling evil coming right down my street, like the dark finger of God, casually tracing a line on the earth. The world was always unchanged when I reemerged, and the next hour or so was spent putting back the treasured items I'd saved from threatened obliteration while enduring the teasing of my family for my over-size, misplaced fear. Then came the afternoon of Lolly Carmi-chael's seventh-birthday party.

Any party at the Carmichaels' was a dress-up affair, even seventh-birthday ones, so I found myself sitting in the back of our family's green Pontiac in a pink, full-skirted dress with my feet trapped in black patent-leather shoes, riding to the event in a sulk, on a beautiful day in May. As we neared Lolly's house, I felt a bit vindicated when I spied dark clouds rolling in, threatening rain. At least we wouldn't have to endure outside games trussed up in these clothes. But my glee was waning as we pulled up the drive to a giant's footfall of thunder. Egg-size drops of rain spattered my pink shoulders as I ran up the stairs, my beribboned present tucked un-derneath my arm. The front door flew open, and Mrs. Carmi-chael, face white-tight, called past me to my mother.

"Geneva! Get in here! There's a tornado!"

My worst fear in the world, and I was away from home in a pink dress. Mama ran inside, and we scrambled to join the rest of the party all huddled together in the center of the family room, away from the windows. A rainbow of balloons floated near the ceiling, a big number 7 written on each one in gold. A stack of presents teetered on the dining-room table, pink punch waveless in a cut-glass bowl. The tornado siren blared just then, sending shiv-ers up our bare legs and causing Mary Ann Archer's mother to blurt out, "Oh, Jesus!" in a voice as shrill as the siren itself.

"Hush up, Jessie," my mother hissed.

Just then, as one, every balloon in the room popped, a sound that shattered our stoicism and uncorked Jessie Archer's full-throated pleas to the heavens. We scattered like frilly buckshot into every nook and cranny of that house. I grabbed Lolly, who'd fro-zen to the spot, wailing, and made for the basement along with the more sensible members of the crowd, my mother included. We left Mrs. Archer standing right in front of the window, hands raised in either terror or supplication, I never knew which.

If you stick a microphone in the face of someone who's been through a tornado, you can bet money they'll say the familiar line, "It sounded like a freight train." It almost seems a scripted description. But I can empirically say there's a reason for that. From my hiding place that afternoon in Lolly Carmichael's basement, that is precisely the sound I heard as I sat with my head down and my hands clasped around my knees as though bound to a railroad track with no hope of escape. I could hear it coming, hear it hit like a battering ram, hear it continue on, leaving the Carmichael house totally, eerily silent as we waited to breathe again.

Mama was the first one back up the stairs. Throwing open the basement door, she gasped when she saw the trunk of a tree sticking like a tongue depressor through the gaping mouth of the living-room wall. The air smelled sickly strong of pine, and looking up, I could see a nonchalant blue sky already pushing the darkness away to the east.

We found Mrs. Archer sprawled across the hooked rug of the family room, her right leg twisted behind her like a strand of spaghetti, her hands still raised to the ceiling, loudly praising God for her salvation, to which Mama replied as she picked up the phone to call for help, "God nothing, Jessie. If you'd been listening to God, you'd have been downstairs with the rest of us with not even a run in your stocking." Mrs. Archer had a slight limp for the rest of her days.

Maybe once you've faced down something so frightening, it loses its power over you. I've never been afraid of tornadoes again. And my reaction to the news of my mother's death this morning was not as dramatic as it probably should have been. After all, at eight years old I'd spent an endless afternoon believing her dead. I'd already experienced the shock, the hideous fascination, of her passing. The fact that her death had ended up false didn't lessen all I'd felt that day. Those same feelings now returned to meet Abigail's news, squeezing themselves through telephone wires to grab me around the throat, but being somewhat familiar, their power was lessened. So I didn't sway; I didn't gasp. Instead I asked Abby for the answer to what was, for me at least, the strangest part of the story. What on earth was my mother doing out in the muscadine arbor? In rapid-fire fashion, Abby told me that's exactly what *she* wanted to know. She delivered her account with an urgency undiluted by the drawl of her words, which shot through the phone like honey-coated bullets.

"I don't have a clue, Lila. I mean, I thought at first maybe she'd gotten hot and stepped outside to get some fresh air. It's been pretty sticky, though there was a nice breeze last night. But Lord, that air conditioner was running full blast when I got here this morning, so I know she couldn't have been hot. It was cold as a meat locker in this house. And I swear, I don't even know if her bed's been slept in. I mean, it's hard to tell, 'cause she won't make it up every day anymore. Not unless Jackie's coming over to clean. You know how Mama never wants anybody, not even her cleaning lady, to think she needs a cleaning lady, so she always straightens things up before Jackie gets here. They said she'd been dead for about four hours, which means it had to have happened around two in the morning, 'cause I got here at six. I called her before I went to bed to remind her about her hair appointment at eight— she likes to get it done real early so the heat won't make it fall before she gets back home—and to tell her I'd be picking her up at the crack of dawn so we could have breakfast out like usual. You know how she loves to eat breakfast out."

"Yes. What *happened*, Abby?" I was trying to hurry this story along even though I knew I hadn't a hope of succeeding.

"Well. Everything seemed fine on the phone. She sounded a little peevish, but I'd interrupted a rerun of that John Wayne movie she likes so much, so I figured that was why. You know, the one where he's out looking for that little girl the whole time and when he finds her, she turns out to be an Indian? So anyway, I drove on over this morning real early so we could go to the Pancake Parlor like she likes to. The coffee wasn't on, and the house was as quiet as the grave. Sorry. Wrong choice of words. I'm still upset. Well, you can imagine.

"It was when I was coming back down the stairs from her room that I noticed the door to the pool wasn't shut all the way. Now, you know Mama locks this house up like Fort Knox every night before she goes to bed, always has done, so this hit me weird. I went outside and looked around the pool, but she wasn't there, so I went on through the hedge to the garden. I didn't see her, but there was her housecoat, you know that satiny one she wears on Sunday afternoons when she takes her nap? Well, that housecoat was hanging on the garden fence, right by the gate. And you know how Mr. Plackett keeps the grass a little longer out past there? Well, I could see what looked like a line heading straight out across the field where the grass was all pressed down like somebody'd been walking through it. I just started following—I was calling her the whole time—until I got down to the creek. I could see the arbor from where I was then, but I thought, *Well, she's not out here after all*, and that's when I saw her feet sticking out like in *Wizard of Oz* or something. Lila, I haven't shook like this—you should see my hands—since Aunt Jo up and died on that cruise that she and Uncle Audie won in that raffle down at the mall. Same sort of thing, just like Aunt Jo. Sudden death. Course, we know that Aunt Jo died of food poisoning. Food on those cruises just sits out all day, you know, and I don't suppose those doctors on those boats are all that good or they'd have a real office and not be working out in the ocean in the middle of nowhere."

I couldn't muffle my sigh. "Aunt Jo had a heart attack on that cruise, Abigail. There was an autopsy. Remember?"

"Yes, well, it had to have been brought on by all that bad food. Anyway, we're all going to have to wait on another autopsy now to find out what happened to Mama. I'm just going to go on home till you and Henry get here. News'll be getting out, and I can't face having to tell this story over again and again without y'all with me. How soon can you get here?"

"It'll have to be tomorrow, Abby. I've already missed the morning ferry, so I'll have to catch the afternoon one. But I'll drive into
Portland tonight and be on the first flight out in the morning. I'll
be there by early afternoon."

"Well, okay. I'll never understand why you still live way up
there on that island. Mama didn't get it either." I heard a loud sniff.
"I don't know what I'll do without Mama. She was my best friend,
Lila. You know that, don't you?"

Abigail's voice still swam through my head a good while after
I'd hung up the phone, its sugary tones as southern as a Savannah
praline. Though I had absolutely no doubt that she would be the
one to miss our mother the most (she'd been correct when she said
they were best friends), I couldn't help but recoil from that part of
her that so obviously relished the drama of the situation. Every
primary-colored sentence had screeched to a halt at an exclamation point that, given the bare facts of the situation, was at least
unnecessary if not a little distasteful.

As with so many of the women in my family, there were no
subtleties in my sister's life; all her choices, from adjectives to ear-
rings, were outsized and theatrical. It's possible that the seeds of this
behavior were planted by maternal ancestors desperate to be heard,
otherwise mutely invisible women in hoop skirts who learned early
to manipulate by drama, exaggerating whatever means of commu-
nication they could grab in their lily-white fists in order to solidify their gauzy shadows and prove that they mattered. I'd spent my
childhood observing this particular brand of femininity, unable and
unwilling to participate. Now I found it almost profane.

The cloth from which I'd been cut was as wildly divergent from
the one that had produced my mother and sister as satin was from
tweed. I find it funny now to remember how hard Mama worked
to fashion my personality into something she could more easily
recognize. Henry was given a pass, one of the perks of being a son.
But southern daughters are supposed to take after their mothers,
and when I was little, mine watched me like a hawk watches an

unaware rabbit, alert for any similarities in our natures on which she could pounce—no matter how trivial or superficial they might be—just some little something that could, perhaps, connect us with the same silken thread that tied her so closely to Abby. Did we like the same movie stars? Or eat the same thing for breakfast? Was I ever going to laugh at the same things that she did?

But I wasn't my sister; my eyes were not blue. I never wanted to wear what Mama chose for me; I hated my hair in a ponytail; I preferred saddle shoes to the shiny patent-leather Mary Janes she was convinced every little girl should want to wear. What an effort she made to change me, and when it was clear those surface alterations would never occur, she began to mistake my solitary nature for sullenness, my laughter for mockery, my silence for a judgment I didn't start to feel until much later. I'm not sure exactly when she gave up, probably around the time Daddy died. I don't remember her telling me what to wear to the funeral. I do remember my baby sister looking a picture all that hot afternoon, in a brand-new dress the same color as Mama's.

I suppose Abigail's own identity card was permanently stamped that day Mama died the first time. I'd felt awful for Abby about that. Every retelling of that fateful afternoon at the pool naturally included the part where she'd stuck her leg out to send Mama right off into eternity and I was afraid she'd feel bad listening to it over and over again. But it was soon apparent that Abigail had inherited not only my mother's cowlick and loathing of the color green but the familial penchant for drama as well. Mama and Abigail loved the spotlight, and a story in which one of them actually died at the hand, or the leg in this case, of the other and lived to tell the tale was a crowd pleaser, and they both knew it. It was obvious Abigail liked playing the pivotal role in the story. She beamed every time it was told.

Of course, it didn't take long for Mama's first death to become as much a part of her biography as her two semesters at Georgia Southern and her double-jointed pinkie finger. That story singled her out, and Lord knows she liked to be singled out. She never let anyone forget that she had been to the other side and back again, and what began as about forty seconds of floating facedown in a backyard swimming pool with her blue shirtwaist billowing up over her head like a cartoon thought eventually became a journey down a long white tunnel full of all the people she'd ever known who'd gone on before, each one waving her back down the way she'd come.

"'Go back, Geneva!' I swear to goodness that's what I heard them say. 'Your work here isn't over.'" Like an underpaid thespian, Mama would add a little dose of pathos each time the story was told, and as she told it every chance she got, it should be easy to imagine how operatic it soon became. I can't help but wonder what all those people were telling her this time out. I guess they were waving her in.

TWO

Growing up in the South is not for the faint of heart. An enigmatic place at the best of times, it is paradoxical to the core. Finding your way through the various switchbacks and roundabouts that make up the overgrown maze of its personality can be a bewildering experience and one that often takes a lifetime, at least. Just when you think you have it solidly in your sights, it slips around a corner, leaving only the faint fragrance of a fading magnolia hanging in the muggy air. At the very moment you feel confident in its definition, it can, without warning, fashion itself into a creature of myth, sending you back to huddle over your history books and crystal balls, once again in search of the truth about this place you call home. It's a land where heart-stopping beauty and heartrending ugliness flourish in tandem, a land of kindness and hate, of ignorance and wit, of integrity, blindness, and pride. It's a land I left, tired of the struggle, after eighteen years and never once looked back. But the South is as tenacious as mint in a garden. Though the surface of my life may appear cleansed of its consequences by the whitewashed winds of Maine, I'm not fooled.

The roots of its influence still run through me like vines, entwining memories and creeping under the doors of my dreams.

It was from just such a dream that I was snatched by Abigail's phone call this morning. Once again I'd been sitting safely in the muscadine arbor, the air around me redolent with the fragrance of home. Gardenia, magnolia, and pine. Honeysuckle. Fresh-turned earth. That arbor had been my own personal haven; even Henry had understood to wait for an invitation. I didn't know that my mother even realized it existed. To imagine her lying dead inside it was frankly impossible, even though I knew it to be true.

With my suitcase yawning open on the unmade bed, I stood at the window, coffee cup in hand, staring out at a calm gray sea on which lay the first peach ribbons of dawn. Looking inside my closet made it easy to tell how long I'd been away. Over the years my wardrobe of linens and cottons had gradually given way to one of woolens and tweeds. I didn't own a pair of sandals, and my grandmother's pearls hadn't seen the light of day since my high-school graduation. I hadn't seen a southern summer in years.

The rules that dictated fashion have loosened over the years, but when I was a little girl, the South was a place where women dressed up. Sunday morning at eleven o'clock, for all its ecclesiastical significance, was a fashion parade of fitted suits, red lipstick, and silk shantung. Stockings were worn in the car-pool lane. These women even dressed up to buy dresses, something that always tickled me and still does.

I was twelve when I saw my first *Vogue* magazine, and it scared me half to death. The women who looked up at me from within its glossy pages were nothing like the white-gloved females who populated my life. Something told me their patience for being ignored was every bit as short as their skirts. The look in their eyes was defiant. They radiated a confidence that seemed to reach up off the pages and slap me awake. Those pictures set a match to my interest in fashion and what it could communicate, an interest that soon had me sketching out patterns, dreaming in color, and even practicing some original designs on Abigail, who was always a more-than-willing model. It also led me to the Rhode Island School of Design as soon as I graduated high school, with Henry, who was besotted with art history, following me a couple of years later.

Franklin Breedlove was a professor of philosophy at Brown, our neighbor on College Hill. I met him one spring afternoon when Henry talked me into going to a hockey game, something for which I had scant interest outside of its allowing me to spend time with my brother. Though I'd been at the school for over two years, I'd never attended a single game and had only a cursory knowledge of the sport in general. I certainly wasn't familiar with the chant of "Go Nads!" that sprang up all around me the moment the home team skated out onto the ice. Nor was I prepared to see the many large, proudly waving placards that featured a horizontal hockey stick with two nondescript circles at the end of its handle. I looked over at Henry in shock.

"What the . . . ?" I said.

"Yeah, great, isn't it? Well, *what*? You knew the team was called the Nads, didn't you?"

"I thought it was the Gnats."

Henry roared. "The *Gnats*? God, Lila. This is Providence, not Savannah. It's the Nads! *Go. Nads!* Get it?"

"Oh, yeah. I get it."

It was, in fact, impossible not to get, especially when the team mascot, Scrotie, made an appearance, leaping and prancing up and down the boundaries of the rink, all of seven feet tall and ana-tomically correct. I collapsed into a fit of giggles that I couldn't seem to control, giggles that became more inappropriate when the Nads began to lose. I finally had to get up and leave.

With my hand over my mouth, still laughing, I inched my way past glowering students who clearly found my mirth traitorous. Standing in line at the concession stand, hoping a strong cup of coffee might give me enough solemnity to allow a return to my seat, I heard another laugh right behind me. I turned around and looked into a pair of smiling eyes that were so blue they made me shy. Kind, intelligent, and twinkling with humor, those eyes caused a quaver somewhere near my heart that was so alien to me it felt almost like fear. Looking into them rendered every boyfriend I'd had up until that point irredeemably trivial.

Franklin told me he often wandered over on Saturdays to watch the hockey game, particularly when the weather was nice. "It makes a pleasant break from grading essays on the difference between hedgehogs and foxes." He was knee-weakeningly handsome in that tweedy, bearded way that some men seem to achieve without effort, and I was a goner the moment I met him. I accepted his invitation to lunch that afternoon without hesitation, and we were married the weekend I graduated.

It had been almost a cliché, and no doubt it had appeared as such to our clutch of family and friends. Fatherless young college student falls in love with handsome, older, widowed professor. We had endured the sidelong stares and polite questions with all the grace we could muster. Franklin told me that time was the only agent we could employ to convince everyone of what we so empirically knew: that we were just meant for each other. And sure enough, eventually, after a quiet wedding, after relocating to his family home on Wigeon Island off the coast of Maine, after many blissful days—he had been proved correct: I came to love his friends as they came to love me. Franklin spent his retirement writing the nature books he'd always wanted to write and enjoying a modest amount of success. We traveled a good deal, filled our house with dogs of every shape and size, and were entirely guilt-free in our happiness, perhaps knowing it was destined to be shorter than what most married couples can expect. I spoke to him now as I continued to stare into my closet, searching for the appropriate outfit to wear to my mother's funeral. "Well. Can you believe this?" I asked.

I could feel the familiar gaze of my husband and turned from the window to meet his eyes, peering out, as they exclusively did these days, from the oil painting that hung opposite the four-poster bed we'd shared for almost twenty-two years. Franklin had sat for this portrait when he was just twenty years old, before most of his life had happened, before I'd even been born. A halcyon moment in time captured by an artist who never knew what sweet comfort his work would bring to a woman decades later, a woman who would one day remove the painting from its lifelong home above a living-room mantel to carry, large and unwieldy in its carved wooden frame, up the stairs to her bedroom; a woman who would that night struggle to hang it up in a spot where her eyes could easily find it from anywhere in the room.

It was into this painting I now stared. It possessed far more potency than any photograph. Truth and soul seemed caught in the brushstrokes of color, as if the very essence of the man depicted had been preserved on the canvas. I could find his charm, just there, in the slight tilt of his handsome face, a bit of his wit in that mischievous glint in his eye, even his kindness in the way his hand lightly rested atop the furry head of his favorite dog.

Twenty-two years is not an insignificant amount of time, but far too short for a happy marriage. Thankfully, Franklin's passing had been quick, and as peaceful as any one of us can pray for. A sudden stroke at the end of a summer's day. I had been as prepared as a much younger wife could be, though not nearly enough, as it turns out. Time is a god we all must serve, enduring its vagaries the best we can, but it still strikes me as strange how the days Franklin and I had together now seem as brief as a finger snap, while the three years since his death have formed a lifetime.

"You're too young to be a widow." That's what everyone said, though my widowhood was something I'd always known would arrive far before I was ready. *"You'll marry again."* Truth was, though, I had no interest whatsoever in the prospect. As far as I was concerned, I had once fallen into a rare love, a love grand enough to fill all my days—past, present, and future. *"You'll change*

your mind." This was always the summation I let pass with no more than a smile.

With its rocky shoreline and winter snowdrifts, so foreign to my southern soul, Maine gave me a connection to nature I'd never experienced in the South. My heart leaped with each new season. I adored the autumnal orange of the maple trees, their vibrant color so perfectly echoed in the fires that roared in the old stone fireplaces of our seaside home. I marveled at the flowery beauty of summer, each color-washed garden all the more magnificent for its brevity. The winter snows—so deliciously novel throughout the first years I lived here, never lost the ability to thrill me at the sight of their first feathery flakes in November. High on our spruce-covered hill, we were often snowed in. I taught myself to weave, thereby uncovering a nascent talent that soon became a passion and, later, the career in fashion I thought I'd ignored. After Franklin died, I stayed put, despite my mother's expectation that I would "come to my senses" and head back home. This was my home now.

These days, from my attic studio overlooking the rocks and the sea, I design and create one-of-a-kind woven garments that fill the shelves of boutiques all across the East Coast. Thanks to a talented, somewhat overzealous business partner, my work is suddenly both well known and highly sought after. Busy, self-sufficient, and solvent, I have slowly managed to crawl out from beneath the heavy hands of depression that threatened to bury me after the loss of my husband.

My days are good ones now—my mornings spent rambling the woods with the dogs, nights working late in the studio by moonlight. And while, Lord knows, I'd still rather have Franklin beside me, there's something to be said for living alone, on a schedule you make up yourself. I go to bed when I want to; I eat, or not, when I please. It's probably true that solitude can enhance your eccentricities, but it's also true that since there's no one around to point them out to you, those eccentricities can soon become a comfortable part of your personality, leading you into a contentment born solely of not giving a damn.

It's only recently that I've begun to feel a restlessness moving about me, inarticulate whispers of doubt; light, almost imperceptible taps on my shoulder that prompt my soul to look around blindly for what is missing. It's a feeling not unknown to me. Franklin always said I suffered from *hiraeth*, an old Welsh term for the homesickness one feels for a home that never existed, but I haven't felt these stirrings for a very long time. Now, with him gone, I occasionally wake up in the night uncertain, listening to the wind in the trees outside my window play songs whose lyrics I can no longer remember. Abigail's phone call now seems to have rung through the house like an augury I've willfully ignored. It was a summons back to the place where parts of my soul remained stuck, in spite of all my best efforts to free them, and this time I couldn't avoid it.

I stared at Franklin's painting, half hoping for some appropriate reaction to the news of Mama's death. I told him the whole story as I continued to pack. "She was out in the muscadine arbor. Remember, I told you about that place. I spent a lot of time out there when I was little. But it's hardly big enough for a child. What could she have been doing out there in the middle of the night?" But he just smiled at me benignly, as he always did these days.

THREE

On the landing outside my bedroom, I saw Molly and Desmond in the window seat, their bright eyes fixed on the blossoming morning. Achingly blue and cloudless, the sky held the distinct promise of a beautiful day. I almost envied these two. To have nothing on the agenda save romps in the summertime sun seemed wholly preferable to the plans I was now making.

"Come on, guys," I called. "I'll let you out. Where are your buddies?" The two fluffy sheepdogs leaped down from their perch by the window to follow me, feathery tails held aloft like flags on a parade float.

Coming down the stairs, I spotted Fidget and Rattle, the two terriers, sitting side by side with their noses pressed against one of the living-room windows, frozen still as stone at the sight of a gray squirrel on the terrace wall. I paused on the stair to take in the view. I never tired of this room. Encompassing almost the entire back of the house, it had a row of bronze casement windows that framed a stunning vista over the fir trees and down to the sea. It had been my favorite room from the moment I'd first stepped inside.

Franklin brought me up here to see the house on a cold, wintry day in January, hopeful I would love it as much as he did, enough to make it our permanent home. Snow-bandaged spruce trees lined the drive, and a piercing wind blew up from the sea, hitting my bare face like fistfuls of quilting needles. The dark windows of the old stone house looked down as I approached, staring at me as though they might instruct the doors to refuse me entry if they deemed me the slightest bit unworthy.

Apparently passing their test, I had followed Franklin inside and found myself astonished at the beauty of the place, hidden for years underneath the mismatched, utilitarian furniture of a vacation house. The once antiseptically white walls had, over time, faded to a yellowish, sickly gray, and the pristine wooden floors slept undisturbed beneath an unsavory beige carpet besmirched here and there with mildew and mold. Like an elderly aunt surprised by an early-morning knock at the door, the old house seemed embarrassed by the state of its appearance. But I loved it at once, loved it all, and knew without question I wanted to live here forever.

I'd sat for hours cross-legged in front of the newly cleaned windows with a color chart in my hands, diligently matching the changing blues of the sea, the myriad greens of the woods, the lavender grays of the rocks, to create a palette for the house that married it seamlessly with the landscape outside. Franklin and I had furnished the rooms with deep reading chairs, wide writing desks, antique lamps, and wonderful paintings. I loved this place with a passion.

Now I walked into the flagstoned kitchen at the front of the house and opened two of the tall windows to let in the crisp morning air. Letting the dogs out the back door, I watched as they raced one another down the hill toward the rocky shoreline. It was a race the sheepdogs, large as they were, never seemed to win. I grabbed a bowl of fresh strawberries from the refrigerator and plopped the biggest one into my mouth as I switched on a CD of Vivaldi. The lilting notes seemed the perfect soundtrack to the colors of the morning and the prescribed antidote to my dread of the coming day.

A flash of red shot through the green outside, visible here and there between the spruces. A familiar truck was coming up the drive, churning gravel as it went. I put my coffee cup on the counter and headed for the front door, opening it just as a woman jumped down from behind the wheel. Tiny and lean as a whippet, she exuded an energy that was almost electric. I heard a thundering sound as all four of my dogs rounded the house, heading toward her in a herd of wagging tails. She clapped her hands and squatted on the pine-needled ground, where she was soon lost in a squirming cloud of fur.

"Hello, guys! Desmond, please don't bite my sleeve. Fidget! Miss me?" I could hear her laughing beneath the happy pile of dogs.

"If I were less secure, I might be jealous, you know," I called out, grinning, from my place at the door.

The woman bounced up as though on springs. She brushed the front of her jeans with the palms of her hands and cocked her head, squinting in the early-morning sun. Her salt-and-pepper hair was held back with a pencil and in serious need of a brush. "You better be grateful they love me so much. Especially as they're coming to live with me for a while."

Thirty years ago Maureen Adams had arrived in New York City with little money and a talent for design. After two years at Parsons School of Design, she'd taken a summer job at a PR firm, where she found the required hype ridiculously easy to invent and the money ridiculously good. With a sharp eye for subtle details, she soon learned the business better than those who taught her. Barely twenty-two, she closed the book on her design aspirations and opened her own agency, and by the time she was thirty, the services of Adams and Company were considered crucial to the success of any gallery opening, movie premiere, or entrepreneurial launch. Her status and success were underlined by a penthouse overlooking the park and a personal driver handsome enough to eventually leave her employ to become a Calvin Klein underwear model. Whenever a career was in need of revitalization or redemption, Maureen's number was dialed. She knew how to excavate a reputation from the shade of obscurity or disgrace without a hint of judgment or disgust. It was her job. She did it well.

Skilled as she was, no one guessed how much Maureen had grown to hate her work until the April afternoon she picked up the phone and called the FBI to turn in one of the city's top developers (her longest-standing, most lucrative account by far) for money laundering and fraud. She gave them information on everything from offshore accounts to shady associates, all collected over several months of secret suspicion. The Bureau was happy to take her call.

The resulting trial was a sensation. When it was over, Maureen sold the penthouse and vanished like the scent of new money. She washed up on the other side of Wigeon Island in an old farmhouse with fifty-five acres of pastureland and a flock of Corriedale sheep. We met not long after I'd married Franklin, at a fund-raiser for the island library, both recognizing possible kindred spirits in the other. When I started to weave that first winter, it had been Maureen who encouraged me to create designs of my own using the wool from her sheep. She would spin it; I would dye it in the natural colors from plants gathered up on the island. Before I knew it, we had planted a dye garden full of alkanet and tansy. She had dried cochineal beetles shipped in all the way from Oaxaca, Mexico, and I learned to crush them without flinching, my hands turning scarlet in the process.

Given her background, I suppose it was only a matter of time before Maureen saw the potential in what we were doing. We became partners; I was the designer, she was in charge of promotion, and Wigeon Island Woolens was born. She designed a striking ad, placed it in a couple of high-end magazines, and the orders started coming in like high tide. Soon we'd employed a half dozen island-ers to help with the spinning and dyeing, and I was weaving every-thing from shawls and scarves to sofa cushions and baby blankets. With a showcase magazine article in *Town & Country* last fall, we had more work than ever before, all thanks to Maureen's tenacity and vision. With things left up to me, I would be knitting by the fire every night with my dogs; running an entire textile company would be nothing more than a figment of my imagination. Mau-reen was a walking, laughing reminder to me that the trajectory of one's life is never set in stone. She was also a very good friend.

Now, with the dogs circling her legs like Morris dancers, she gave me a hug, and I felt the stressful thoughts of the morning evaporate. "Have you booked the ferry?" she asked.

"Yeah. I'm on the three thirty this afternoon. I'll drive on into Portland and stay the night there. My flight leaves at six, so I'll need to get some sleep if I can."

We headed back into the house, the dogs following us as one. "I'm sorry to leave you right now, Maureen. I know how busy we are. Most of the designs are already drawn up, but I do need to get with the girls and show them some things before they start work-ing."

She waved me away. "Oh, don't worry about that. We've got plenty of time. This is the spring line, and as long as we've got them all on the shelves by February, nobody will be screaming."

Maureen had flopped down in one of the fat chairs by the living-room windows and pulled Fidget into her lap. "Be thinking of new designs while you're traveling," she said as she rubbed the terrier's tummy. "Orders are coming in like crazy. I told you that article would push us to a whole other level. Of course, the fetch-ing photo of you and the dogs didn't hurt." I made a face and laughed. She looked up at me, her eyes soft with concern. "I'm really sorry about your mother, Lila. You okay?"

When I'd phoned her early this morning, I'd just said my sister had found Mama dead when she came to pick her up, omitting the stranger aspects of that grim discovery. A certain private weariness still made me reluctant to reveal the entire tale. "I'm fine, I guess. I just need to get through the next few days. It's been a long time since I've been back home without Franklin. And . . . funerals. You know?"

"Yes. I do know. They're hard. But we all have to go through them at some time or the other. I'm just sorry it's your turn. And don't worry about anything up here. The dogs will have the run of the farm, and you know how they love that. The work will get done. We'll take care of everything, so don't waste any energy thinking about this place. It'll all be here when you get back. And besides . . ."

Just then the sun bounced a beam of white light off the sea down below, piercing the window and muffling Maureen's voice into nothingness. The brightness went straight into my eyes, making me squint while at the same time cracking open a memory long forgotten, a memory with the vision of a tall young girl flashing inside it like silver sun on blue water.

When she was sixteen, Mama had been a lifeguard at the Wesleyan City Pool. I'd found this out by accident. She'd had a sick headache one Sunday afternoon and dispatched me to her bedroom to find some aspirin, and as I pushed aside bottles of nail polish and old copies of *Guideposts* magazine in the top drawer of her night table, I glimpsed the scalloped edge of a black-and-white photograph peeking out from a rubber-banded stack of recipes for congealed salad. It didn't require great effort to slide the photo from its hiding place, and as I had permission to be there in the first place, I hardly saw it as snooping. It was almost as though the photograph wanted to be found.

I didn't recognize her at first. Tanned and smiling, in a blinding white bathing suit, she stood in the center of a row of young men with her hands hanging loosely at her sides, by far the tallest of the group. In front of her feet sat a large trophy on which could be seen the inscription GENEVA TOLLESON, WESLEYAN LIFEGUARD OF THE YEAR, 1953. Her blond hair shone in the sunshine, and the expression on her face was one I'd never seen before: unguarded, happy, carefree. I felt like I was holding a clue to a mystery I'd not known existed until that very moment. It was as if I were looking at someone I'd never even met. And, of course, I was.

Despite the large swimming pool that glistened in the courtyard behind our house, I'd never once seen my mother dip a pink-polished toe in the water. But Lord knows she'd been determined that we should learn to swim. Both Abigail and Henry took to the water like dolphins, jumping and plunging into its chilly depths with fearless abandon as soon as the weather got the slightest bit warm. But I'd hated it. Mama was convinced I just needed to be properly taught. So for three whole weeks out of a precious summer holiday, I was enrolled in swimming lessons at Wesleyan City Pool. The English language does not contain enough words to adequately describe how much I hated those lessons.

I hated the way a wet bathing suit felt on my pale little body, all squishy and clingy and cold. I hated the way the summer sun smashed into the concrete surrounding the pool, causing my eyes to sting. I simply couldn't grasp the appeal of standing shoulder to shoulder with strangers in a pool of chlorinated water in the vain attempt to master an activity I saw as both pointless and downright uncomfortable. The only part I ever mastered fully was floating on my back with my head far enough out of the water to keep it from finding my ears. I didn't pass the final exam. Mama was very quiet all the way home, and we never spoke of it again.

Now, on the very morning she died, I remembered that afternoon when I'd found the photo of her. That day, in an effort to reconcile the face looking up at me with the woman sitting downstairs, I'd glanced across the room at a framed picture of my mother, an eight-by-ten enlargement of the one she'd chosen to be included in the most recent church directory. Perfectly coiffed and with a practiced smile, that face was a palimpsest of the grinning girl in the photo I'd held in my hand. I'd stared at her face for a long while, pricked by regret over how much I'd hated those long-ago swimming lessons. With feelings of sadness and guilt I could never articulate, I'd carefully placed the photo back where I found it, taking only the aspirin bottle with me as I quietly closed the night-table drawer.

Was this what I had to look forward to this week? A locked box of memories flying open unexpectedly at any given opportunity?

". . . so we've moved them down into the lower field, and everybody seems much happier." The memory in which I was lost snagged on the sound of Maureen's voice, still in the middle of the conversation I'd briefly vacated, and dissipated like mist. "And we all have . . ."

She paused. "You haven't heard a word I've said, have you?"

"Huh? Sure I have. Of course I have."

"Then tell me what I said. Hmmm? Can't, can you? For all your many talents, you really are a terrible actress, Lila. Everything you feel is written all over your face the second you feel it."

I groaned and clutched a pillow to my chest. "Trust me, it's been a lifelong problem."

Maureen grinned at me and shook her head. "Listen, it's weird for any of us to go back to the place we grew up. We all feel like that same kid we once were. If we were nerdy, we feel nerdy again. It doesn't matter if you're a nerd with a trillion-dollar bank account. If you were the fat kid, you can be a supermodel now and still be the fat kid the minute you go back. It's just the way it is. Funerals are stressful enough. Don't go making it harder on yourself. In my experience people are usually so busy worrying about how *they're* perceived that they rarely take time to focus too sharply on anybody else anyway."

"Maybe. But you've never lived in the South. When you're the slightest bit different, you stand out like a monkey in a chorus line. It's no coincidence that Thomas Wolfe was southern, you know. When he said don't go home again, the man knew what he was talking about."

"He didn't say 'don't' go home again, he said you 'can't.'"

"Same thing. It's a different world down there, Maureen. Seriously. You gotta understand, these are people for whom applying for a passport can be considered unpatriotic."

"Oh, stop it."

"No, really! For their entire lives, they never travel out of a four-state radius from the very spot they were born, and if they ever do, it'll be on some church-sponsored tour of the Holy Land when they're in their seventies or something, bouncing along inside a tour bus with fifty people who look, dress, and eat exactly like they do, and the whole time a sermonizing tour guide is validating every misguided thought they've ever had about the people who've lived for centuries on the land where Jesus walked so they can all return home comfortable in the notion that they've been right about everything just like they thought they were."

Maureen snorted. "You're exaggerating and you know it. And you're also being a bit harsh, don't you think?"

I giggled and pitched the pillow I was holding at her. "Yes! I'm being completely harsh. But I'm only halfway kidding. And that's the worst part." I groaned. "I feel so damn guilty for thinking these things every time I go home. These are, by so many definitions, really good people. I am certain they'll surround us the moment we get there, with food, and love—anything we need to make the next few days easier. I just feel like that goodwill is conditional. Like if they really knew who I was—who Henry is—things might be different."

"Trust me, you're just getting yourself all worked up over nothing," Maureen said, shaking her head. "It won't be like that. It's been years since you've spent any real time there. You are a grown woman, Lila. You'll handle this just fine. Besides, Henry will be with you. You've always told me he makes everything better." She plopped Fidget down on the hardwood floor, and he scurried off toward the kitchen in search of his breakfast.

I stood up and followed him to find the dogs waiting patiently by the pantry door. "You're right," I called back over my shoulder as I dragged the large bag of kibble from its place in the pantry corner, the four dogs performing a spirited roundelay at my feet. "Thank God for Henry. None of this stuff has ever bothered him the way it does me. I'll feel better when I'm with him."

"See, there you go. So it's all going to be fine, right?" I could hear Maureen's grin in her voice.

"Oh, it's going to be a breeze." I laughed and set the dog bowls down on the cool stone floor.

Later, after several cups of coffee, a bit of local gossip, and a good long hug that squeezed out a few tears before I pulled away, I helped Maureen load my four impatient dogs into the bed of her red pickup, then watched as they drove back down the drive. I could still hear the excited barking after they'd turned onto the main road. She was right, of course. Everything would be fine up here. But my worries were free-floating, and I could feel them gathering like storm clouds around a little southern town called Wesleyan.

AS I TURNED to go back inside, a breeze blew up from the ocean behind the house, beckoning me down to the terrace. I followed the path through the spruces, my footsteps silent on the mossy ground, till I reached the high flagstoned porch that rested in the branches of the trees. Here and there the feathery limbs parted to allow me a view of the placid blue sea below. With the dogs gone, the house was strangely still, like a classroom after dark. Knowing I still had another few hours before I had to leave for the ferry, I sat in one of the porch chairs, laid my head back, closed my eyes, and allowed the streets of Wesleyan to float up before me, lined with ancient oak trees and simmering in the heat of the sun.

Most southerners feel some sort of holy gravity in the soil they call home. When everything else is lost, they can still point to one place on a map and say, "There. See? That's who I am." But that kind of attachment was something for which I still wished. Wesleyan was where I grew up, where I was taught to tie my shoes and ride a bike, where I learned how to make biscuits and sweet iced tea, and where, at eight years old, I found out that things can go wrong. It hadn't felt like home to me since the day my father died.

I used to wait all year for *The Wizard of Oz* to come on television. My favorite scene was when Dorothy opened the door of her black-and-white house to that saturation of undiluted color. I knew somewhere in my soul that scene spoke of something far greater than the culmination of a windy journey from Kansas to Oz. It touched a longing I could never voice, one that would keep me awake long after the movie was over as I lay in bed inside a shaft of southern moonlight every bit as ashen as those Kansas plains, pondering Dorothy's choice. After all those emerald-green wonders she'd seen? After dancing scarecrows and cowardly lions? After all that magic, all that mystery, Dorothy Gale still chose to go home? That always seemed utterly ridiculous to me.

I'm not one of those people who remember the names of my high-school acquaintances. I've never come home for reunions. I haven't grieved when a landmark was torn down or when the words to the school song were changed to better reflect the times. I didn't fret as year by year, foot by foot, the ever-widening highway gorged itself on the front lawn of the elementary school, gobbling up the rows of pink azaleas, the velvety green grass, the benches and the swings, till it eventually reached all the way to the door. Oh, I pretended to care when an indignant (the school song) or heartbroken (the azaleas) Abigail called to tell me of these unwelcome changes. It feels like I've always pretended when it comes to Wesleyan. Whenever I'm there, I know, deep down in my soul, that I am still looking for Oz. It's a quest most people in Wesleyan could never comprehend. They would forgive their homeland anything.

The grief of the southerner lies in this unwavering love of place. A love that is boundless and visceral, it forms the bedrock of his every belief and action from the moment he feels a marsh wind cross his face or hears the midnight choir of cicadas tuning up at twilight. Take him away from the South and the scent of a magnolia blossom on a summer's night can damn near make him cry. But the love the southerner feels for the land of his birth is continually under threat, for the region's history runs counter to its beauty in a brutal fashion, and we have to find a way to make peace with that fact. Some of us never do. Some choose to ameliorate our past by painting the pages of history books with the concentrated colors of excuse and denial. Others, like my sister, simply ignore it altogether.

For all I could neither understand nor relate to about Abigail, the one thing I envied was her connection to home. It was deep and authentic. Her blood was in the very soil around Wesleyan in a way mine was not. There was nowhere she'd rather be than in the town of her birth. The lights of Paris, the relics of Rome, the mountains of Cape Town? None of these gave her the slightest temptation to question her place on the earth. No grass was greener, no air was sweeter, no sleep was sounder than what she had at home.

I was tied tightly to Maine by the love I'd had with my husband, but as I opened my eyes to the golden morning light, I knew I was stitched to this spot by the memory of Franklin, not Franklin himself. Though I did love this place more than any other I'd known, sometimes, on those nights when I couldn't sleep, I could feel the threads unraveling. Once again the old longing for home was whispering, but for the life of me I just didn't know where home was.

I'd tried to ignore Wesleyan for years, futilely counting on distance and time to erase its shadowed map from my mind. But no matter how happy my life was here in Maine, no matter how far I'd traveled or how much love and success I'd enjoyed, Wesleyan was still there, biding its time, waiting to be dealt with. If I'd doubted that, Abigail's phone call had given me all the proof I needed. Once again I felt the familiar dread at the mere thought of boarding that southbound plane, and I knew it had nothing to do with the loss of my mother. Was her death going to be the sad catalyst I needed to put that place behind me once and for all? I didn't know. But one thing was certain: by this time tomorrow, I would be facing Wesleyan, and all that it stood for, head-on.

FOUR

I was asleep when the plane wheels thudded down on runway number three at the Atlanta airport. Looking out the tiny scratched window, I could see heat rising from the black tarmac; the men unloading the luggage stopped every few seconds to wipe sweaty foreheads with the backs of their hands. Unwilling to participate in the usual passenger competition to be first out the door, I chose instead to check my lipstick and erase the obvious signs of sleep from my face. I was the last one off the plane.

Squaring my shoulders, I threaded my way into the throng of travelers following signs to the main terminal. Henry had promised to wait for me at a coffee shop there, and as his plane was scheduled to arrive a full hour before my own, I was hopeful that sixty minutes of strong coffee would be able to adequately erase the effects of three hours of in-flight drinks. My brother did not like to fly.

I was moving at a clip and vaguely light-headed when I rounded the corner and spied the green and brown Starbucks sign just past the security lines. I pulled up beside a souvenir shop full of peanuts and peach jelly with my heart beating faster than usual while my eyes scanned the rows of wooden tables arrayed inside the wide, clear windows, slowly moving from one to the other till there, in a pool of sunlight, they found Henry.

It's never wise to wonder if you'd be friends with your family were you not bound together by blood. Like a waterlogged door that can never close properly again, once entertained, that question can permanently change things, making it easier for you to notice the faults and the foibles of the people you're tied to for life. But when it came to Henry, I had no doubts. There was no one on earth I'd rather be with than my brother.

There are experts who'll tell you that happiness is inherited, that a microscopic wad of DNA determines one's view of the world. If that's so, then a very jolly fellow must nest high up in our family tree, someone who shares my brother's dark eyes and crooked smile. For as long as I've known him, Henry's disposition has always been sunny, his glass forever half full.

For some reason his jovial nature gives me more personal satisfaction than perhaps it should, as surely it's something innate. But I've never seemed to shake the feeling of responsibility I'd always felt toward my little brother. Without any official directive, from the first moment he came into my life, I've considered it my job to protect him, to keep the monsters away, and sweep a clear path for him to walk. This feeling only intensified after Daddy died. It's always been a commission I took seriously, and one I've loved. No one was happier than I was when Henry finally realized his dream of opening his own art gallery. Just looking at him now simply filled me with joy.

It's really true that men age better than women. It had hardly been a year since I'd last seen my brother, but in that time he'd acquired a splash of gray just above his temples, a change guaranteed to send any woman straight to a salon but one that only served to make Henry more attractive. He always managed to look both effortlessly casual and impeccably dressed simultaneously, and today was no exception. I smiled when I spotted the spectator brogues.

Suddenly struck with a vague sense of recognition, I felt, if only for a moment, that I was gazing at nothing less than a reincarnation of Daddy. Age had not only gifted Henry with an unexpected amount of handsomeness, but it had also bestowed upon him an almost mirror image of our father. The sight dropped a pebble into my memories. They began to ripple through my mind: Henry finding me in the muscadine arbor the day I thought our mother had died, Henry's big dark eyes staring up at me as I read him a ghost story on a rainy night, Henry beside me at Daddy's funeral in his little gray suit.

We had been preacher's kids, those creatures known to elicit both dread and envy in all who walked the hallways of the church. It's believed, and probably rightly so, that more than any other type of child, the offspring of pastors, preachers, vicars, priests—any religious authority, really—are somehow more mischievous, more prone to the sort of trouble that thrives in the warm environment of constant attention and tacit forgiveness. Maybe this is deserved. Certainly Henry did his best to fit that description.

The Christmas he was nine, the church decided to retire the old blow-mold crèche that had sat on its front lawn every December since before my parents were born and instead have a live nativity scene, complete with all the requisite animals assembled around a Holy Family that would include six-month-old Fletcher McClatchey as the Baby Jesus. Naturally, this was cause for much excitement in the congregation, not to mention in the McClatchey family. Unbeknownst to anyone, however, late on the afternoon of the first performance, Henry had sneaked inside the enclosure and untied the pair of quietly dozing camels. During the event later that night, no one seemed to notice the huge creatures shuffling farther and farther away from their designated positions, until just as the children's choir began its wobbly rendition of "O Holy Night," they made their break for freedom. Not a soul who was there will ever forget the sight of several of Wesleyan's finest, along with Joseph and the Three Wise Men, chasing those two galloping camels up the middle of Second Avenue. They were almost to the highway before they were caught. Few people found humor in the situation at the time, but I remember wishing with all my heart that Daddy had still been pastor. He would've laughed for days.

As a child, whenever I thought about God, he had my father's face. Watching him standing tall in the pulpit on Sunday mornings, washed in a celestial light that streamed in through the necklace of tall stained-glass windows, speaking the words of Jesus—joy, love, forgiveness—it was easy for a little girl to confuse the two. Daddy was speaking of God, but he himself was the corporeal embodiment of all those things to me. And when he died, he took God with him. I turned all my attention toward watching over my little brother, whose heart, I knew, was at least as broken as mine. Abby was too small to realize much of what it meant when we told her that Daddy would never be coming back home. He'd already been gone two years when he died, and to a little girl like Abby that's pretty much forever anyway.

Mama seemed to rise to her role as the grieving widow with her usual aplomb, determined that our lives wouldn't change. She wore red lipstick to the funeral. I can't remember if I saw her cry during the whole of the service. She just seemed angry, even checked her watch a couple of times while Reverend Weaver was speaking. Dry-eyed and unblinking, she stared a hole right through him the entire time, her face as stony as the statue of Little Gracie down in Bonaventure Cemetery. Henry and I held hands when Mrs. McGee sang "In the Garden," and I still remember how cold his hand felt in mine.

Afterward, when everybody was eating all the food brought over by the neighbors, I let Henry come with me to sit out in the muscadine arbor till it got dark. Nobody missed us. We talked about Daddy awhile, till Henry said he couldn't help worrying about how bad it must have felt to die so far from home. Then we just sat there, watching the ladybugs crawl up and down the vines in the shade.

Families change when a parent dies, and not always how you'd expect. Sometimes they turn brittle, splintering off into dark places, like a pencil stuck too far in the sharpener. Sometimes they just get quiet. Their conversations float on the surface, never venturing into the deeper waters to reach the fears and gray questions that keep each one of them awake in the dead of night, eyes wide open in the darkness of their separate rooms lined up along the same hallway. Little things that don't matter become stand-ins for things that do. It's just easier, I suppose, to be angry over who got the gooseneck rocker when Aunt Jo died than it is to admit you're scared because you don't know why Aunt Jo had to die in the first place. She was only forty-six years old.

But you don't realize all this when you're young. You just think adults don't talk about things because they're not really important, or maybe they don't think you'll understand. So you start to push the scary questions away, deep down inside yourself. It's not until you're older that it dawns on you that adults are afraid to ask the questions themselves. My family got very quiet when my father died, and nobody ever told me, or Henry, why.

He saw me approaching before I entered, his face breaking open into a sunny smile as he waved a mock salute through the window. As I wheeled my bag behind a chair, he slammed his palm down on the table and stood. "Damn, I've missed you!" he bellowed. He gathered me up in a strong hug, and I felt my shoulders loosen as I breathed in Henry's smell of coffee, chocolate, and peppermint.

"How many drinks on the plane?" I asked, barely managing to get the words out as he squeezed all the air from my lungs. The peppermint was Henry's trademark disguise when he'd been drinking a bit more than he should.

"Now, don't you start," he said, holding out my chair as he gave me that mischievous grin I remembered so well. "Hell, this is a special occasion. I mean, it's not every day a man's mother is found facedown dead in the middle of a muscadine arbor in the heart of the Southland. Lord, it's so Tennessee Williams! 'No sign of foul play.' That's what Abby said the police told her. You never think *that'll* be something somebody tells you when your mother dies, do you? I mean, she was seventy-five years old! What sort of 'foul play' are they talking about?"

"I don't know, Henry. I guess it's just because of where they found her. You've got to admit it looks somewhat unusual. What could she have been doing out there? Do you have any idea at all?"

"God, no. I never understood anything about her, though, so I'm the last person to ask. I was just sitting here remembering how I used to catch her glaring at us when she thought we weren't looking. You remember that? We'd look up and catch her, and she'd rearrange her face like lightning. What *was* that, Lila? I swear, call me paranoid, but it was only ever with the two of us. Used to make me nuts."

"Yes. I can call up that face if I want, which I never do, thanks."

Henry turned to watch the crowds rushing past, and I was flooded with the old protectiveness I'd always felt toward him. It had been a subtle feeling, so subtle that I sometimes thought it grew from my imagination like a weed, well tended by Mama's chilly, appraising stares and vague dismissals: I was never really certain she liked us very much. With Abigail she was wide-open hugs and conspiratorial laughter, but a chasm stretched out between us, blockaded by an almost casual aloofness and distrust. As with everything else in our family, we never talked about it; I never questioned her. What child wants to find out why her mother loves her least?

Henry turned back to me. "You need some coffee? You look a little peaked. Maybe a muffin? They're big as gorilla fists but really tasty." Without waiting for an answer, he bounded up and over to the counter to order for me, bringing back a hot, fully caffeinated coffee along with a chocolate muffin. He was right, it was tasty.

"Your hair's longer," he said. "I like it. And you've got some sun on your face. Some of your freckles are back."

"I appreciate you not calling them age spots."

"You? Never." He sighed loudly as he watched me eat. "I know Abby's going to stick it to me at some point about not coming down at Christmas. 'Mama's. Last. Christmas.' That's what she'll call it, I have *no* doubt. Complete with eyes closed and that catch in her voice. And what can I say? The truth? 'Abigail, I didn't come home for Christmas because I wanted to actually experience a *merry* one for once in my life.' Yeah, right. I can see myself saying that. But it *was* a merry Christmas, the best one I can remember since before Daddy was killed, complete with eggnog and carolers and snow and a big, fat fire in the fireplace. All that Hallmark stuff. And don't let anyone kid you. That's possible if you just make up your mind to have it and don't get guilted into going through the motions with all those people who just end up making you feel bad. And yes, I am talking about the f-word. Family. So shoot me."

"Thanks very much."

"Oh, I don't mean you, and you know it. Besides, you must agree with me. You haven't had a Wesleyan Christmas in several years yourself."

"True. But I did invite Mama and Abby up to Maine last Christmas if you remember. It wasn't my fault they refused to come."

"Well, after the last time I'm not surprised. Are you?"

Franklin and I had always spent every other Christmas in Wesleyan. He got along better with Mama than either Henry or I ever had. He'd help her with Christmas dinner—peeling potatoes, basting the turkey, making iced tea. He'd listen to all the local gossip with what passed for genuine interest. Franklin, who'd been raised high Catholic, sat beside her on the fifth pew of Second Avenue on Christmas morning, belting out "O Come, All Ye Faithful" like a Baptist. He was actually capable of making her laugh, something that confounded the life out of Henry, who said he was convinced that Franklin just saw Mama as some sort of case study. "Mark my words, he'll write a history of our family one day and nobody will believe it's nonfiction."

The first Christmas after Franklin's death, I was still bent beneath grief, with neither the energy nor the heart to climb onto a plane to anywhere. So I had invited Mama and Abigail up to Maine. Mama hadn't wanted to come. Abigail told me this as soon as she got me alone, but she didn't have to; it was glaringly evident in the silence Mama had worn like clanking armor all the way from the airport.

Truth was, I'd known before I'd even asked that she wouldn't want to come. Children were supposed to go home to their parents for Christmas; parents didn't travel to them. But I also knew that she'd come if Abigail did, and my sister wouldn't have missed it. A Christmas out of town would not only provide Abigail with a whole new audience of potential admirers but it would also enable her to supplement her wardrobe with beautiful winter clothes, something the warm weather of Wesleyan had always disallowed. Sure enough, Abby had jumped on the invitation like a bulldog and on December 23 floated down the jetway of the Portland airport dressed in more red than Rosemary Clooney in *White Christmas*, with my less-than-delighted mother following closely behind.

It should have been a pleasant holiday. It's hard to find a more Christmassy setting than snow-covered Maine. But despite the picture-perfect surroundings, my mother's shell of disapproval refused to crack. Complaining about the cold, she'd rebuffed any invitation for forest walks, even when Abby, bedecked in rabbit fur and angora, pleaded with her to come. She'd sat still as a silk flower while Henry told funny story after funny story at the dinner table. Her cool politeness was unrelenting. It created a tension in the house as tight as an overinflated balloon.

"What'd you say to her?" Henry demanded one night after he'd snuck into my bedroom bearing two steaming mugs of hot chocolate.

I'd scooted over and made room for him to sit on my bed. "I didn't say anything to her. I don't have a clue what she's so pissed about. She's even icy to Abigail."

"True. Though Abby's so tickled to be prancing around in the snow that I don't think she's really noticed at all. Not much of a Christmas for you, though, is it?"

"To be honest, it wasn't going to be very festive for me no matter what. In a weird way, this is somehow better. I guess I should ask Mama what's the matter with her, but I kinda feel like she's just waiting for one of us to do that so she can blow up about something."

"Well, I think Abby's talked her into making her red velvet cake for Christmas dinner, so maybe that'll cheer her up. She's mighty proud of that cake, and really, no one can make it like her. We'll compliment it a lot, and that'll probably snap her out of it."

Sure enough, Mama spent the next afternoon baking her cake, and she did seem to loosen up a bit when it was done. With drifts of snow-white frosting at least two inches thick and shiny green holly leaves all around its base, it sat on the kitchen counter like a sultan's crown, a masterpiece of southern baking. Mama was proud, we could tell. But the respite was short-lived, and everything went to hell on Christmas morning.

We'd only just arranged ourselves in our traditional places— Henry and me together on the sofa, Mama in the big chair by the fire, Abigail on the floor by the tree in a pair of red satin pajamas, ready to perform her annual role as gift presenter—when Molly the sheepdog rounded the corner from the kitchen, her expression joyful and her furry white face adorned with the vestiges of what once had been a truly spectacular red velvet cake. All three of us had fallen out laughing, but Mama took one look at the dog, burst into angry tears, and by two o'clock was on her way back home, with Abby trailing behind carrying their unopened presents like a sad little sherpa. I shook my head to erase the memory.

The two of us sat in silence, me slowly sipping my coffee,

Henry tapping his fingers on the table in a well-remembered rhythm.

"Do you think it's possible she'd started to go round the bend just a bit?" he asked in a secretive whisper, bending low over his coffee and looking up at me. "I mean, you know, I've heard that old people start to wander off sometimes. Could that have been it, you think?"

"Well, Abby's not mentioned anything like that to me."

Henry snapped back up and said, in a louder voice, "Yeah, well, let's face it. Would Abby even notice? You can't sit there and tell me you've never wondered about our dear sister's . . . shall we say, *sense of direction* herself."

Knowing he'd asked the question without really expecting an answer, I considered it anyway. Once again I heard Abigail's voice in my head, still crystal clear from yesterday's early-morning call. I could just see her, standing in my mother's kitchen as the blue lights of the police car raced round the room and back again, her one hand holding the phone, the other placed protectively over her pearl-draped throat. If Henry and I wore the distinct resemblance of our father, Abigail was the very picture of Mama. Blond as light, fair as day, her eyes the startling blue that makes for movie stars. We were the dark bookends on either side of her fairy tale.

I've often wondered what her life would have been like if Abigail had not too soon learned the ineffable power that walks hand in hand with beauty. It seemed as though she was wielding it with an uncanny ease by the time she was five years old. Her teenage years were a pastel blur of cheerleading, parties, and boys. When she was seventeen, the magazine of the same name even put her on the cover of their "small-town girl" issue, an honor that cemented her irrefutable reputation as the prettiest girl in town. While I pored over college applications in my desire to further not only my education but my distance from home, the talk when it came time for Abby to graduate high school centered only on whom she might marry. When it was decided there were no feasible candidates in Wesleyan, she was shipped off to one of the South's largest universities, where she majored, as many beautiful girls had done before her, in sororities and corsages. She exited after two years to glide down the plushly carpeted aisle of Second Avenue Baptist Church in a flurry of white while the man of her dreams awaited her at the altar, wearing a light gray tuxedo and an insincere smile. The marriage lasted three months longer than her college career.

She took back her maiden name when she came home to Wesleyan and began work as a receptionist in Dr. Pitt's dental office. Only an afterthought now, her beauty, shy and a bit tired, hid behind a few extra pounds and a mountain of overcompensating effort as she tried to remind herself and others of its once-undeniable glory. Just out of her thirties, she had not yet begun the too often unavoidable slide into bitterness to which other faded beauties are so susceptible. Abigail still believed her time would come. You had to admire her optimism.

Henry leaned back in his chair and stretched. "Well, you ready? We better get this show on the road."

We stared at each other for a moment, then began gathering up our things. "Did you reserve a car?" I asked.

"You bet I did. I got us a convertible. A black one, considering the circumstances."

FIVE

The part of me that might have been uncomfortable rolling into town for my mother's funeral in a black convertible was eclipsed by the part that was grateful the car wasn't red. Henry put the top down the minute we closed the trunk on our luggage. I twisted my hair into a knot to keep it from tangling and let the wind blow me into relaxation as we hit the highway, blessedly free of traffic snarls on this late morning, and headed south.

"So Andrew stayed home?" I asked. Henry and Andrew had been together for more than twelve years and were known to frequently protect each other from the more prickly parts of each other's families. I knew that Henry had a good relationship with Andrew's mother. She lived on the coast of East Texas, near Galveston, and the two of them often visited her there. His father was dead, like ours. Andrew had never set foot in Wesleyan, though they'd both visited me in Maine many times. I was very fond of Andrew and found him to be a perfect match for my funny, sweet-natured brother. Their oceanside cottage in Rhode Island was a place full of laughter and love.

"Yeah. I asked him to. Way too many land mines in this particular situation, don't you think?" Henry grinned at me, his hand
draped lazily over the steering wheel.

"Well, maybe." I kicked off my black Tod's and wriggled my
toes.

I'm sure there were plenty of people in Wesleyan who at least
suspected that Henry was gay, probably starting with his first-grade
teacher. Looking back, it had been evident to anyone open to the
possibility, which meant, of course, that both my mother and sister
hadn't a clue. How many times I'd thought about telling them but
didn't, believing it was Henry's truth to tell and for me to do so
would be breaching some sort of essential confidence. But how
can something so obvious be a secret? It's sort of like convening a
family together, everyone wide-eyed and nervous at the prospect
of what you're about to reveal, and then telling them you have
brown eyes. Can't they see that for themselves? Should you have to
tell them? Henry and I had never had "the conversation." In spite
of the occasional girl he'd dated in high school, I'd always known.
He'd always known I knew. I'd always stood at the ready should
anyone attempt to make him feel less than he was, and as I was so
often standing in the Second Avenue Baptist Church, this was a
full-time job.

After a few minutes with no other sound but the wind, Henry
smiled and said, almost to himself, "You know, I used to think the
only thing good that ever came out of Texas was grapefruit. But
Andrew changed my mind about that."

I nodded and grinned over at him. In that moment I could easily see Henry at four or five, once again dressing up for Halloween
night as a girl, his favorite costume by far. He'd always been greeted
with laughter and exclamations on his creativity by everyone who
opened the door to our shouts of "Trick or Treat!" and if he was
ever teased—an occasional occurrence that caused me to fly into a
fit of pique on his behalf—he'd simply laugh and say, "Oh, Lila,
they're just trying to be funny." Later that night he'd fold up the

pleated skirt and wipe off the lipstick, putting them away for another year.

Exits with long-forgotten names flew past as we made our way
out of the city, the distance between each one growing with every
passing mile. Henry turned on the radio, and the opening notes of
"Under the Boardwalk" slid from the speakers, as reminiscent of
southern summers as the scent of garden roses or the tinkling bell
of the ice-cream truck.

The past often rides on the notes of a song, and as this one
wove its way around the car and out into the open air, it carried
with it all the carefree vacations we'd taken to our favorite Florida
beach before the loss of our father changed everything. Henry
turned the radio up, and it took no effort to see through the eyes
of the little girl I used to be, holding Daddy's hand, trying without
success to match his stride in the sand as we strolled along in the
watery pink light of a setting sun. Henry and I would stare out at
the dark stripe of horizon as the sea stole the sand away beneath
our bare feet, grain by grain, as though we stood together in an
hourglass, sidestepping to firmer footing every minute or so. The
wind would whip and whisper. And Daddy would tell us stories.

"Look," he'd say. "Way out there. As far as you can see, and then
a bit more. Can you see it?"

"See what?" I'd ask, my little eyes squinting as they stared at that
mysterious place where sea becomes sky.

"Oh, there's so much to see," he'd reply. "There are creatures,
way down in the water, creatures taller than buildings, creatures
that can fill up the sky. Monsters and heroes, angels and witches,
good things and bad things."

"Will the monsters come get us?" Henry would ask, his mask
of confidence betrayed by the crack in his voice.

"Not while I'm here they won't," said Daddy.

I would stare and stare, my eyes stinging, my heart throbbing
halfway in hope and halfway in fear. And just as the night took
over the day, I would squeal, "I think I can see it, Daddy! I see

someone walking out over the sea! Someone really big! Can you see him?"

"Of course I can, honey. You bet I can."

The stories Daddy told us erased a flat and monochrome world forever; they sparked and crackled as they unlocked door after door in the halls of my mind, doors that could never be closed. Later, after he died, it was to these rooms that I'd run, finding comfort in the color inside them. I had no doubt that this song had brought back the same memory to Henry and was just about to ask him when he said . . .

"You don't think Mama could have been meeting someone, do you? You know, like, *a man* or something?"

The imaginary sea in front of me drained in an instant. My eyes flew open. "You have got to be kidding me," I said. The image of my nightgown-clad mother traipsing off in the middle of the night to meet "a man" way out in the back of the garden—in a rather child-size muscadine arbor, no less—was what I finally needed to crack my control right down the middle. I started to laugh.

"Well, now. I mean, you hear of this sort of stuff." Henry sounded defensive. "Andrew's Aunt Rachel is a lot older than Mama—she's in a nursing home over in Dallas—and his cousin tells us she has a new boyfriend every month or so."

"Yeah, I bet she does. Let me guess, they all die on her, don't they?" I was laughing with gusto now.

"Come on, Lila. I'm serious." Henry started to smirk, and we were both soon overcome with the kind of laughter made thera- peutic by being forbidden, the kind best for wringing tension out of your nervous system like dirty water from a mop.

"Let's see now. Who could it have been?" I was enjoying my- self. "Maybe Mr. Byrne?" The thought of the rotund choir direc- tor from our high school wedging himself into our garden arbor provided a highly picturesque mental image.

"The choir director! Yes! Perfect. Or hey, I know. Old Dr. Reed! Course, with him on that walker, he'd've had to start heading down there around lunchtime to make a midnight rendezvous. Who knows? It could have been Jackie."

The thought of our mother having a clandestine relationship with her cleaning lady kept us going for a good five miles and led us into even more outrageous suppositions as to the possible reason she'd expired in such an unexpected setting. Our levity was no less welcome by being somewhat forced, but it became a bit melted around the edges the closer we got to our exit and had evaporated completely by the time we ascended the ramp, leaving behind the monotonous gray of the highway for the winding path of dappled sunlight that is State Route Four in the month of July.

It really doesn't matter the amount of time that passes between visits to your hometown. It's as if a sleeping sensibility awakens in the very marrow of your bones to answer a call made even more insistent by its silence. It's a call from within, a visceral response to the way sunlight lies across a certain green field or the sight of a mockingbird all alone on a fence post. Henry and I both heard it. He turned off the radio, and we rode along in silence, looking out the car windows at scenes from our past, each of us alone with our thoughts.

The back roads of the South are, like the South itself, a medley of disparity. The storybook sight of fat-bellied cows, like soft brown polka dots on lemon-lime fields, can momentarily lull the passerby into believing he is traveling through paradise. But just as he begins to nestle down into that thought, a vision of bone-aching poverty will appear before his eyes and make him shudder. Handmade signs spring up out of nowhere, scrawls on politics or religion that far too often advertise their creator's bigotry as well as his devotion. Roadside crosses rise out of the dirt at the exact spots where loved ones have crashed, and died. And all the while there is the sweetest aroma aloft on the air, a batter of white flowers and mimosa, baking slowly in the sun.

The town of Wesleyan sits in an island of green, almost equidistant between the lanky brown pines of Atlanta and the moss-robed oaks of Savannah, close enough to each to feel a persistent pull of both the mountains and the sea. It is red clay mixed with sand. The night breezes that swirl into the windows of Wesleyan carry the fragrance of both honeysuckle and salt, an evocative mixture that calls from two directions at once, generating a homesickness that never quite leaves. Regardless of my indigenous roots, this setting seemed to spawn a dislocation of the soul that had plagued me since I was old enough to recognize it.

There were the inevitable changes, of course, and these became increasingly apparent as we approached the center of town. Parisian-inspired awnings stretched across the wide windows of several new restaurants, and a candy-colored cupcake shop now sat next to Harlan's Hardware on the corner, all evidence of the ongoing gentrification that continued to flex its tentacles out from Atlanta in a concentrated effort to lure the free-spending millennials, an age group equally desired and distrusted by the older merchants and politicians still holding tight to the reins of Wesleyan.

"Oh, here we go," Henry said, cocking his head in the direction of the town square. "How's that for a welcome-home sight for you?"

Confederate bunting was draped on the iron fencing that surrounded the leafy park. Several faded brown tents had been erected in the corner near the gazebo, and I could see about a dozen men in gray woolen uniforms standing around in clumps of twos and threes, their pasty white faces glowing with sweat in the airless heat.

Henry stopped the car at the red light and stared over at them, shaking his head. "Personally, I blame Margaret Mitchell."

It's true that Miss Mitchell's epic tale of the Confederacy managed to obscure reality with roses so completely that even today what many southerners believe about that time adheres closer to her book than to history. When the movie version was released in 1939, the myth of the Confederacy as "a pretty world where gallantry took its last bow" mingled with Vivien Leigh's green eyes and Clark Gable's rakish grin to become solidified as fact, a fact so revered and romanticized that twice a year men of a certain age still come from all over the state to gather beneath the live oaks of Wesleyan Square, set up camp, and spend the weekend masquerading as Civil War soldiers, breathing life into the losing side once again.

"'Look for it only in books, my friends,'" said Henry. "'For it is no more than a dream remembered, a Civilization gone with the wind.'"

"I can't believe you remember that." I hadn't thought of those words in years but could still see them cursively laced across the screen of our television whenever that movie was shown. For every gray-blooded southerner, they encapsulated a yearning for a world that, in truth, had never actually existed.

"Of course I do. We had to memorize those immortal words back in third grade. Didn't you?" Henry drummed his fingers on the steering wheel, impatient for the light to change.

"Nope. I guess I was spared." I laid my cheek on the palm of my hand and shut my weary eyes. The iron-hot afternoon sun pressed down on my forehead; all I could see from behind my closed eyes was orange. I was beginning to feel a bit carsick. "Hey, how about we put the top back up on this thing?"

"You're probably right," Henry said, pulling away from the light and into the gas station on the corner. "We're due for a pit stop anyway. I'd like a Coke, too. You?"

"Love one." Slipping my feet back into my shoes, I opened the car door and got out, stretching my arms up over my head as I made my way to the bathroom to check what damage had been done to my appearance by the rollicking winds of the convertible.

A pale woman stared back at me from inside the grimy mirror. I put my hand to my face and turned this way and that. Yeah, Henry was right. Too many sunny morning walks along the rocky coast had lured some of my childhood freckles out from their hiding places just below the surface of my skin. A dusting of them now covered my nose, vague little reminders of the girl I used to be.

Henry was leaning against the car when I got back, holding a plastic cup out to me. "Looks as if they've got that kind of ice you like," he said. I noticed the *i* in "ice" was longer than it usually was. Our southern accent might lie dormant when we were in other parts of the country but was known to reemerge without warning in sympathetic surroundings. I grinned at him and took the Coke.

SIX

Henry bears the name of our Scottish great-grandfather, a man neither of us ever met and the man responsible for building one of the grandest houses in Wesleyan. But by the time Daddy and Uncle Audie were born, William Henry Bruce had sold all his newspapers and radio stations to a media conglomerate in Ohio and moved to the South Carolina coast, where he promptly died, leaving the house to my grandparents, along with enough money to secure the futures of several generations to come. Audie and Penn Bruce grew up in that big white house, and when our grandparents passed on, Uncle Audie and Aunt Jo moved in, living there happily until that fateful cruise from which Aunt Jo never returned. I hadn't been inside the place since her funeral.

Built in the Greek Revival style once so favored by southerners as the ultimate example of graciousness and taste, the house still stands at the end of a willow-lined drive off Quarles Avenue downtown, its six white columns remaining proudly at their posts along the wide front porch. From the outside it's hard to see the changes, though I suppose the tennis courts that now lie like crossword puzzles where the rose gardens used to be are a hint. Inside, the high-ceilinged rooms have endured the sort of devolution required to transform a historic old house into a luxury condominium. It's long since been named Windward Grove, and I'm told there's a waiting list for purchasing a residence there. But the citizens of Wesleyan still call it the Bruce house, even now.

Despite the legendary romance of names like Monticello, Andalusia, and Rowan Oak, people in the South don't usually christen their houses anymore. Places tend to be known by the name of the family who built them and lived there first. Folks can live in a house for a hundred years, but if the very first name emblazoned on the mailbox belonged to a Mr. Cochran, then it'll be the Cochran house for the rest of time. So when my parents moved into the shady old McKinley house on Davenport Drive and promptly hung a brass plate by the door that read GREENWOODS, there were some in Wesleyan who had no choice but to consider them uppity, especially given the fact that Penn Bruce had grown up there and should have known better.

Nobody had much to say, though, when my mother had this newly coined sobriquet printed in Venetian-gold lettering on her crisply monogrammed stationery. No, they were too busy noticing that my birth announcement, printed on that stationery, had arrived only seven months after Mama and Daddy's big church wedding. I was passed off as premature, and everyone in town eventually adopted the name Greenwoods for the old Tudor house under the red cedars that Ernest McKinley built for his family in 1925.

I never thought of Greenwoods as particularly grand, though I was aware it was considered precisely that by more than a few. To me it was just home, large to be sure but comfortable, and hardly a palace. Certainly nothing on the same scale as the Bruce house on Quarles Avenue, a fact that squatted between my mother and Aunt Jo like a toad till the day Aunt Jo died. Greenwoods was quirky, with nooks and crannies that hid like secrets down each hallway and round every corner. I considered myself lucky to be privy to all these. I knew the best place to read (under the back staircase), the best window from which to climb out and sit on the roof at night (the side window in Henry's room), and of course the best place to get away from everyone else (the muscadine arbor in the very end of the garden).

Greenwoods sat back off the street at the end of a curving brick drive, too far for the neighbors to ever see clearly inside its mullioned windows when they drove by at night, no matter how much they might have wished to. With its polished wood floors and high, paneled ceilings, it was a well-mannered house, one in which raised voices were as unseemly as white shoes after Labor Day. Lamplight fell through the windows at night, painting triangles of gold on the dark green lawn. Perhaps a shadow would occasionally drift across the damask curtains, but no one could ever manage a good look inside to see what sort of furniture we had or if it was really true that there was an N. C. Wyeth hanging on the dining-room wall.

The painting had been passed down through my mother's family tree, limb by limb, eventually coming to rest in our home when her Great-uncle Rufus, a man she'd never met, died at ninety-three. It had arrived with much fanfare, and rather high shipping costs, on a winter morning when I was six and was an item much loved by our entire family, for reasons as individual as we were. Mama loved it for the envy it inspired in her art-literate friends, whereas Abigail merely thought it was pretty. It reminded Henry of the ocean, his favorite place on earth, and for Daddy, raised on the Wyeth illustrated classics, it called up the tales of *Treasure Island* and *The Scottish Chiefs.* For me the painting became a friend, a sweetly silent audience to my days, always—but not quite—present, like a guardian angel.

Mr. Wyeth had chosen not to give her a name, preferring instead to simply call her *Girl on a Sand Dune,* so when I was ten and dreamily wandering through my Jane Eyre phase, I christened her Charlotte. Always winsome, always young, she stood on the shore in a white dress with a book in her right hand while seagulls flew overhead in a balmy summer sky. Her left hand was held aloft, and in it she clutched a white hankie that whipped in the ocean breeze. She was waving—forever waving—hello or good-bye, I never knew which. She greeted us when we came home; she bade us farewell when we walked out the door. Now I found myself looking forward to seeing her again.

Streets shot out in every direction from the town square like spokes on a wheel, and we followed the one most familiar. Even with the air conditioner running full blast, having the top back up on our rental car made the day seem much hotter. The heat radiated like echoes off every road sign. A stray storm had just preceded us, and steam now rose from the surface of the road like an unnatural fog, swirling round the tires of the car as we turned into Greenwoods. The white crepe myrtles lining the drive seemed to wince in the sun as we passed, and a large group of sulking blue hydrangeas eyed our arrival with tepid enthusiasm from either side of the porch. Strangely, there seemed to be no one at home.

"Huh. I figured there'd be cars lined out to the street by now," Henry said as he switched off the engine. We both sat staring out at the silent house.

"I guess everybody's gathering over at Abby's," I replied. I could tell by the look of relief on Henry's face that he was as grateful as I for the chance to settle in and prepare for the crowds of friends and neighbors no doubt already encamped at our sister's bungalow on Rumson Road.

"Why don't I carry in the bags, then run to the store and pick up some stuff to have here to eat," he said. "I know there's nothing but white bread and Little Debbies in there. You can have a rest. I'll go get us some real food. You know, like fruit and wine and stuff."

"Especially wine?"

"You bet. We're gonna need it."

Henry opened the door and got out. "Lord, it's hot," he said as the humid air flowed into the car, heavy as cane syrup. While he unloaded our bags, I fished my phone from my handbag and sat there staring at Abigail's number. Coming back down the stairs, Henry saw me through the car window and opened my door.

"Hey, don't call her right now. You need some time. Listen to me, take advantage of the empty house. It's cool in there. Go on in and splash some water on your face, have something cold to drink, maybe even close your eyes for thirty minutes or so. She'll never know. We can call her together when I get back."

He was right, I knew that. I nodded and got out of the car, letting my phone drop back into my bag.

"Good girl," said Henry. "I won't be long. Want anything special from the store?"

"Ice cream."

"Already on my list." He got back in and closed the door. As the black car disappeared down the long drive, I placed my hand on the heavy doorknob and turned it.

SEVEN

Every house is haunted. Some are haunted in the traditional way: by spirits generally more mischievous than malevolent, who take delight in closing the open door, rocking the empty chair, or snuffing out the flaming candle, unfortunate souls who failed to squeeze enough enjoyment out of their paltry allotment of days to sufficiently satisfy their eternity. Most, however, are haunted by our own memories: bits of ourselves, individual and unique, left behind and lying dormant for decades but with the power to quicken and breathe the moment we step back inside. These personal spirits can live in the house of our childhood or the church where we married. They wait for us with the patience of angels, alert to the sound of our step, the certain sweetness of our perfume, the touch of our hand on the door. Like rainbows through beveled glass, they coalesce in the stillness, ethereal as a dream yet visible to our eyes only. We alone may catch glimpses of ourselves at long-forgotten ages, running down the hallways or sitting with a book at the window. We alone can see our parents as they once were, young and hale. Fleeting, hardly real, the sounds of our youth can return on a breeze—the music, the laughter, the tears. These spirits gather in the corners of once-familiar rooms to whisper and sing, a murmuration of memory meant for just one.

Knowing this, I stood in the entry of my childhood home, all alone there for the first time in decades, and I waited. The sweltering heat of the outside day hadn't possessed enough power to push inside these silent rooms. I kicked off my shoes to feel the coolness of the black and white marble tiles on my bare feet. The only sound was the ticktock of the mantel clock in the back sitting room, an insistent metronome that had provided the soundtrack of this house for longer than I could remember.

As is true with so many gracious southern houses, nothing had changed. I stepped down into the long living room. The rays of the afternoon sun lanced the windows, landing in puddles of light on the polished pattern of the old hardwood floors. The pale yellow walls were aglow. Two down sofas still sat facing each other—each still invitingly plump, each still clad in its dress of soft floral linen—and the antique baby grand still sat by the window, a well-thumbed Chopin minuet propped up on the rest, advertising my mother's musical expertise. The room smelled like lemons, a gift from the two fading magnolia blossoms arranged on the Biedermeier secretary to the right of the dining-room door.

From here I could see Charlotte waving, beckoning me onward, so I continued into the dining room. This was a feminine room. It was painted the palest of pinks, like the inside of a seashell, and its mood could be influenced by the whims of light, dim and dismal on days of rain, luminous when kissed by the sun. Hepplewhite chairs stood at silent attention round the long table, and plaid silk curtains, extravagant as ball gowns, framed a view of the rose garden outside. It took little imagination to see Mama and Daddy seated in their usual places at each end of this table, with my brother and me on one side, our baby sister on the other, in her high chair with the painted lambs.

It hurt to know I was the only one left alive who could clearly recall happy times around this table, the weeknight dinners and Sunday lunches when Daddy's booming laugh and Mama's lilting giggle punctuated every conversation. All the laughter stopped when Daddy went away; we never ate in this room again. Both my siblings were too little when this happened; their memories were the unreliable ones of early childhood—more color than clarity, more sensory than sure. Now, with Mama gone, those days belonged only to me. The memories might be a bit faded, but they still came back to me when I called them.

We always ate dinner by candlelight, Daddy insisted. And there were always fresh flowers. I remember seeing him outside in the garden in the early-evening light, cutting roses while Mama set the table. Like most southerners, Daddy was a born storyteller, and every meal was another opportunity for him to spin a tale. I loved being his audience and looked forward to sitting around this table every night the way some kids look forward to birthdays.

I know Henry can only see Mama as the woman she was after Daddy left—distant, cool, and unreadable. But she hadn't always been that way. Or maybe I only remembered her by the light my father had cast. So warm and comforting, that light had been so bright it threw everyone else into shadow. And when it went out, everything changed.

I pushed open the door to the kitchen and went in to find the only room at Greenwoods that looked different from the one I had known. Instead of the red-and-white kitchen of my childhood, with cherries on the wallpaper and linoleum on the floor, I was met with a large open room of white. Painted-white cabinets above white subway-tiled walls. Pale gray marble countertops surrounding stainless-steel appliances. I could see the hand of Melanie, my childhood best friend, now local designer, in the sleekly serene decor.

At the end of the room yawned an expansive bay window through which could be seen the small courtyard where we used to eat breakfast every weekend in spring and where I could now see chartreuse dwarf cedars, underplanted with white vinca, rising out of mossy stone pots arranged here and there. Inside, a large round table sat in the window encircled by six high-backed chairs upholstered in pale green linen. A bowl of Granny Smith apples, each one the color of new grass, sat in the center of the glass-topped table, the perfection of the arrangement so precise it forbade any temptation to pick up an apple and eat it.

Just then my tired eyes caught a glimpse of movement through the glass door on my left. I looked out to see a disheveled Abigail, cheeks bright red from the heat, struggling with an armload of flowers and grocery bags as she tottered up the screened breezeway leading from the drive. The humidity had caused her blond hair to rebel against the sleek chignon she'd attempted, and her lips were moving as though in argument with someone both irritating and unseen. Knowing she wouldn't expect me to be standing there, I quickly tried to think of how best to move without startling her, but as I slowly backed up, the door banged open and there stood my sister, her blue eyes as wide as a wet cat's. Abby let out a high-pitched squawk and dropped the groceries on the dark wooden floor. I heard the muffled sound of a dozen eggs cracking inside the brown paper bag.

"Holy shit!" screamed Abigail.

"I'm sorry! I'm so sorry! I didn't mean to scare you, Abby." I lunged toward the flowers and caught a few of them just before they hit the floor. "I didn't see you till it was too late." I was losing the effort to suppress a giggle and turned my head so she couldn't see. Hearing her blurt out such a colorful phrase was rare to say the least.

Placing the flowers on the table, I swallowed my laugh and turned to help her gather up the grocery bags. Both of us bending down on the floor, our eyes met, and I saw the tears well up inside Abigail's like the first raindrops before the storm. I reached out to hug her, and sure enough she burst into an explosion of sobs.

"Oh, Abby. Come sit down. What are you doing here? We

thought everybody must be over at your place." My sister relin-
quished the rest of the flowers, still crying, and I led her over to a
chair. She took her straw handbag—large and covered in gingham
raffia flowers—from off her shoulder and rummaged around for a
tissue. Finding one, she angrily blew her nose and waved one hand
in the air, scattering the scent of Estée Lauder's Youth-Dew like a
censer full of sugar water.

"Oh, well! Who cares? Right? I mean, who really cares?"

"What's the matter, Abby?"

"What's the matter? What's the *matter*?" Abigail's voice rose an
octave with each word. "I'll tell you what's the matter. Not only
did I find my mama dead yesterday morning at the crack of dawn,
but before noon passed by, I found out that she told Wendell Landers she doesn't want a funeral! Yes, that's right. Don't you look at
me like I'm crazy. That's what Wendell told me. Called me up
straight from the funeral home. The phone was ringing when I
pulled into the drive yesterday. Of course, everybody knew by
then that Mama'd died. Wendell heard it from Eugenia Gunnels at
nine thirty, and how *she* found out, I *don't* know. Course, they
probably all knew ten minutes after Corky left here yesterday if he
called his mother. Hilda Bacon would've told everybody in town
before she woke up good. But Wendell said he wanted me to
know all this before we started planning anything. Seems Mama
came to see him a couple of months ago, by *herself*, and told him
that when she went, she did not under any circumstances want us
to have a funeral for her. No music. No speaker. No visitation. No
nothing! Nothing but flowers. She wanted flowers sent here to the
house if people felt the need to do anything. Wendell says he told
her that she'd have to put all this in writing. Said he didn't want to
be responsible for it if she hadn't written it down somewhere, and
so she shows up a couple of days later with this letter saying just
what he said she said. I told him I wanted to see it with my own
eyes. I just took the phone off the hook last night in case he was
right. I wanted to see for myself before I had to talk to anybody.

So I drove straight over there first thing this morning, and he *was* right, Lila! It's all in her handwriting. I've got it here in my bag."

Abigail dug around in her purse and drew out a piece of yellow paper. Holding it in front of her like it was on fire, she said, "Just listen to this now: 'I, Geneva Bruce, do hereby declare that when my time comes, I *do not* want any type of funeral service to be held. No visitation at the funeral home either. If people want to, though, they can send flowers around to the house. I want to be cremated and my ashes scattered in the muscadine arbor in the back. But I *do not* want a service.' She's underlined the *'do not'* part." Abigail finished the last sentence in a strangled sob and looked up at me, baleful as a basset hound.

"I mean, what on *earth*, Lila? *Everybody* has a funeral. I've never in my life heard of anybody who'd died and didn't have a *funeral*. Even criminals have funerals. Even *atheists* have funerals! You should have seen the look Wendell gave me. I mean, it's like a slap in the face to him. I know he's counted on our family's business for years. Everybody uses his funeral home. Course, maybe he can still handle the cremation part, I don't know. I've never known any-body who's done that either. Well, there was Daddy. But Mama said that couldn't be helped."

Abigail started to cry in earnest now, and I put my hand on top of hers. She took a shuddering breath and pointed to the flowers, white roses and red chrysanthemums, now scattered across the table. "W-W-Wendell said I'd better just take these. Mama's Sunday-school class had already sent them over in a vase, and Wen-dell said since there wasn't going to be any visitation or anything, he reckoned we would want them here at the house. It was so embarrassing, Lila. So I just drove back home, grabbed the god-damn flowers up out of that vase, and left. Figured I'd just ride around till you-all got here. I drove over to Sunnyvale for these groceries"—she waved a hand over several cans of tuna that had rolled out of the paper bag by the door—"'cause I don't want to see anybody we know. I mean, what am I going to *say* to people?

What am I gonna say to Reverend Rice? And what are we gonna *do* with her? Where's she supposed to *go*? Course, we don't even know how long they're going to keep her for this autopsy thing. I don't really think they should make us do that if we don't want to. It's ridiculous. I swear, this is all too much for me. I didn't shut my eyes all night long."

"They have to do an autopsy, Abby. There was no apparent cause of death, and it was unusual circumstances. So they have to."

Abigail snorted loudly and stood up. Grabbing the grocery bags, she started putting things away, slamming cabinets and drawers in frustration. When she got to the carton of broken eggs, she just stood looking down at them expressionless for a quiet thirty seconds, then walked over to the trash can and began to slowly drop them in, one by one. Each egg made a tiny splatter as it landed among the coffee grounds and junk mail. I could see her making an effort to control herself. When she spoke next, her voice was shaky.

"I guess it doesn't much count what I think about the damn autopsy. They're gonna do it no matter what. That's what Corky said anyway, and he's a policeman so he ought to know. I tell you, Lila, seeing her feet sticking out of that arbor was the most awful thing I've ever seen in my life. I swear I just froze there for two full minutes, and I don't even think I was breathing. She was just laying there, facedown in her blue nightgown, the one I gave her for Mother's Day. You know how she expects a new nightgown every year for Mother's Day. Just laying there, all sprawled out. Holding this old spoon." Abigail pulled a large silver-plated soupspoon from her skirt pocket and held it aloft. The pattern on the handle caught the light, and I recognized it immediately.

"What? What was she doing with a spoon? Did you tell Corky about that?"

"Huh?" Abby sniffed. "Well, no. No, I didn't. I mean, it was just an old soupspoon. It's not like it was a *gun* or anything. I figured she'd gotten a big spoonful of ice cream before she went outside. She does that sometimes. I think she figures the calories don't really count if the ice cream's not in a bowl." She chuckled softly to herself for a second, then teared up again.

"So she was holding it? She had it in her hand?"

"Yes. I *told* you. It was in her hand. That's how I knew she must have been eating something, and I'm thinking it was ice cream because that's what she usually did at night. Black Walnut. That was her favorite. Why are you looking at me like that, Lila? I didn't do anything."

"Well, Abby, I mean, you should have left her like she was. You shouldn't have picked up anything at all. Certainly you shouldn't have taken something out of her *hand*. You should know that."

"For pity's sake, Lila! You're acting like one of those cops on TV. Like it was a crime scene or something." She was starting to wail again. "Poor old soul. Way out there all by herself in the middle of the night. I just hate to think about it." Tears rolling down her cheeks, Abby pulled the cuff of her blouse up to wipe her eyes, turned, and ran out of the room. I heard footsteps pounding up the stairs and then the slam of a door as my sister disappeared into the bedroom of her childhood.

I stood, walked to the counter, and picked up the large silver spoon. I twirled it over and over in front of my face, letting the rays of the now-setting sun make the silver dance. Abigail's explanation seemed plausible enough, I supposed. But something wasn't right. This particular spoon had a history. Still holding it in my hand, I turned to the refrigerator. My reflection was aqueous in the gleam of the stainless steel. I opened the freezer and looked inside. A few frozen waffles, some green beans and frozen peas, even a box of orange Popsicles. But not a carton of ice cream to be seen.

EIGHT

With the soupspoon still in my hand, I headed back into the darkening entry hall and switched on a lamp. Hoisting my suitcase, I went up the stairs, past the large arched window on the landing that overlooked the back garden. Violet shadows were now pooling beneath blue-green trees, and the water in the swimming pool was as black and clear as a staring eye. I noticed it was as cleanly translucent as ever, even though I doubted a toe had been dipped into its chlorinated water for years. The holly-bush hedge that encircled it like a Christmas wreath had grown to an impressive height. The expert hand of Mama's gardener, Mr. Plackett, could be seen in its razor-sharp sculpting. Its top was as smooth as a southern boy's crew cut.

The same white gate still sat in the long side of the hedge, opening onto the garden and out to the grassy field. My memory took over where my eyes failed me, ironically making the view all the sharper. I knew that the garden was wilder here, bordered by old woods and carelessly sprinkled with oakleaf hydrangeas; their white blooms would soon be shining in the dark. There were pathways here, too, little trails that led into and out of the woods, trails I had followed and knew like my handprint. At the far end of the field, the land sloped downward, leveling out just before it reached the creek. On the other side, in a tiny clearing carpeted with clover and wild violets, sat the muscadine arbor.

The arbor stood about six feet tall, though the vines that entwined it made it look much larger than it was, particularly when covered with the summer fruits that hid like secrets behind the olive-green leaves. It could be entered only by pulling the vines apart. You had to duck down pretty far to clear the entrance but were greatly rewarded once you managed it. Within those arbor walls, I had sat transformed by my imagination into Cleopatra and Guinevere, Titania, Ariel. This had been my kingdom. I had never dreamed it would one day become a tomb.

I reached the top of the stairs, the long hallway receding into darkness on either side of me. Abby's bedroom door was shut tight. I turned left and tiptoed down to my old bedroom at the end of the hall. My mother had redone this room soon after I'd left for college, knowing perhaps, without being told, that I'd never live in it again. Green-and-white toile covered the walls and dressed the tall windows, setting off the mahogany furniture and dark wooden floors. The high antique bed was Colonial, with carved pineapples perched atop each of its four posts. Two large wing chairs covered in green velvet sat in front of the deep-silled windows. I threw my suitcase into one and collapsed into the other.

As upset as Abigail was, she was right about one thing: funerals were fundamental in the South. Not to have one would seem strange to more than a few of my mother's neighbors, not to mention her friends. However, it was difficult to ignore the seed of relief that had been planted in me the moment I heard about Mama's plan to ignore this sacred rite, and I could well imagine the sheer joy Henry would express at the news.

Though meant to be a hallowed time set aside for people to mourn and laud the recently deceased in equal measure, southern funerals, at least the ones I'd attended, consistently fell short of the mark. More often than not, they were a time not only of great emotion, which is at least expected, but also of enormous tension and even, occasionally, uncomfortable revelation. Secrets are spilled at southern funerals. Death, particularly when its inevitability has been ignored and denied for generations, possesses a power to snap diffidence and dignity right in two, causing those left behind to be overcome with the need to unburden their consciences before they themselves are found sleeping in a slick, shiny coffin in their best Sunday suit.

Junior Hines found out he was adopted at his mother's funeral. Becky Lee was informed by those with good reason to know that her just-dead husband had been having affairs with not one but two of her best friends for the past fourteen years. Peter Wood asked his wife for a divorce at his father's funeral, and right before they lowered Sonny Culpepper's mother into the ground, his Aunt Lois told him she was not really his aunt but was in fact his sister.

Rather than spawn a loving memorial for the life he's just finished, the poor individual so recently deceased seems too often to serve chiefly as a catalyst for the purging of the soiled and tattered souls of his friends. Perhaps this was something my mother wished to avoid. The cremation part was a bit unusual, but maybe she'd chosen that because Daddy had been cremated. Mama did have a thing for symmetry. Of course, having her ashes scattered in the muscadine arbor when Daddy's were in an urn under a dogwood tree at the Second Avenue Baptist Church cemetery broke the set completely apart.

NINE

I had just begun to doze when I heard Henry's car in the drive. I figured he could unload the groceries on his own. When I woke an hour later, the room was dark and the house was still. No sound from Abby's room. I slipped along the hallway as quietly as I could and headed down the stairs. I needed to fill Henry in before Abigail reappeared, and I knew exactly where to find him.

The library was not original to the house but had been added on sometime in the forties when the McKinley children entered their teenage years and old Mr. McKinley found himself desirous of a room of his own. Its entrance was a fairly nondescript wooden door off the back hallway that judging by appearances alone could just as easily have opened onto a coat closet but in fact led to my favorite room in the whole of the house. Lined floor to ceiling with dark wooden bookshelves, long ago filled to capacity with enough intriguing titles to last anyone a lifetime, the library was always quiet, always cozy. I thought of it as a winter room, for even in the heat of July it seemed as though snow should be falling outside the diamond-paned windows and a fire should be roaring in the grate.

It was a room for lamplight, a room for stories. My father had supervised the decoration here, and in a nod to our Scottish heritage the windows were dressed in the Clan Bruce tartan, a deep red-and-green wool that, to my eyes, had always made the room feel much more holiday than heraldic. The Bruce family crest hung above the fireplace, its azure lion keeping watch, and no doubt approving, as Daddy read us tale after tale of Scotland, including the stories of Robert the Bruce, the legendary hero who was reported, but never quite confirmed, to be our ancestor.

If the validity of our direct connection to that illustrious Scot was in question, our father's devotion to our Scottish heritage never was. He'd always tell us that one day he'd go back. "That's where we came from," he'd say with a wistful look in his eye. "Your great-grandfather was born there. We are in the soil, the very air of that place, kids. You'll see what I mean when you go there yourself. And mark my words, I'll get back one day. If not in this life, then in the other." It used to unsettle me to hear him say that, though it did add an extra layer of mystery to every Scottish tale he told.

Four tall leather chairs sat facing one another in the center of the room. Daddy had found them at an auction, their caramel-colored leather scuffed and worn by years of readers who'd sat in them before, perhaps with a glass of whiskey balancing on their knee and a book of Burns poetry in their hands. This was exactly how I found Henry now, in the chair closest to the window.

"Did you get some rest?" he asked without looking up.

"Just a little. Abigail arrived just after you left."

"Whoa, boy. I wondered if that was her car out there. What's she doing here?"

I flopped down into the chair opposite him. "Well, there's a wrinkle in the proceedings," I said, rubbing my eyes.

"So soon? We just got here." Henry sat, expressions changing like a flip book, as I related our mother's burial wishes.

"No funeral. Well . . . wow."

"Yeah. 'Wow.' Abby's off the rails about this, Henry."

"I can imagine. Where is she anyway?"

"Well, she ran out of the kitchen in tears a couple of hours ago. Up to her room and slammed the door. I've been tiptoeing down the hall like a cat burglar. I wanted to talk to you before I got into it with her again. What do you think?"

"About what?"

"Henry, don't be obtuse. You know about what. Do you think we really shouldn't have a funeral? Nothing?"

"That's what Mama wanted, Lila. I'd never have thought of it, but I can't say I'm sorry about it. Surprised, yeah. But not sorry. You know I've never been a fan of funerals. Especially the kind they have around here. The muscadine-arbor bit is pretty weird, though. Don't you think? I mean, she died in there and everything."

"I think it's *all* damn weird." I hadn't told Henry about the spoon and wasn't sure I was going to. "But I don't know, Henry. I think we might have to do something here, you know, at the house. A reception or something. If for no other reason than Abby. She's pretty torn up, and you know they always say that the funeral is to help the living as much as to honor the dead."

"Who says that?"

"Oh, hell, Henry. I don't know. Somebody must have said it sometime. Anyway, the point is that I think it'll help our sister if we have a few people over to say good-bye to Mama in a way Abigail can understand. Just some coffee and cake or something. People can tell us how sorry they are and we can all get on with things. I think Abby would like it."

Henry sighed theatrically. "Oh, well, that's okay with me, I guess. Mama surely won't know anything about it anyway. Least I guess she won't. And it won't be a funeral, so we won't have to get

anybody to sing or preach or anything. And we won't have to listen to all her friends saying how 'wonderful' she looks laid out in
a coffin. Hell, there won't even *be* a coffin, will there?"

"Guess not."

"Wow. Well." Henry picked up his book again, then looked at
me. "How are we going to get the word out, though?"

"You forget where we are, Henry. This is Wesleyan. A couple
of phone calls to the appropriate ladies and the whole town'll be
here in five minutes."

TEN

Whenever Mama played the piano at church, Honoria Wood turned the pages, which pretty much summed up their relationship. They'd known each other since kindergarten, and although I'd never heard my mother utter one good word about her in all the years of my life, it was well acknowledged that Mrs. Wood was her best friend. Very different in appearance (with her tight white perm, Honoria was at least four inches shorter than Mama and, shall we say, a good deal more nourished) but very alike in the things that mattered. They shared similar views on politics, religion, and race, that trifecta of litmus tests for southern values, and whether bound by guilt or devotion, they were both in the fifth pew on the left side of the Second Avenue Baptist Church every single Sunday morning.

Like my mother, Mrs. Wood was a widow, her husband having succumbed to some unmentionable cancer long before he turned fifty. Her son, Peter, now divorced, was devoted to the old lady, and the two of them could often be found dining together on Friday nights at the S and S Cafeteria over in Simeon; both were fans of the sweet-potato casserole there. Honoria and her three squashed-faced Persian cats lived about two miles from Mama, in the same brick two-story in which she'd been born. My mother hated those cats.

Not waiting to weigh the pros and cons of my newly hatched idea, I went straight to Mama's writing desk in the sitting room and found her address book. There was Mrs. Wood's number, next to her birth date. Even though they saw each other every week, the two old ladies never missed sending birthday cards, something I found oddly sweet. I picked up the phone and dialed.

"Hello?" Her voice sounded just as I remembered, not a trace of age seeming to have eroded either its curiosity or its strength.

"Hello. Mrs. Wood? It's Lila Breedlove. Uh, Lila Bruce? I just wanted—"

I was cut off before I could finish the sentence.

"Oh, darlin'. I am so sorry. So very sorry. I just don't know what to say. I saw your mama last Thursday at book club, and she seemed just as right as rain. I couldn't believe it when Hilda called me. Just could not believe it. Several of us have been trying to get hold of Abigail since yesterday, but she's not answering her phone. Is she okay? Do they know what happened?"

"No, ma'am. Not yet. There's going to be an autopsy. I've only gotten in this afternoon, and I haven't really talked to anybody but Abigail so far. She's over here at Mama's house right now, and she's . . . well, she's pretty upset. As you can imagine."

"Oh, that poor child! She and your mama were closer than sisters. Well, I know you were, too, dear. It's just such a shock for all of you. For all of us."

"Thank you. Mrs. Wood, I was calling because . . . well, you may or may not know this, but Mama didn't want a funeral, and—"

"No funeral?" she interrupted. "You sure about that?"

"Positive. She put it in writing and left it with Wendell Landers. He gave her instructions to Abigail this morning."

"Well, I never. Why on earth would she have done that, you reckon?"

"I really don't know. Trouble is, we feel compelled to honor her wishes about it. And I'm a little worried about Abigail. She's not taking any of this very well, and I think she needs to be around people and—"

"Of course she does."

"Yes, well, I was wondering if perhaps you could help me invite some of Mother's friends over for a reception or something. Maybe day after tomorrow? I could call a caterer and have some food here and—"

"Caterer? *Caterer!* Lord, you don't need to call any caterer. We'd all love to do this for you kids, you know that. It'd be an honor, Lila. Don't you worry about a thing, dear. I'll get on the phone tonight, and we'll have it all together in a jiffy. No trouble in the least. What about flowers?"

"Well, Mama requested if anybody wanted to do anything special, they could send flowers here to the house. I realize that's pretty out of the ordinary, too. But, well, she—"

"Liked flowers. I know." I thought I heard a teaspoon of feminine scorn in the old lady's laugh, but I could have been mistaken.

"Thank you so much, Mrs. Wood. I'm really grateful. Henry and Abby will be, too."

"You don't have to thank me, Lila dear. We all love you, you know that."

"Yes, ma'am. I do."

Having placed the handset back onto the receiver, I walked into the darkened kitchen and saw that Henry had made me a salad and left it on the counter with a glass of red wine. I reached for the wine with gratitude; each large sip felt like a reminder of just how exhausted I was. After nibbling at the salad for a few minutes, I headed back upstairs, pausing briefly at the library door to thank

Henry and let him know that Mrs. Wood was on the case for the reception.

"We don't have to worry about getting the word out now," I said. "The ladies of Wesleyan are officially engaged. I'm going on up to bed. I'll check in on Abby before I go. If she's sleeping, I'm just going to let her be till morning."

"Good idea. Sleep tight."

Ascending the shadowy staircase, I stepped into the dark hallway and padded back down to my room. It felt odd to be in here with nothing recognizable on which to hang a memory. Not a shred of evidence remained of my long tenure—no school uniform hiding in a drawer, no pink prom dress hanging in the closet. If not for the prevailing fragrance of the house—a mélange of lemons, lavender, and old paper that can always be found in varying degrees lingering in the corners of gracious old homes in the South—I could have been anywhere.

I swung my heavy suitcase up onto the bed, unzipped it, and rummaged around for my pajamas. I would unpack properly tomorrow. Tonight all I wanted was a hot bath, a cool bed, and a long, dreamless sleep. Pulling the heavily lined curtains closed, I saw only my reflection, the shapes of the back garden now gloved by the blackness of night. My memory was clear, however. I knew that just beyond the sweet gum tree by the holly hedge lay the remnants of a vegetable garden I'd tended the summer I was ten.

It had been a casual effort, my produce deriving chiefly from discarded watermelon seeds and tomato cuttings wheedled out of our green-thumbed neighbors. I had no professional garden tools. I pruned with embroidery scissors and dug in the red clay with an old silver-plated soupspoon, a spoon that to anyone else's eye was identical to all the others in my mother's Sunday set. But there'd been a dent on the side of the handle, a small imperfection that had caused Mama to remove it from the drawer of the sideboard and put it in the gardening shed for me.

This spoon now lay on the table beside me; I'd recognized it immediately. This same spoon was the one my mother had in her hand when she died underneath the muscadine vine. The thought hadn't seemed to occur to anyone but me, but I wondered: had she been using this spoon for the same purpose as I had, so many years before?

ELEVEN

It rained in the night. One of those warm rains that falls softly, like sheets of sheer tissue, covering the ground with a silver mist that rose up in the warmth of dawn. The dense fog would burn off completely by ten, but at seven it pressed gray hands against my window, promising a sticky and stifling day.

After a brief glance out the window, I crawled into bed again and pulled the sheet up under my chin. I was lying there, the lullaby of the slowly spinning ceiling fan luring me back to sleep, when I heard footsteps. I could tell by their careful tread that whoever it was was walking on tiptoe, which ruled out my sister. I sat up, listening. The steps stopped outside my bedroom door, and after a long second or two I heard a faint and tentative knock.

"Lila? You up?"

I recognized that voice immediately, the long, cottony twin syllables of my name as identifiable as a fingerprint.

"Melanie. Yes, I'm up. Come on in."

She opened the door a crack, just far enough for me to glimpse a heavy-lidded blue eye, as familiar to me as my own. As the door slowly opened, it seemed to erase years with each inch, and when she walked into the room, it was as if we were kids again.

Melanie Barnett Abernathy had been my best friend all through childhood. She was the girl who had everything—her beauty undeniable, her intelligence incomparable, her kindness deep and wide. These qualities were evident to every one of my friends from the first day we all met, lined up single file in the summer heat for the toddler class at Bible school. They were never questioned, never argued, never rivaled. As we grew up, Melanie carried the weight of these God-given blessings so lightly it never occurred to any one of us to be resentful or jealous of her. The fact that she chose me for her closest friend had always made me feel special, and even now, decades later, my heart lifted at the sight of her pretty face grinning down at me. She sat on the edge of the bed, flipped off her sandals, and pulled her legs up beneath her.

"Lord, Lila. What a fix."

"Mmmmm. Not the way I thought it would happen, that's for sure. Sprawled out in the muscadine arbor in her nightie." I looked up at Melanie, and we both started laughing the sort of laughter that ripples on the razor's edge of tears.

"God, we are awful. Just awful." She wiped her eye on the cuff of her navy linen shirt. "Did Mother get it right? No funeral? Really?"

"Really. And that's as much a surprise as where she died."

"And she never mentioned anything about that before? Why wouldn't she want a funeral?"

"Melanie, I have absolutely no idea." I rubbed my fist into my eyes. "You know we weren't close. I mean, she didn't like me all that much, remember? Or Henry either, for that matter. Why would you think she'd talk to us about something that personal? But she liked Abby, and Abby was as blindsided by this as we were, so I don't think she told anybody why."

"Lila, I hate it when you say she didn't like you. She loved you, you know that. She just, well . . . I don't know. Maybe you looked too much like your father. You ever consider that?" She got up and walked over to the window, pulling back the green toile curtains and filling the room with a pearly light. "Think about it. Maybe the reminder was just too painful after he died. And as for Abigail . . . well, she looked like Geneva. Always has. Maybe that's why your mother got so close to Abby—she didn't remind her too much of Penn. That's what I've always thought anyway." I watched as she meticulously fluffed out the curtains so that they fell in perfect pleats, then stood back to admire her work.

She was the opposite of a fair-weather friend. We both forgot birthdays, though we never missed sending each other a Christmas card, hers always containing a family photograph that revealed the almost magical maturation of my goddaughter, Neely. We talked on the phone frequently, even if our face-to-face meetings were rare. And with a prescience to be prized by clairvoyants, Melanie always divined when I needed her, showing up at my door with a solid support that had never yet failed to right my world whenever it threatened to slip off its axis.

The last time we'd been together for any length of time was just after Franklin died. She'd come up to the island to stay for a few weeks with me, weeks I barely even remember. She cooked me cheese grits and took me on long walks up and down the shoreline, picking up perfect rocks along the way only to pitch them into the sea before we headed for home, all the while telling me outlandish stories of her decorating clients back home in Wesleyan.

"You can't keep secrets from your decorator," she'd said. "We see it all. I can tell you who the hoarders are, who sleeps in separate beds, who has five different kinds of vibrators in their nightstand drawer. I could probably blackmail the whole town if I ever took the notion." And I had laughed in spite of myself.

Then, on nights when the grief tore my soul apart and I saw no worthwhile reason to stay on the planet, she would pull out a bottle of whiskey and pour us both a glass, all the while telling me of the goodness of life. I don't know whether or not she believed all she said, but she kept me tethered till the blackness became charcoal and the charcoal turned to gray. She left before the light returned, but she did so secure in the knowledge that I was out of danger, and I'd always be grateful for that.

Now, standing by the window in a nimbus of early-morning light, she cocked her head to one side and said, "You look good, Lila. Really good."

"You look good, too. No surprise there, of course. Same as always." Throwing off the covers, I swung my legs over the side of the bed and stretched my arms to the ceiling. "Oh, God. I don't feel nearly adequate for this day."

"I know. It's not going to be fun, but you'll get through it. I'm here to help. And there's Henry. Have you seen him yet this morning?"

"No. I figured he let you in. He's not up yet?"

"Nobody's awake but you, I think. Didn't see anybody when I got here. Abigail's car isn't here." Melanie sat down in the green velvet chair by the window, smoothing out the wrinkles in her white linen pants. I recognized the lacy pink woven shawl she had draped round her shoulders as one of my designs. "I used the key Geneva gave me when we did the kitchen over last year. Forgot to return it. It was still on my ring. Should I go wake Henry?"

"No, let him sleep a while longer. I can't imagine where Abby's gone this early. Did your mother tell you about the soiree we're having here tomorrow night?"

"Oh, yes. Honoria called her yesterday evening. She's been cooking all morning. In between phone calls, of course. I swear, Lila, this is going to be bigger than any funeral Geneva could have imagined."

"Maybe that was her plan all along. She did love attention, you know."

"Now, now."

"And as to your theory about why I wasn't quite my mother's favorite . . . You look exactly like your father, too, you know, and I can't help but notice Catherine's always doted on you."

It was true. Melanie greatly resembled her dad. Charlie Barnett had also been gifted with the arresting combination of Cherokee-dark hair and sea-blue eyes, as well as an irresistible charm that had endeared him to everyone in Wesleyan from the time he was a child. As their children were destined to be, he and my father had also been lifelong friends, though those lives had been cut short for both of them. Only two years before Daddy was killed, Melanie's father had hung himself in the woods by Bobbin Lake.

"Yes, well." Melanie sighed. "Everybody's different, I guess. I gave up trying to figure people out a long, long time ago. You should try it."

"I do my best. Tell me now, how is sweet Neely?"

"Your goddaughter is good. She'll be tickled to see you. Only three months to go. I still cannot believe she intends to make me a grandmother. I tell you, it's hard to lie about your age when you're one of those." She made a face.

"Spare me. You can always lie about your age. People would believe you if you claimed to be thirty."

"Yes, but you and I know that I'm not." We both grinned at each other. "Lord, Lila," she said, "how did we get to be forty-seven? It seems like last week we were lying on the floor in this very room, listening to Billy Joel records and reading *Glamour* magazine. And now I'm going to be a grandmother!"

"Do I get to call you 'MeeMaw'?" I laughed.

"Only if you never want me to speak to you again." She turned back toward the window and listened. "I'd better get downstairs in case people start coming by. I'll put some coffee on. It's all about to start."

She crossed the floor and placed a cool hand on my shoulder. "Don't look so worried. It'll be over before you know it, and you can head back up to your precious island." She turned and left the room, closing the door behind her with a soft click. I listened to her footsteps evaporate into silence.

For all its rigid constancy, time can be so malleable in the face of memory. Something as simple as the smell of old roses can bewitch it completely, causing it to twist and turn back onto itself until entire decades are lost and you feel as though it hasn't advanced one hour from that bright morning when you were six, standing alone in the garden sun to watch an orange butterfly flicker among the white flowers. Run your fingers along the blue satin hem of a baby's blanket, hear the song that was played at your wedding, or see the face of a childhood friend, and time can crumple and crumble into nothing at all. Seeing Melanie again had tugged that invisible cord leading back to the girl I once was, and I welcomed that girl's presence. I would need her resilience today.

TWELVE

The van from Chadwick's Flowers pulled into the driveway at nine. Melanie and I were just finishing our second cup of coffee when we saw Travis Chadwick, middle son and summertime delivery boy, struggling up the breezeway with his freckled face completely obscured by an armload of white lilies. He made several trips back to the van as we watched the kitchen slowly fill up with flowers.

When he unloaded the last lavish arrangement, Travis said, "There's more coming. Mom's called in some extra help to get it all done by tonight. People aren't doing the usual stuff, like wreaths and sprays either. They're ordering things like this instead." He held aloft a large vase of scarlet peonies and Bells-of-Ireland. "We've already been to the wholesaler twice this morning, and I bet we're not the only florist coming. You know McKay's will be here. I'll see you later this afternoon. Y'all take care." He headed back down the drive, then turned. "Oh, yeah . . . and I'm sorry for your loss," he said.

He uttered his final sentence in the perfunctory manner of

those who work in the business of bereavement, and I felt a twinge of discomfort at the feeling of relief bubbling up inside me. Not having to spend this hot afternoon at Landers Funeral Home picking out coffins and choosing appropriate hymns was an indisputable gift. I was just more hesitant to admit it than Henry was. And Abby wouldn't see it that way at all, of that I was certain.

Melanie and I set about finding appropriate places for this first wave of flowers. I'd placed the last vase on the polished sideboard in the dining room when I heard another car pull up out front. I watched through the window as an elderly man negotiated his way out of the driver's seat, his considerable girth putting up a fight as he wiggled and wrenched himself into a standing position. He slammed the door and paused to lean against it while he took a white handkerchief from his suit pocket and wiped his brow. I could see him heave a heavy sigh, his belly rising and falling like a dumpling in hot oil.

Dr. Samuel Peters had been my mother's physician for as far back as I could remember; their friendship began long before I was born. Always a natty dresser, with a head of white hair worthy of a southern politician, he stood there in our drive in a navy-blue linen sport coat and tan trousers, a pale pink shirt stretched tight across his tummy, its white buttons straining with the effort. I watched him head toward the front door, waddling like a mallard, and as he reached out to ring the bell, I opened it wide.

"Lila, honey! Look at you! How long has it been?" His voice was as kind as I remembered, the concern on his face more than evident.

There was no polite way to sidestep the hug, and I knew instantly that his copiously applied cologne, as emphatic as noise, would later necessitate a change of clothes if I were to avoid a headache. Pulling back as quickly as I could, I held him at arm's length and smiled.

"It's been a long time, Dr. Peters."

"Oh, please call me Sam. Like your mama did." He stepped

gratefully into the coolness of the hallway and took my arm. "I'm so sorry about her, Lila. I really am. I'm happy to see you but so sorry it has to be in these circumstances."

I steered him through the dining room and into the bright light of the kitchen, where he greeted Melanie with the same tactile warmth he'd directed at me and accepted her offer of a freshly filled coffee mug.

"Are you here about the autopsy results?" I asked.

The doctor sat down heavily at the round table and sighed. For a long moment, he stared into the depths of his coffee cup as though looking for something he'd lost. Melanie met my eyes and gave a slight shrug. Finally he spoke.

"Well now, Lila. There's no need for an autopsy, honey. I know what killed your mama."

"You do? How? What?"

"I was afraid something like this would happen. I told Geneva flat out she was being unfair to you kids not to tell you. But you know your mother, Lila. She'd made up her mind, and there wasn't a man alive who could change it. It was her heart, hon. She'd ignored some pretty serious symptoms for a while. By the time she let me run some tests, she must have had several heart attacks already. The damage was evident—and extensive. I told her plainly the next one would most likely kill her. That's why she wrote that letter to Wendell about her funeral. She knew it was coming sooner than later.

"I knew when I saw her last week she didn't have too long, and I tried like the dickens to get her to tell you all about it. But . . . well. She didn't. I hate it she passed this way, without giving you kids a chance to prepare for it and all. But there's no need to go through an autopsy. With her heart like it was, any strong exertion would have been dangerous, even fatal, and they tell me she'd gone way out in the back, all the way across that little creek out there? In the middle of the night. What on earth was she doing? You girls know?"

"No, sir, we don't." I felt strangely embarrassed. "I wish she had at least told Abby." This was going to be one more hurdle for my sister to clear, and I didn't want to be there when she tried.

"Well, I know. Frankly, I think she was dead wrong not to. But I could only push her so far. Marjorie told me to call you-all myself, but of course, professionally speaking, I just couldn't. Felt like the least I could do now was to come over here this morning and tell you the truth. I didn't want you to think she'd met up with some kind of . . . what'd Corky call it? Foul play? I called him yesterday as soon as I heard. Told him to put that kind of talk away. There wasn't anything unusual about her death. No, she was sick, Lila. Real sick. Wouldn't have had too much longer if she'd stayed in bed every single day. Though I sure wish I knew why she decided to take herself off way out there in the middle of the night. She knew the risk. I'd told her, plainly."

He delivered this news almost apologetically, as though he'd possessed the power to change things and had somehow shirked his duty, and I couldn't help but feel sorry for him. "You're very kind to come and tell us all this in person. It does answer some questions for us, and I'm grateful. I do hope you'll come to the reception here tomorrow evening. I know Mother would want both you and Marjorie here."

Dr. Peters barked out a laugh. "I'm not so sure about that, seeing as she didn't want a funeral. But that business of requesting flowers like Wendell says she did . . ." He laughed again. "I'll tell you what I told Marjorie: Seems to me she just didn't want one of those churchy funerals. Seems like you kids might just be doing precisely what she intended. A big to-do. Here. In her honor. With a whole lot of flowers. Yes, that sounds like the Geneva I knew. And you bet Marjorie and I will be here. Wouldn't miss it for the world."

He looked up at me, his eyes soft. "Your mama was a formidable woman, Lila. But I guess I'm not telling you anything you don't know already." I nodded and gave him a small smile. As though waiting for that slight encouragement, he continued. "Did I ever tell you about the day I decided to become a doctor? No, I wouldn't have, I guess. But your mama was there—in fact, she was the reason.

"A bunch of us had gone down to the beach for the day. This was long before she met your daddy. All us guys were playing volleyball, and all the girls were lined up on beach towels getting some sun. There'd been this little boy running around playing in the sand, and all of a sudden his mama looked up from her book and started screaming bloody murder, pointing out into the ocean. We all turned, and there was his little head, bobbing up and down like a cork, way out past the waves. I think we saw him for about two seconds before he disappeared under the water.

"Then, out of nowhere, there was this blur going past us, fast as lightning. It was Geneva. I don't think I've still, after all these years, seen any human run that fast. Straight into the water, out past the waves, till we could just barely make her out. Nobody said one word. We all just stood there frozen to the spot, watching. Pretty soon—it felt like an hour, but it could've only been minutes—we saw her blond head shining in the sun. She was swimming back with that little boy tucked up in the crook of her arm. Carried him out of the water and plopped him down on the sand. He coughed up a good bit of water, but he was all right. His mama was wailing, of course, and praising Geneva to the high heavens, but Geneva wasn't having it, which was unlike her, as you know." He laughed. "She was never one to shun the spotlight. But this time was different. She wouldn't take any praise, just told the lady she was glad she was there to help and went back to her beach towel.

"Seeing that little boy saved like that . . . well, it stayed with me. I knew that's what I wanted to do with my life from that day on. But I never heard Geneva talk about it again.

"That was your mama. When things were tough, she just did what she had to do. Didn't involve anybody else, she just got on with it. I remembered the look I caught in her eye as she was running headlong toward that ocean. I only ever saw that look on her face a couple of times after that. Once at your daddy's funeral and then again when I told her how sick she was."

Chuckling wryly, the old doctor rose, and I quickly stuck out my hand, deftly dodging another odoriferous hug. "I'll see both you girls tomorrow," he said. "You call if you need anything, you hear? Anything at all. I'll see myself out. Give my love to Catherine, Melanie." He went out the back door, the glass rattling when he shut it tight.

"Well," I said.

"Well," Melanie replied.

THIRTEEN

The door to Henry's room was closed, but I could hear him humming inside. I knocked lightly.

"Come in, but I warn you, I'm not decent."

I opened the door anyway, and there was Henry in his boxers with his arms stretched up straight above his head.

"It's yoga," he said, grinning in my direction. "Well, my version of it. I just stretch and stretch and bend over and bend over and stretch some more. Every morning. Keeps my clothes fitting and my skin glowing. Or at least I think it does. Andrew thinks I'm nuts. What's that? Coffee? Bless you, sister."

I handed him the cup and sat down on one of the twin beds. Looking around, I noticed that this room was basically unchanged since the last time I'd visited. Like my own room, though, no apparent traces of the former occupant remained.

The room looked northward, its three tall windows staring out at the perpetually green cedars that graced the front lawn, giving the house its name. One small window faced the side of the house, allowing effortless access to the roof outside. This had been forbidden and so, naturally, frequently used. Most summer nights would find Henry and me lying on our backs on this roof while its black tiles slowly released the heat they'd soaked up during the hot afternoons and handfuls of lightning bugs made the treetops electric. I wondered how long it had been since this window had been opened.

"So," I said. "You're a boxers man."

"Yep. Breezy." He looked at me from between his legs, and I laughed.

As I began to relate the conversation I'd just had with Dr. Peters, Henry listened, shaking his head as he bent at the waist, his arms as straight as propellers. "Well, I can't say I'm surprised. Mama always kept her cards close to the vest. I would've thought she'd have told Abby, though. And really, didn't Abby notice something was wrong?"

"You know Abby. If she thought Mama looked sick, Mama probably explained it away somehow and Abby bought it. Of course, like Melanie just said, denial is a powerful thing."

"Melanie's here? Man, I'd love to see her. It's been years. Let me pull on some trousers, and I'll come downstairs."

While he got dressed, I stood up and went to look out the window. The fat blue hydrangeas that clustered together around the front steps were in their full morning glory. They would wilt completely by noon.

"Henry?" I kept my back to my brother as I spoke.

"Hmmm?" He was lacing up his shoes.

"You remember when we were kids and I used to have that little vegetable garden?"

"Yeah." He stood in front of the mirror, buttoning his linen shirt. "Pitiful excuse for a vegetable garden."

"Right. Well, Mr. Plackett never really wanted me to mess with any of his good tools, so Mama gave me some stuff from the kitchen I could use. I chopped up the ground with a bent-up cake slicer. Made seed rows with a rusty melon baller. And she gave me a big old soupspoon to dig with. It had a funny little dent in the side and she wouldn't use it anymore, so she gave it to me. I remember it."

"So?"

"So. When Abby found her yesterday out in the arbor, Mama had that spoon in her hand. It's the same one. Abby took it. I recognized it the minute I saw it. And it's been making me think. Why would Mama go all the way out there in the middle of the night carrying that old spoon?"

I could feel Henry's eyes on my back. "Well, I don't think she was gardening. Do you? Are you saying she was digging up something?"

"I don't know what I'm saying, exactly. It's just something that's been nagging at me."

"Well, let's go out there and take a look. I'm always up for an adventure."

We heard a car door slam hard. I craned my neck to see who it was and could just make out a corner of Abigail's silver Camry in the drive down below. I turned around. "Oh, boy," I said. "Abby's back. We better hurry up and get down there. Melanie didn't sign up for this."

FOURTEEN

Coming through the den, we could see Melanie sitting at the kitchen table, her eyes wide open and fixed. The look on her face was difficult to decipher but appeared, at least to me, to be an uncomfortable mixture of disbelief, aversion, and fear. I followed her stare across the room and had no doubt that my expression instantly became a mirror of her own.

There, flying around the kitchen from refrigerator to cabinet and back again, in a whirl of color and scent, was Abigail, an Abigail who appeared to have utterly changed in the span of the last sixteen hours. Her baby-blond hair was now a fiery shade of red and cut into a knife-sharp bob that slashed like a rapier from the nape of her neck to the tip of her chin. Her shirt seemed at least two sizes too small, and in the deep V of its neckline a rather stupendous cleavage had been unleashed and was now looming Rushmore-like over a three-inch-wide black belt cinched tightly around her waist. The hem of a tight floral skirt hit her just above the knee, and she was teetering dangerously on too-high heels as she poured sweet tea over a full glass of ice, all the while midstream in a sentence largely devoid of punctuation.

"And so I said to him, I said, 'Just go ahead, Mitchell, just go on and do it,' and of course he didn't want to at first, what with me being all emotional and stuff, but I told him that had nothing to do with it, that this was something I've been wanting to do all my life—you know, I've always felt like a redhead inside—but Mama would've pitched a fit if I had. God knows what everybody else is gonna say, but you know what? I don't give a rat's ass, I really don't. Oh, Lord! Henry!"

Having just noticed her brother standing openmouthed in the doorway, Abigail ran toward him, arms outstretched. Henry took a slight step backward before being engulfed in her voluminous embrace.

"Look at you, Henry! Just look at you! I swear you look just the same as the last time I saw you. God, men just don't age, do they, girls? Lord, Henry, can you believe all this?"

Henry mumbled something that sounded, at least syllabically, supportive. Abigail's stream of verbiage continued.

"I wrote up the obituary this morning real early—well, I really did it last night 'cause of course I couldn't sleep. Took it over to the *Journal* this morning and they were real nice. Sharon Lovejoy's daughter, Mary Lynn, you know, the one with that eating disorder? No? Well, she's real skinny still, but I think she's doing better, at least that's what I heard. Sharon! You know Sharon." She'd mistaken our shock for ignorance. "She goes to our church? Used to work over at the skating rink? Well, she might be after your time, I forget I'm so much younger than you two." I heard Henry cough. "Well, anyway, Mary Lynn is working at the *Journal* this summer, front desk, so she took the obituary for me. She said it'd make the paper this afternoon. So that's that, I guess."

"Abby. Why don't you sit down." Henry pulled out a chair and took my sister by the arm, steering her gently toward the table. Some of her iced tea sloshed out onto the floor.

"What for?" she asked, looking suspicious.

"Well, first off . . ." Henry looked over to me.

"Abby, Dr. Peters stopped by this morning while you were gone."

Abigail's head snapped around.

"He told us Mama had been sick. Very sick. It was her heart. Apparently she'd already had a few heart attacks. Dr. Peters had told her she was in danger of a life-threatening one, but she just didn't tell anybody. Not even us. There wouldn't have been anything you or me, or anybody, could have done."

Abigail just sat there, expressionless, running a bright red fingernail around the rim of her glass. "Okay," she said after a long minute. "Okay. Right. Anything else?"

We watched her warily, waiting for the penny to drop. "Abby, did you have any inkling she was ill?" I asked her quietly.

She slapped her thighs with the palms of her hands and stood up. "Nope. Not a clue. Anything else?" She flashed a pageant smile at the three of us.

"Well, um . . . yeah, there is something," said Henry. "We've sort of organized a little get-together here tomorrow evening. Kind of a party, I guess. You know, like a wake? For Mama. All her friends, you know? And I thought I'd call Uncle Audie and see if he'd like to come up. If I leave early enough in the morning, I can have him back here before it starts. That is, if he feels like it."

Just then the front doorbell sounded and Melanie excused herself to answer it. Abby continued to stand by the table, staring at nothing particular. Then she sighed heavily and said, "That's fine, Henry. Good, that's good. Then I think I'll go shopping and pick up something new to wear."

"I could go with you if you like." The words were out of my mouth before I could grab them back, and I felt horrible at my fervent hope she'd refuse my company.

"Sure. That'd be fine. Henry can stay here and answer the phones. You mind, Henry?"

Clearly unprepared for this calm side of our sister, Henry merely shook his head. From the front of the house, we heard Melanie call out, "Hey, y'all? I could use some help out here. McKay's has arrived."

We rounded the corner into the front hallway and were met with a colorful wall of flowers, every kind of arrangement of every variety of bloom obtainable by a southern florist in the month of July. Circles of chrysanthemums, vases of roses, wreaths of white lilies, even an inexplicable horseshoe of daisies and fern.

"Damn. It's like the Rose Bowl parade in here." Henry picked his way through the newly arrived garden to shut the front door with one hand and give Melanie a belated hug with the other.

"Henry, it's good to see you. Here, take this." Melanie handed him two large peace lilies potted up with moss and studded here and there with paper doves. "Put these out in the courtyard. In the shade. They'll like this weather, and we can decide where to put them later."

Together the three of us began to distribute the flowers throughout the house. We were rapidly running out of space. "This is just the second wave, I'm afraid," Melanie said, placing a gargantuan basket of purple delphiniums on the piano. "We'll be getting more, I'm sure of it. I'm putting these up in your room, Henry. They'll look good with all the blue in there." She hoisted a cut-glass vase of every yellow flower known to man onto her hip and headed for the stairs, her sandals smacking the marble floor as she went.

"Oh, that's just great." Henry's head disappeared behind another potted plant as he turned in the direction of the garden door.

I was standing there alone in the ocean of flowers when an odd slapping sound started up from somewhere down the back hall. Sidestepping my way through the wreaths and bouquets, I followed it to the little library door, where inside I found Abigail, slamming drawer after drawer in our father's old mahogany desk, her glass of iced tea tipping precariously toward the polished wood.

"I'm going to invite Jackson to the party. I've still got an address for him in an old address book somewhere. I can overnight it, and he'll get it first thing tomorrow morning. Plenty of time for him to get here if he can. Here, hold this." She handed me the glass, bending over to rummage in the drawer nearest the floor. This unfortunate stance provided me with an even more stunning view of her newly released bosom than the one I'd endured when she was upright.

"Here it is," she said, and stood up.

"Abby? Do you think that's wise? I mean, when's the last time you saw Jackson?"

"Oh, Lord. It's been years." She massaged the small of her back, her eyes closed in the struggle of thought. "I guess it was that homecoming dinner the church had back in '98. We didn't get to talk much, though. Mama was there and all."

"But isn't Jackson married, Abby?"

Jackson Woolf, I knew without being told, was the man my sister should have married. Anyone who'd ever seen them together when they were young would have said the same thing. So much alike they could have been mistaken for kin, their perpetually smiling faces pointed, always, toward the same vista. Both sixteen when his family moved to Wesleyan from Chicago, they had a connection that was almost immediate, and they became inseparable in short order, their obvious happiness something that delighted everyone in town except Mama and the folks at Second Avenue Baptist Church.

Abigail's beauty told a story her heart never wrote, a story that would pluck her from the common crowd and set her on a pedestal. It was the story Geneva Bruce had been determined to tell with her own life before fate snapped that book shut, leaving her a preacher's widow raising three small children. It didn't take long before my mother had pinned her own unfulfilled dreams on the incandescent beauty of the child she most resembled, her younger daughter. But Jackson Woolf was Jewish and therefore never in the running as the lead character in that daughter's story no matter what anyone, including that daughter, might have thought.

Oh, she waited at first, certain their obvious attraction would wane with the seasons. But come each birthday, each Christmas, the presents became more and more serious until, one particularly rare snowy Valentine's Day, Abigail came home with a tiny chip of an engagement ring on her finger, and Geneva—desperate, shameless—pulled out the big guns, detailing all the faults of her besotted daughter's betrothed with a cleverness that masqueraded as kindness, a selfishness cloaked in concern.

"You can't do this to that poor boy," she said. "He would never be comfortable in our circles. You know that. And he's Jewish, Abigail. You of all people know that the Bible says not to be 'unequally yoked.' You know what that means."

Abigail, who in point of fact did not know what that meant, was initially defiant, swearing up and down that Jackson was the best man she'd ever known and that he'd only been *born* Jewish— he didn't go to one of those synagogue things. Mama said that meant he had no religion at all. And finally, when Mama started to cry and said she was sure, deep down in her bones, that Daddy would never have approved of this boy for his youngest, dearest child, that he would be appalled at Abby going against what God would have wanted . . . well, Abigail crumbled like the red rose petals in the homecoming-dance corsage still pinned to her dressing-room mirror.

At first they decided to wait. Just until Abby finished school and Jackson got established in his father's sporting-goods business. But, of course, songs are written to lament the death of such plans, and her second year of college found Abigail flashing a ring of more appropriate proportions, and Jackson, brokenhearted and bitter, had moved far away.

I'd never forgiven Mama for this, and now, as I looked into Abby's puffy, painted face, I could see that despite her "best friend" relationship with our mother, she'd never forgiven her either. Not really. She answered my question without meeting my eyes.

"Well, he *was* married. But I heard not long ago that they divorced. Nobody round here ever met his wife . . . well, his wife that was, you know. He moved up to Memphis when we . . . well, he moved up there. That's where his daddy opened up that second store, and apparently he's done really good. Jackson took the business online some years back and supposedly made a fortune. He's even some sort of politician—I can't remember what kind. Mayor? Maybe school board, I don't know." Having located the address book she'd been searching for, Abigail was flipping through it furiously. "I've kept him updated here in this old book, Mama never looked at it, and I just thought since this has turned from a funeral to a *party* that I might as well invite him."

"Abby, I just don't know about that. Given the history, would coming to Mama's funeral be something he'd feel like doing? I mean, after the way she, I mean . . ."

"Broke us up? Took away the only chance at happiness I ever had?" Abby gave a brittle laugh. "That's what you're wanting to say, isn't it? And you're right. Well, personally I think maybe that's exactly what he'd enjoy doing. Come celebrate! Come celebrate the end of our beginning. Believe me, I'm not asking him to come mourn. 'Cause I know I sure won't be!"

The righteous anger on Abigail's face threw a hot flame into the room, one that singed my soul. "Abby, you're tired. You've had a shock. Well . . . several shocks. Why don't you sit down and rest a minute. We'll go out and get some lunch. Maybe go over to Allen's and get you a new dress for tomorrow night, like you suggested. Okay?"

Once again an eerie calm came over my sister's face. She just stood there, staring down at her hands. "There was just so much I didn't know, Lila. I thought we were so close and all, and now I find out she knew she was about to die and she didn't even tell me? That she'd planned out her funeral—well, her non-funeral, you know what I mean—and she didn't even care enough to share anything about it all with me? I was always there for her, you know? Always there. I feel like, well . . . I'm fine. Really. I'm fine." She pulled a bottle of red nail polish from her pocket and sat down in one of the high-backed leather chairs. She shook the bottle, opened it, wedged it securely between her knees, and began to touch up her nails, methodically covering over every tiny chip until they were perfect. "I'll tell you one thing, though. I would've liked it if Andrew had come on down. I swear, I just wish Henry would get over it."

I stared blankly at her while fat droplets of water slid off the sweaty glass of tea in my hand to disappear into the Scottish sea of tartan beneath my feet.

"How do you know about Andrew?" I whispered.

"Oh, come on, Lila!" She looked up at me and smirked. I felt both amazed and stupid.

"How long have you known Henry was gay, Abby? Did Mama know?"

"Well, *I've* known about Henry for as long as I can remember. And I've known about Andrew for years. I even talked to him on the phone once, several summers ago. He answered Henry's phone when they were out of town."

I placed the iced tea on the desk and sat down in my father's old chair, folding my hands in my lap to steady them while Abigail calmly blew on a freshly painted thumbnail.

"I told Andrew not to tell Henry about that, and as far as I can tell, he never did, which is pretty admirable, 'cause I bet he's been tempted. I'm just waiting for when Henry feels okay enough to introduce us. It's just so silly. And as for Mama, I never did ask her if she knew that Henry was gay. If she ever suspected, she never let on one bit. Every time he'd visit, she'd ask him if he'd found any nice girls up there in Rhode Island, and he'd say no, that he was still looking for one to fit the bill. He'd always say that with a funny little grin on his face that Mama never noticed, but I did." She met my eyes with a knowing look.

"Like last Easter when I was so frazzled with the egg hunt and finding Mama's hat before church—she'd decided last minute that she didn't like the one we'd bought, so I had to go looking for the one she'd worn last year, and it'd been kinda bent up in her closet, so I had to fluff it out and rearrange the flowers and stuff—well, that morning she said something about Henry coming down to go with her to church and how she wished he'd get married before she kicked the bucket—her words, not mine—and I almost just blurted it out. 'Mama, Henry's queer as a duck, and you're the only one in town that doesn't seem to know that.' But I didn't. Of course I didn't. Mama would've had kittens right there in the middle of all those dyed eggs, and from then on, Easter would have been a bad memory for both of us, not to mention Henry. I really like Andrew, though, despite having never met him. I think Mama would've liked him, too, if she wouldn't have been so worried about what all her friends would say."

I started to speak, but Abby cut me off. "Oh, yes, I know how you hated it when either of us was concerned about stuff like that. I know you don't give a damn what these 'old crows,' as you call them, think. But believe you me, when you're the one people are talking about, it's different." She rested her head on the back of her chair. "Course, they're talking now, you can bet they are. What with Mama found sprawled out like a flounder in the muscadine arbor. Lord help me. So I've made a decision." She raised her head and stared at me, eyes bright. "I've decided not to care anymore. I'm going to do what I want to when I want to do it. It's all a big joke anyway. You were right, Lila."

"I don't recall ever saying anything was a big joke, Abby."

"Well, you sure didn't let what anybody down here thought change anything you ever did, did you? Left town as soon as you could. Married that old man. Sorry, you know what I mean. And from what I've always been able to tell, you never regretted a thing. Well, did you?"

"No. No, I guess I didn't." I could feel the beginnings of a headache. "But, Abigail, please. Please give yourself some time to process all this. I mean, you only found Mama out there day before yesterday. Just take a breath. Don't do anything you'll regret."

"Are you talkin' about Jackson or my hair? 'Cause one of them I've already done, and I'm fixin' to do the other one." She laughed, blowing on both hands, then holding them out for inspection. "Now. Let's go get me a new dress."

She sprang up from the chair, grabbed the address book from the desk, ripped out the page with Jackson Woolf's name on it, and left the room. I sat staring at the door for a long minute, then went to find an aspirin and change my shirt.

FIFTEEN

J. P. Allen's was the only dress shop in town as far as the ladies of Wesleyan were concerned. The "Allen" lady was created by following an elegant recipe that relied heavily on a Kennedyesque formula of graciousness forever flourishing in memory if no longer in reality. The colors were bright and pure. The cuts were sedate. The hemlines always seemed to hit precisely in the center of every woman's knee, no matter her shape or size. It was the sort of place where the customers dressed up to shop for a dress. I found it an amusing relic. Abigail loved it.

The heat rising up off the sidewalk seemed to breathe, and we were grateful to feel the frosted air that flew toward our faces when we entered. The place was exactly how I remembered it. Heavily carpeted, with circular racks of dresses grouped by color. I could just make out the strains of the sort of easy-listening music passed off as classical by the ignorant ear, piped in from somewhere behind the crystal chandeliers that hung like ice clouds above our heads. Despite a rather healthy crowd, the store was strangely quiet, as usual. I always felt the need to whisper in here.

I'd hoped Abigail might have decided to change before coming. But when she came downstairs, still clad in that low-cut shirt of the morning, her shocking red hair shining like an insinuation, I was too intimidated to say a word. Henry gave me a sidelong glance over the copy of *Southern Living* held up before his face like a shield. I merely shook my head and followed Abigail out the back door to her car.

Now, standing in the middle of the venerable old store, I sorely regretted my cowardice. She was attracting the sorts of stares known to morph into gossip with astonishing speed. Abigail, either unaware or uncaring, flounced from rack to rack with a blithe indifference, her newly sprung bosom bouncing along before her like birthday balloons.

Passing by displays of more decorous colors with not so much as a glance, she headed for the loudest palettes in the store, selections clearly meant for the younger patrons, those shopping for bachelorette parties and proms. Here were the backless, the strapless, the split and the slit, and my sister was considering them all. Finally she held up a fuchsia suit that flashed a row of round rhinestone buttons down its center. "What about this?" she asked. I urged her to try it on. Despite the garish color, it looked fairly tame, and I had seen so much worse. But a few minutes later, when Abby emerged from the fitting room with the tight jacket unbuttoned to a dangerous depth, I felt my cheeks flush. This had been the wrong choice altogether.

"I'm not sure, Abby. It's a little too . . . well, too *much*, don't you think?"

Abby twisted around and grabbed the price tag, holding it up to the light. "Hmm, it's a little more than I'd like to spend on a normal day. But hey, this isn't a normal day, is it?" She stood in front of the mirror, turning this way and that.

"No. You misunderstand me, Abby. I meant it's a little too . . . uh . . . I don't know, too revealing? Maybe try buttoning it up a couple more buttons? Or maybe a bigger size?"

"What? Why?" Abby smoothed the skirt down and pulled a panel of the three-way mirror around so she could adequately view her backside. "I think it's fine. I like it. Could be a little shorter, is all." I shuddered inwardly, aware of several pairs of interested eyes gazing over in our direction. "But if I wear some really high heels, it'll balance out. I love the color, too! I've got a lipstick that'll just match."

Despite my suggestions of several thoroughly safer alternatives, we left Allen's with the fuchsia suit, boxed and tied with the store's signature striped ribbon, swinging on Abigail's arm.

After the refrigerated air of the dress shop, the viscous heat draped itself over us like a damp woolen cloak. The sunlight was so bright I could barely see. Feeling slightly woozy, I stopped to retrieve my sunglasses from the depths of my handbag, and when I looked up, I saw my sister, several strides ahead of me, talking to a woman who for many years had resided only in the halls of my memory.

It was obvious she had dressed with a total contempt for the weather, as if any low-level god of summer heat could dare alter her sartorial perfection. On her, the long-sleeved silk blouse looked positively chilly; the crease in her black linen pants was as sharp as the blade of a skate. Her silvery hair was combed in a style that though capable of standing its ground in the face of any wind that might blow, still managed to appear nonchalantly done, and through luncheons and dinners her expertly applied plum lipstick would never dare venture outside the lines of those vaguely smiling lips. In my experience only southern women of a certain age are capable of looking like this on a sweltering day in July.

"Mrs. Barnett?" I joined them just as Abigail appeared to be finishing a sentence. Melanie's mother turned around slowly, giving my sister a cool look as she did so.

"Oh, Lila. It's Catherine. Please! How are you, dear? It's been way, way too long. I am so sorry about your mother. Melanie still at the house?"

"Yes, ma'am. We've just been to Allen's to pick up a few things for the get-together tomorrow night. I do hope you're coming." Hugging her was like putting your arms around a bird.

"Of course I am. You know I'll be there, sweetheart. I . . . um . . . I was just telling Abigail that I saw the obituary in the paper right before I left the house. I found it to be . . . entertaining, which I'm sure was her intention." She shot Abby another chilly, appraising look. "No doubt everybody will get a kick out of it. But I wonder if maybe you might want to change it a little bit before it runs again tomorrow?"

"No, ma'am." Abigail, ramrod straight and squinting in the sunshine that set her newly red hair alight, looked up at Melanie's mother. "Like I was just saying, Catherine, it was all true, and I think it was exactly what I wanted to say. If this isn't the time for honesty, I don't know when it is."

Catherine Barnett stared into Abigail's defiant blue eyes for a long minute in search of something she obviously thought was essential. Finally she said, "Well, dear. If you're sure. Just remember, none of us get to do these important moments over again. And they can stay with us for a long time. If not forever. You just give that a thought, all right? Lila, you call me if you need anything whatsoever, you hear? I'll see you both tomorrow evening." She gave me a quick kiss against my cheek and turned to go, her straight back slicing through the gelatinous air like an ice-cold butter knife. I wheeled to face my sister.

"What on earth did you say in that obituary?"

"What? I . . . well, nothing that wasn't true, I can tell you that for sure." Abigail's chin was raised, an obstinate pose I remembered clearly and one that didn't invite further discussion without the very real possibility of a scene. She spun around and headed for the car, swaying on the high heels she was so plainly unaccustomed to wearing.

GENEVA TOLLESON BRUCE, of Wesleyan, Georgia, died early Monday morning, July 18, 2012. The only child of the late Forrest and Margaret Tolleson of Savannah,

Georgia, she is survived by her three children, Lila Bruce Breedlove of Wigeon Island, Maine; Henry Hamilton Bruce of Greenport, Rhode Island, where he has lived for the past nineteen years with his partner, artist Andrew Gant; and Abigail Christine Bruce of Wesleyan, Georgia. Mrs. Bruce's husband, the late Rev. James Pennington Bruce, passed away in 1973. Mrs. Bruce was a lifelong member of Second Avenue Baptist Church, where her husband, Rev. Bruce, was pastor from 1964 to 1971. She taught the Golden Age Sunday School class every week and played piano for the 11:00 service, all of which makes it very confusing and embarrassing to say that, at her request, no funeral service is to be held at the church. Mrs. Bruce was a difficult woman at times, and it seems never more so than in her death. The family would like to apologize to those friends and relations who would naturally be expecting to express their sympathies in the usual Christian way, but they feel a responsibility to carry out their loved one's last wish. It is her expressed request, however, that those desiring to acknowledge Mrs. Bruce's passing may send flowers to her home at 1414 Davenport Drive, though what the family is going to do with all those flowers, they don't exactly know.

The newspaper lay on the kitchen table, folded so that Mama's obituary stared straight up at the ceiling. Next to it lay a note in Henry's idiosyncratic scrawl. I picked it up.

"Well, it looks like I've been outed. Andrew's on a plane down here. I'm headed to the airport to pick him up. This is fun, ain't it?"

SIXTEEN

Of all the flowers known to line the walls of southern funeral parlors, the unassuming carnation is the most ubiquitous and potent by far. No doubt embarrassing for this shy little flower, its frilly fragrance too often emanates from blossoms dyed in aberrant colors to suit the season—leprechaun green for St. Patrick's Day, military blue for the Fourth of July. Now, from baskets and vases galore, in various shades of yellow and pink, they filled every room of my mother's house with an obnoxious, cloying smell that followed me as I opened the door to the courtyard, brushed the leaves off a chair, and sat down.

The wind was kicking up, a portent to the possibility of another afternoon storm, and it lifted my hair as it spun through the garden and up into the trees. I laid my head down on my arms and closed my eyes, lost in thoughts that allowed only an unconscious awareness of Melanie joining me, silently sitting down in the chair nearest the pool.

How could Abigail have written that obituary? And if she felt the need to write it—to get it off her chest, to release some of her anger—how could she have let it be published? I'd never been close to my sister—that had been Mama's position—but sitting here in the waning light of the garden, I realized that I'd never known her at all. Hurts and resentments that had been invisible to me were pushing up like weeds all around her, and I was worried about what she'd do next. She'd been right, I'd never been one to worry over the disapproval of other people, particularly those I didn't respect. But this change in my sister was so extreme I felt some responsibility to explain it, and that made me dread tomorrow night more than ever.

Funnily enough, I wasn't particularly concerned about Henry. Despite my watchful protectiveness of him while we were kids, I would bet most people in town were like Abigail: they already knew he was gay. Of course, acting like they knew might too closely resemble acceptance, a bridge too far for most of the stalwart faithful of Second Avenue. From my observations everyone got along just fine when "sins" were kept hidden. Place them out in the sun and that was a different matter altogether. No surprise that a Baptist president had been the one to initiate a policy of "don't ask, don't tell." It was practically a tenet of the faith.

I'd seen it happen before. When Donna Callahan fell in love with the band director at Crawford Middle School and left her husband of fourteen years, any affection parishioners might have felt for her flew right out the window, to be replaced by the need to reiterate the church's position on divorce. It was almost as if any close proximity to perceived immorality might throw impassable roadblocks onto their own straight and narrow paths, paths that, it must be said, had suffered their share of switchbacks and variations according to the interpretation of the times. Southern Christians once felt justified by Scripture to have white- and black-only water fountains. Go back far enough and you'll find the righteous owning slaves.

So, much in the same way my own birth was widely accepted to be "premature," despite all evidence to the contrary, my broth-

er's sexual identity was a nonissue as long as it couldn't be confirmed. And since we were preacher's kids, a moniker we would
wear for the rest of our lives here in Wesleyan, our family's place in
the community was unassailable by anything less than the truth.

But our little world, so ordered and respected, was upended the
Saturday morning Melanie's father, Charlie, was discovered swinging from that water oak down by Bobbin Lake. Quail hunters
found him. He was wearing his best gray suit with the blue striped
tie Catherine had given him for Christmas. No one had seen it
coming. He hadn't left a note.

Daddy took it harder than anyone, it seemed. He couldn't even
preach the funeral. People were forgiving about that. It was the
shock, they said. Daddy and Charlie had been best friends since
childhood, after all. But the shock seemed to stick with him, and
within two months he'd taken a leave of absence from the pulpit,
and a month after that he'd signed up to be a chaplain in the army,
requesting to be posted to the war that played continuously on the
six-o'clock news as soon as his training was over. He told people
he felt like he wasn't doing enough with his life, and, being his
parishioners, they tried not to take this too personally.

It was during this time, a mere two weeks before he left, that
Daddy took me to the movies to see *Willy Wonka and the Chocolate
Factory*. Just the two of us. It was a magical story, and I loved it.
When the obnoxious little girl blew up into a blueberry, lifting up
into the air and wailing, I was completely delighted. Turning to
Daddy, certain he found it as funny as I did, I saw he was crying,
his face wet and shining in the flickering light of the film. At first
I thought it was because he was laughing so hard. I'd seen him do
that before, though not in a long time. But it took only seconds for
me to realize that these tears bore no resemblance to the ones
brought on by laughter. Fear washed over me in that theater seat.
Fear like none I'd ever known before, and with it an embarrassment I couldn't understand. It was the embarrassment that made
me turn away without asking him what was wrong, and by the

time I looked back, he was dry-eyed once more. It was as though I'd imagined it all.

No explanations for my father's frightening behavior ever came my way, and I figured it had something to do with him leaving. Of course, being not yet seven years old, I wasn't privy to the conversations between my parents during those days, but I clearly remember the cold chill that wafted from room to room whenever they were about. There were a lot of whispers, a lot of glares. Mama didn't cry when Daddy left. In less than two years, he was dead.

All this, much more than any similarities in personality or proclivity, had solidified my friendship with Melanie Barnett into something stronger than diamonds. Our shared grief and confusion bonded us like sisters at a very early age. Now as we sat in the courtyard of my parents' house a few days after my mother's death, I felt she was the only person I could talk to.

Glancing over, I saw her chewing on the end of a pencil, a set of blueprints spread out on the table before her with a coffee cup holding them down in the wind. She looked over at me and smiled. "I thought you were dozing," she said.

"No. Just thinking." I twisted my hair up into a knot and laid my head back on the chair.

I heard Melanie's pencil tapping on the table. "So," she said. "The obituary. I suppose you saw that?"

"Oh, yeah. I saw it." I shook my head. "I don't know what's gotten into Abby. I don't know what to say to her. I mean, I understand she's upset with Mama for being so sick and not telling her. And then finding her like that. But my Lord, Melanie, she's just morphed into a different person altogether in the span of twenty-four hours. I don't know what to do."

"You don't have to do anything." Melanie set the pencil down with a snap. "Seriously, Lila. I mean, what are you supposed to do? You can't fix it."

"I'm not trying to *fix* it." I sat up straighter. "But shouldn't I at least . . . I don't know, shouldn't I try and ask her what's going on? I mean, did you see what she's wearing? That's not like Abby. You know that."

"Well, maybe it *is* like Abby. We don't know. Maybe that's what she's trying to say. Let's face it, Lila. Abigail lived under your mama's thumb for years. You don't know, you weren't here, but she didn't say boo without Geneva's permission. Maybe this is a reaction to that. I think you just have to let her be, at least for now. Try to confront her and all hell might break loose."

"You mean like that business about not waking up a sleepwalker or they might go nuts."

"Something like that." Melanie grinned and picked up her pencil again. "Where is Abby anyway?"

"She dropped me off and went back to her house. Said she'd see us tomorrow. I don't think she wanted to be here when I read that thing." Melanie laughed. I watched her for a few minutes, making notes on the plans in front of her with a frown of concentration on her face. "What are you working on?" I asked.

"Oh, it's a new addition for a couple out in Simeon. Big new house on the marsh. They say they want it 'shabby chic,' and I'm determined to make it more chic than shabby."

She kept jotting notes, stopping occasionally to stare out into the garden before a new idea sent her bending back over the blueprint and scribbling furiously. I continued to watch her. "You really love what you do, don't you?" I asked.

"Hmmm? What? Well, yeah, I guess I do. I've been at it so long I hardly think about it anymore. But yes, I do like it." She arched her back, stretching, and I remembered she'd been here all day. "I was sort of lackadaisical about it till Neely went off to school. Then I guess I was grateful I had it. I threw myself into it more like a career than a hobby then."

"And that's paid off big time. I'm proud of you."

"Well, thanks. It's fun, really. Everything's new each time out. Except when one of those trends blows through and everybody wants their home to look like everybody else's. Sometimes I think if I hear the words 'granite countertop' or 'open concept' one more time, I'll pull my hair right out. But by and large I do love it."

"I'm sorry, Melanie. I just realized I haven't even asked you how Philip's doing."

"Philip? Oh, well, he's just Philip, you know. His caseload has gotten larger recently with all those building violations down at Laurel Bluff. Big development, lots of money, and they never bothered to get the proper permits in place before they started. Environmental groups swarmed over it like locusts and shut it all down. So now all the homeowners are suing the builder, the builder is suing the environmentalists, and the county is suing everybody. Philip's got more work than he can shake a stick at."

"Are you guys happy?" The question popped out of my mouth before I could grab it back.

"What?" Melanie looked over at me. "*Happy?* Where'd that come from?"

"I don't know. I'm sorry. I just wondered. I'd left town by the time you two got engaged. I didn't know Philip very well. Oh, don't pay any attention to me. It's just all this stuff with Mama and Abby, and Henry sort of, you know, *coming out* with Andrew tomorrow night, it's got me reflective, I guess. Just ignore me."

"No, no. It's all right." She paused, picking the yellow pencil back up and rolling it between the palms of her hands. "Happy. Wow. You know, Lila, I'm really not sure what that means. I thought I was happy when we got married. I know I was happy those first few years after Neely came along. But I have to admit that Philip and I . . . well, we're just two different people. As the years went by, we sort of became like a business, I guess. Each one of us knew what we had to do, and we did it. I suppose we love each other. But I don't think it's the kind of love you and Franklin had. We're just used to each other." She stared out into the deepening shade of the trees. "I used to wonder what it would be like to run off somewhere. Not tell anybody, just take off, oh, I don't know where . . . to Greece—or Padua." She smiled to herself as though I weren't even there. "I've always loved that word: Padua. To start a new life where nobody knew me and nothing was expected of me. You know? Where I could say what I wanted, be who I was." Blinking suddenly, she bent back over her work, now in shadow as late afternoon began to slide in through the trees. "Oh, I suppose everybody feels that way from time to time. As for Philip and me, we're just used to each other, I guess."

I felt instantly, unspeakably, sad. I remembered how life had changed when my father died. I knew that Melanie's must have changed as well, but we'd never spoken about that as adults. I decided to risk it now.

"Melanie, when your daddy died, how did Catherine take it?"

"Good Lord, Lila." She sighed. "You're going back a ways, aren't you?" With her forefinger and thumb, she smoothed the thin lines running between her eyes like exclamation points, lines I hadn't noticed until right this minute. "Well, let me see. She was sad. I remember hearing her crying in the middle of the night for a long, long time. None of us knew why he did it. I've heard people say you have to know, that there has to be some kind of clue, or sign, even if they don't leave a note. But I really don't think Mother had the slightest hint. Dad always seemed so happy-go-lucky, you know? You remember. It hurts like hell to think he was that unhappy and nobody was aware of it, hurts so bad I can't think about it. So I try to remember him like the man I thought he was. There are just some questions that never get answered, no matter how much you might want them to be."

I could see her eyes shining in the waning light. A car horn sounded in the driveway behind us, and the conversation was over.

SEVENTEEN

The houses on Davenport Drive were divided by tall trees and dense hedges that held their branches aloft like stop signs. It wasn't a street that indulged in family cookouts or potluck dinners. No one walked up the long, shaded drives to borrow a cup of sugar, and kids didn't trick-or-treat here on Halloween night. People moved in, people moved out, and we never even knew their names. So when Henry answered a knock at our back door one hot afternoon when I was nine to find old Mr. Gentry standing there with Blarney, we were more than a little surprised.

Blarney was a large-pawed golden retriever who'd arrived down the street at the Gentrys' house as an eight-week-old puppy, a gift for the elderly couple from a son too busy to visit. Chuck Gentry was hopeful the dog would provide the company he couldn't, thereby assuaging the nagging guilt he felt whenever he took his family on a vacation that didn't include a stop in Wesleyan to see his parents. As it happened, Blarney proved too much for the old couple, and one morning, after another attempt at walking the big dog escalated from aggravating to downright dangerous, Mr. Gentry led him up our drive in hopes that one of the three energetic children he'd glimpsed from time to time might be willing to exercise the dog for five dollars a week.

Of course we were thrilled. Despite our near-constant pleadings, we'd never had a dog of our own. Mama wasn't fond of animals, especially in the house, and we all three felt, as Henry so eloquently voiced at the time, "Well then, what's the point?" So we grabbed the offer with both hands, and it soon became true that Blarney was as much our dog as the Gentrys'. He waited for us to get home from school, he went for long rambles with us in the woods, he napped beside me while I read in the muscadine arbor. He was also occasionally spirited up the back stairs for sleepovers with Henry, though Abby and I pretended not to know about that.

Now as Melanie and I stood looking out the kitchen window at Henry pulling Andrew Gant's suitcase from the back of the rental car, I remembered why I credited that dog with Henry's happy love life. I simply couldn't look at Andrew without thinking of Blarney, something that irritated Henry no end. It wasn't just the unruly golden hair shared by both, it was the open smile, the happy energy, the sheer big goodness of the man. I watched him lope up the drive with his familiar easy grace, and I was suddenly flooded with gratitude at his presence even as I once again thought of Blarney the golden retriever.

Andrew's family had never been one of those who rode out a hurricane. Even the rumor of one sent them running inland like greyhounds the minute they'd finished boarding up their rambling old house on Galveston Bay. He'd learned early on never to be a slave to unnecessary worry. "If you've done all the good you can do," he'd say, "just step aside and let fate take over."

He'd first started painting in high school, entering his drawings in local competitions at the behest of his father, a professor of twentieth-century art who knew talent when he saw it. By the time Andrew graduated from the Slade in London, he was already selling his work for sums that more than paid back his parents for his artistic education.

He liked to say the wind blew him into Henry's art gallery on Forthlin Avenue and in truth, had it not been storming that morning, he never would have opened the door. But it was, and he did, and if Henry knew who he was at the time, he never let on. That had been nineteen years ago, and they both said it seemed like last week.

The two of them were like puzzle pieces whose curved and crooked edges fit perfectly into each other. Being in their company never failed to lift my spirits, even if I'd not known that my spirits were low. Now just the sight of Andrew made me feel better. I opened the door and met him in the breezeway.

"Sister!" he bellowed, and I grinned at the nickname he'd bestowed on me the first time we met. "You are more ravishing than the last time I saw you. I swear, I always forget how much you look like your gorgeous brother."

"Andrew, I'm so glad you're here!" He gave me a bear hug, and unexpectedly, I began to cry.

"Whoa. What's this, now?" Andrew held me away to look at my face before folding me back in his arms like a toddler. "This just about your mama, or is it something else?"

"Oh, it's everything, I guess. I'm just a big baby. I'm all right, really." I stood back and accepted the starched linen handkerchief he removed from the pocket of his tweed sport coat.

"You're going to roast in that thing down here," I said.

"You are absolutely right about that, sis." He pulled it off and threw it casually over his arm, and we went inside, Henry following.

"I tried to tell him," Henry said. "But he loves that jacket. Won't listen to me."

"I dress for the weather I want, my boy. Not the weather I have. Though I have to admit, this is brutal." Andrew laughed and stuck out a hand to shake Melanie's. I made introductions.

"Good to finally meet you, Andrew. I've heard wonderful things about you for years." Melanie smiled, the same smile that had dazzled strangers since childhood, and by the look on Andrew's face, it had lost none of its power.

"Really?" he asked. "And here I was thinking I was utterly unknown around these parts."

"Not unknown, just a pariah." Henry chuckled and headed for the stairs, suitcase in hand.

"Um . . . well, you're not unknown to everybody." A faint pink blush rose high on Melanie's cheeks. "Not to me, at least. And you're certainly not a pariah. Can I get you something to drink?"

"To be honest, I am about to starve. I just jumped on the next plane when Henry called and didn't eat breakfast. And the lunch on that thing was unspeakable."

"Oh, well, we have plenty to eat here. I know my mother sent over a casserole, and I think I saw some fried chicken that must have arrived when I left to run some errands around noon." Melanie walked over to the refrigerator and opened it.

"Yeah, that's from Mrs. Wood. I let her in. She brought some potato salad, too. Looked kinda greenish to me." Henry had come back down and was now peering into the pantry as though it were full of lab specimens. "Damn, there's some repellent stuff in here. Who on earth eats hominy?" He held the offending can out behind him. "And a can of Spam? Good Lord, did Mama really eat this stuff?"

"I tell you what," Andrew said, "we passed a nice-looking restaurant on the way in. Michel's or Michael's, something like that. Why don't we go there? My treat. Everybody needs a break about now, right?"

"Oh, that's the new place," said Melanie. "It's Micheline's. Italian, I believe, and it's supposed to be really good. Yeah, let's go out. I've had my mother's casserole." She wrinkled her nose. "I'll drive. What do you say?" She grabbed her handbag, threw it over her shoulder, and the four of us trooped out to her car, our spirits a little lighter to be in one another's company.

THE OLDEST RESIDENTS of Wesleyan are the oak trees that line the stick-straight roads of the town square, their ancient roots cracking and buckling the sidewalks into rolling waves of concrete. Like giant, contorted old members of a primeval choir dressed in tattered gray robes of Spanish moss, for centuries they have remained the ever-watchful witnesses to the major events and tiny trivialities that play out under their velvety arms. They were here long before everything and will be here long after nothing.

Micheline's Cucina Paradiso, with its bright red awnings eagerly broadcasting newness if not originality, sat underneath these oaks, its lantern light illuminating their lowermost branches, turning gray into gold. Floral tablecloths covered eight tiny round tables clustered beneath the mossy limbs like little rose bouquets. Despite the heat we opted to sit outside.

Though it's always been a prescription known to achieve unpredictable results, people still choose to soothe extreme stress with alcohol, and we saw no reason to look for other remedies tonight of all nights. A couple bottles of quality red had us laughing before the salad course, and we didn't stop throughout the entire meal. Finally free to candidly discuss Abigail, we all shared our shock at the sudden change in her.

"What I still can't believe," said Henry, his arm draped lazily across the back of his chair as we waited for dessert, "is that you never told me you talked to Abby. I mean, for Pete's sake, Andrew. I didn't even realize she knew I was gay, and here she was talking to my partner like it's something she did all the time."

"I *told* you on the way down here," replied Andrew. "It was when we were in London three years ago. I answered your cell by mistake. She made me promise not to tell you. She said you'd tell her yourself when you were ready. And frankly, I could see from that one conversation that she was just like you'd always described her. I didn't want the drama, particularly when we were on vacation. Plus, if you'll remember, your mother was still around, and I had no fondness for the idea of cracking open the entire can of nuts. So I just left things as they were. Who'd it hurt?"

"Nobody, I guess." Henry shook his head and took a long sip of wine. "I just find it hard to believe she knew all these years."

"What, you think you're that unconvincing as a gay man? In those shoes?" Andrew pulled back the tablecloth to reveal Henry's brown-and-white spectators.

"I'll have you know these are the height of elegance. Cary Grant wore shoes like this." Henry held his foot up for inspection.

"I rest my case," said Andrew, raising his glass in the air.

Between the laughter and the wine, the tension of the past two days began to subside, and we were soon talking about Mama. In particular, where she'd happened to die.

"What is a muscadine anyway? I don't think we have them in Texas." Andrew was looking at me as he asked this question.

Henry spoke up before I could answer. "They're the sweetest things you ever put in your mouth. But don't ask Lila. I could never get her to eat one."

"Well, that's where you're wrong," I said. "I did eat one. Once. But it was too early in the season and the skin was too green. The thing was as bitter as gall. Sets my teeth on edge just to remember it. And I went off them for good, I'm afraid."

"Oh, you just made your mind up too soon." Henry shook his head. "I'm telling you, when they're dark purple and fat with all that sweet juice, there's nothing better in the whole world. Muscadine wine? Muscadine jelly? Man, just the best. But my favorite way to eat them is still fresh off the vine, when they're warm in the sun."

"So maybe your mother could've been going out to pick some?" Andrew looked at me quizzically.

"Well, that's the thing. You *pick* muscadines. You don't dig them up." Everyone looked at me. "I mean, she had this soup-spoon with her, and . . ."

"And . . . what?" said Andrew, taking a forkful of tiramisu off Henry's plate and ignoring his look of disapproval. "What is it you think she was doing?"

"Oh, I don't know." I didn't meet his eyes. "Probably nothing. More than likely it's just what Abigail said. She'd gotten a spoonful of ice cream or something and took it out in the garden with her. Only I checked. And there wasn't any ice cream in the freezer, and . . . well, this spoon was the one I used to plant things in that little garden I had when I was a kid. Mama knew what it was. She knew where it was. She never kept it in the house. It was always out in the shed."

"Well, I'd bet she didn't just suddenly get a hankering to plant some beans at two in the morning," said Henry.

"No." I was beginning to feel both sorry and relieved I had brought this up.

"Has either of you gone out to the arbor to see?" Andrew looked back and forth between the two of us.

"No." Henry and I spoke in unison.

"Well, hell. Why not? I say we go right now." Andrew raised his hand to call for the waiter. "Let me pay this exorbitant check, and we'll get out there."

"But it's already dark. And it might rain. And I, well . . . I'm probably just jumping to conclusions. You all surely don't want to troop way out there this time of night." I looked from one slightly flushed face to the other, not knowing myself what I really wanted to do and feeling more than a little ridiculous.

"You, my dear, are exhibiting a perfect example of passive-aggression. The southern version, which is, as we all know, the most extreme and purest form." Andrew made a face at me and pushed back his chair.

EIGHTEEN

A thin sheet of clouds stretched across the face of the full moon like a silk lampshade, casting a sterling-silver light on the back garden of Greenwoods and trapping any lingering heat of the day that might have been tempted to escape. The shadows of the poplar trees spread out over the meadow in long, dark rows, little tributaries of black waiting to be crossed on our way to the muscadine arbor. Whispering and giggling like kids, we grabbed a flashlight and a spade from the shed, unlocked the white gate in the holly hedge, and stepped through into the garden.

"Is this the right way?" Melanie stumbled a little on the wet grass.

"Oh, yeah, it's a straight shot." Henry moved to the front, flashlight in hand. "A pretty good bit to go yet, though. You should take off those shoes, Mel."

Melanie hesitated, taking a long look at her delicate sandals. She slid the strap off one ankle, and a shoe hit the ground. "Help me remember I put them under this bush," she said as she laid the shoes together beneath a hydrangea.

Far removed from their glory of old, the garden beds now held only a few tomato plants and a smattering of scarlet zinnias whose edges were ragged and chewed by the sun. We picked our way through to the lush grass that flowed like a green sea from the edge of the red clay garden path. Seeing the look on Melanie's face as her bare toes sank into the soft grass, I kicked off my shoes as well, and after a few steps Henry and Andrew followed suit. It was hard not to indulge the desire to run.

Here and there ghosts of little pathways headed off into the woods, but we avoided those and kept to the straight line that led to the arbor. Eventually the ground began a downward slope, though much less dramatic than in memory, and soon we were at the creek, its clear, cool water showcasing the algae-bearded rocks sound asleep on its bed. Clearing the creek in a jump, we climbed the slight rise and found ourselves in the meadow.

"It's been so long since I've done this," I whispered. "I mean, seriously, like thirty years or more. I used to come out here every single day when I was little."

We continued on, single file, with Henry in the lead. The woods were thicker now, their dark borders creeping in ever farther, paring our path bit by bit until it barely resembled the one I used to walk. But then, like the parting of a green curtain, they pulled themselves back, and there down the slope of a small hill, centered in what still remained of the wild meadow, sat the muscadine arbor.

The touchstones that stand in our memory rarely match up to reality. They suffer from the distortion of time, with a tendency to become bigger and grander whenever we call them to mind. Schoolrooms, once so cavernous, are when visited today much smaller than we realized. People, like hours, are shorter than we knew. But as I stood there staring down at the arbor I'd known so well as a child, I was astonished to see it was much larger than I remembered. Grotesquely overgrown, its wild branches reveling in the neglect of the past decades, it appeared almost to breathe, in and out, in the silent midnight breeze. The doorway, never obvious to the incurious visitor, was now completely obscured. I could see where my mother had broken some branches getting in. Her nighttime visit and subsequent demise now seemed more peculiar than ever.

"So. Here we are," said Henry. "Who's going in?"

"Well, I'm certainly not," said Andrew. "Not in these trousers." He pointed to his pristine tan pants, their cuffs now stippled with dew. Melanie's silence told us quite plainly she wasn't even considering the idea.

"No. I'll do it." I spoke quickly, without thinking, but realized as I did that it was supposed to be me. "Just hold the vines back, will you? I don't want to get scratched up any more than I have to."

Henry and Andrew pulled back the intertwined vines, breaking some in the process as Mama had done three nights before. "This is about as big as we can get it." Henry held an armload of green branches off to the side, revealing a three-foot-high hole. It released a fragrance of fresh earth that I remembered well. I bent down, my hands on my knees, and peered into the darkness.

I took a deep breath. "Okay. Here goes." I took the flashlight from Henry, got onto all fours, and crawled inside.

If the overall appearance of the arbor was bigger than I remembered, the interior most certainly was not. No longer could I stand up inside it. The riotous vines reached almost to the brown earth now and would soon close the arbor up completely. Wiggling myself into a sitting position, I pushed the insistent tendrils away from my face and pointed the light toward the loamy ground around me. Nothing appeared to have been disturbed. If my mother had been intending to unearth some secret here, she hadn't succeeded.

"Hand me the spade," I said.

"What did you find?" Henry asked. I could hear the nervousness in his voice.

"I haven't found anything yet, Henry. I thought I'd just dig around a bit and see what happens."

A hand stuck through the opening, and I took the red-handled spade. A botanical highway of thumb-thick roots ran just beneath the surface of the ground, snaking and twisting its way in an unbroken web that left few promising places to dig. My spade hit a root every time I stuck it in the earth. Until it didn't.

In a spot at the back of the arbor, almost to the other side where the exit was now so strangled with overgrown vines that one couldn't possibly crawl through, the spade sank into the ground with ease. Surprised, I scooted closer, wiping tiny leaves from my face as I went.

"What's going on?" Henry was bending down, trying to see through the foliage in the dark.

"Just a minute." I laid the flashlight on the ground and began to dig in earnest now, a little mound of damp brown earth growing bigger and bigger beside me. Then my spade hit something that rang like a bell in the silence.

"What was that?" Henry hissed.

"Would you just give me a minute? I'm not in the most comfortable position here, you know. It's probably just a rock or something." But somehow, deep down, I knew it wasn't a rock.

The sound of Henry's feet circling the arbor like a hound dog grew faint, replaced in my ears by a low hum of anticipation that became louder as I continued to carefully remove the dirt from whatever it was down below. I ignored his increasingly insistent demands to know what was happening until I heard him say, "That's it. I'm coming in there."

"You stay right where you are, Henry Bruce," I barked. "There's not enough room in here for me, much less for the both of us."

I picked up the flashlight and pointed it down into the hole, then dropped it with a thud, my hand over my mouth to muffle my gasp. Slowly I reached to pick it back up and shone it down into the darkness, my fingers still flat on my lips. The macabre, grinning face of a snowman stared up at me, his coal-black eyes fixed onto mine, the red and green of his scarf only slightly foxed and faded. Like a piece of creased, yellowed paper found in the pocket of an old coat, a memory began to unfold, and I could once again see Mama packaging Christmas fudge for me to take to my teacher at school. Of course. This was a Christmas tin. And by the whimsical lines of its design, it was several decades old at least.

Wiping the dirt from the snowman's face, I worked my fingers around the edge of the tin till it loosened, and carefully I lifted it out. It was about nine inches long and no more than three inches deep. I knew I should wait and open it in front of the others, but I couldn't seem to stop myself. I wiggled the top back and forth, back and forth, and the lid began to move.

"Don't you dare open that thing without me!" I jumped and turned to see Henry's face, wide-eyed and flushed, with a scratch on his cheek, sticking through a hole in the arbor, Andrew and Melanie holding back the tangled muscadine vines for him to see in.

NINETEEN

"Oh, all right. Pull those vines back a little more. I'm coming out."

Holding the snowman tin to my chest, I scrabbled across the floor of the arbor, twisted around, and crawled out on all fours. Sitting cross-legged on the damp ground, I looked up into three stunned and expectant faces.

"I cannot believe there was really something in there," said Melanie. "Do you honestly think this was what your mother was coming to get?"

"Has to be," said Andrew. "I mean, what else? Lord, I do love a mystery. Let's open that thing!"

"No." I spoke with a firmness that surprised even me. "We're not going to open it here. Not like this. Let's take it inside." I looked up at Henry and he nodded, then reached down to pull me to my feet.

No one said a word as we went back over the hill and through the meadow, each one of us deep in thought about what had just happened. As I watched their backs walking away, I knew none of them had really expected to find anything in the arbor. It had been a bit of a lark, that was all. But now that I held this mysterious tin under my arm, I was afraid my mother had been trying to find something vital before she died. Something hidden. Something secret. Something with the power to change all our lives.

When at first Henry couldn't find the keys to the garden door, we all laughed, a bit too self-consciously for any one of us to convincingly say we weren't tense. The keys were finally found in Andrew's sport-coat pocket, and we followed him inside, not looking at one another. I laid the tin on the round kitchen table and stood back.

Under the bright lights of the kitchen, the Christmas tin, so obviously of another time, looked even stranger than it had in the moonlight. The jolly snowman's face had been scraped by the claws of a muscadine root that had year by year, by the smallest of increments, removed fractions of paint from its surface, leaving him scarred as a pirate. He looked even scarier than he had in the dark. The four of us stood round the table staring down at the tin as though it were ticking.

In one quick move, I picked it up and opened it, much the way one rips off a bandage. We stared. There, inside, tied with fuzzy garden twine, was a thin stack of envelopes. The wax from the twine had drawn a brown line down the center of the one on top, and its stamp was indistinct with age. The handwriting across its face was eerily familiar, much as one's own childish hand is recognizable, but strange when one views it as an adult. I lifted the stack of letters out of the tin, surprised to see that my hand was shaking. We all sat down.

While the others watched, I slowly untied the twine. The tiny clutch of letters seemed to sigh as it loosened, each envelope separating from the others and floating down on the table. Picking one up, I looked around. Henry's face was white, no doubt a carbon copy of my own. The letter was addressed to my mother. Heart beating fast, I opened it and began to read it aloud.

October 14, 1973

Dear Geneva,

I have tried, you cannot know how hard I have tried, to change. There was a time right after Henry was born, when I thought I could put my true self into a box and shut it away for a lifetime. I now know this is not only impossible but unnatural. Charlie showed me that. I am responsible for his death. We were both living a lie that was going to get us in the end. It was only a matter of time.

I understand about Abigail. And I don't blame you. Loren gave you what you needed when I couldn't. She is a beautiful child, and you know I love her like my own. If you could see fit to let her keep on believing she's mine, I'd be grateful. She never has to know. But I'll leave that up to you. It should be your choice.

I'm not sure where I'll go now. You've made it impossible for me to ever come home, I know that. Maybe that's for the best, for all of us. I love the kids too much to ruin their lives, and let's face it, that's what the truth would do. Especially in Wesleyan. It's better to live in their memories as someone they can look up to. That's all I hope for now. It's all I have left. I pray you'll let me keep that.

I won't write to you again. Maybe one day you'll understand that I did the very best that I could. I do love you in my way, very much.

Penn

Cold adrenaline flooded my veins, and I felt as though I might faint. I didn't want to look up.

"Wait . . . what . . . what does this mean?" Henry's voice shook a little as he spoke. "Let me see that thing." He snatched the letter from my hand. "Look here. This is dated October? Of '73? Daddy died in September of that year. I mean . . . right?"

The silence in the room held too much emotion and split open with the sound of Melanie's voice, small and thin as a child's. "What does he mean about my father? Read that part again? The part where he says he's responsible for Daddy's death? What does that mean?"

Andrew spoke up, his voice steady and calm. "Okay, guys, let's all just take a breath now, shall we? There's a couple more letters here. Let's just take a look at those, okay? Henry, you want to read them?"

In a quiet voice, Henry read out the next letter. It was another one from Daddy, written in 1971, when he'd just arrived in Vietnam. From the date it was mailed, I knew he hadn't been there long. I also knew it was less than a year from the day Melanie's father, Charlie, had hung himself. The letter was fairly mundane, mainly an account of the journey and arrival at his post. It sounded nothing like a letter from husband to wife and was devoid of the emotion in the other, final, correspondence we'd just read.

The last letter had been written much later, dated 1979, and by another hand. The writing was thin and spidery, unlike our father's, but I felt I had seen it before. The address in the top left corner confirmed my hunch. This was from Uncle Audie, written a few years after he came home from that fateful cruise with Aunt Jo.

May 4th, 1979

Dear Geneva,

Is it possible we could have a talk? I know I haven't seen you in a long while, and I apologize for that. After all these years, I have had a letter. I don't think I have to tell you who it's from. I have tried to understand how you must have felt during those years. It couldn't have been easy, I know that. But I don't think I can ever forgive what you did. I'd like to hear it from you as to why, and how you've been able to live with your decision, because I can't get it out of my mind. Sometimes I think I just might go mad with the pain of it.

If you'd agree to see me, I'd be grateful. If I don't hear back from you, I will take it as a no. I've enclosed a picture I thought you might like to see. It might make things easier, or at least more clear.

Audie

The photograph inside was faded, its ghostly figures nearly erased by time. As though my eyes had the power to set them free, they rose from the slick, shiny paper in which they'd been trapped to stand before me, solid as flesh. They could not have been out of their teens, two laughing, dark-haired boys, their arms thrown across each other's shoulders in the ease of familiarity, one looking straight at the camera while the other stared at his friend with an expression that could only be labeled as love. The recognition took my breath. Charlie Barnett and Penn Bruce. Long before I was born, long before judgment, long before pain.

I stood up and walked to the window, where I could see the stunned expressions on the faces behind me reflected in the dark glass. Bits of my life seemed to have broken off from the whole, like a long-completed puzzle that's been pushed off a table. My parents had been the mirror through which I saw myself. In mere minutes their memory, once so solid and secure in my mind, had splintered into pieces I no longer recognized. There was a new creation to be made of these shards, I realized, but at the moment they seemed too sharp to gather up.

Henry got up and stood beside me, our eyes meeting in the glass. We stared at each other for a long while without speaking. Finally I said, "We need to go see Uncle Audie. We need to go now. Right this minute."

TWENTY

The memories of my uncle were muted, like an old Polaroid left out too long in the sun. Always impeccably dressed, with tortoiseshell glasses that appeared to be permanently glued to the bridge of his long, crooked nose, he seemed forever removed from the rest of us at family gatherings. Widely regarded to be the most formidable trial lawyer in town, for us he'd been too easy to overlook, his detached personality pale in comparison to that of his rather flamboyant wife. Loud and exuberant, Aunt Jo simply dominated every scene they were in so completely that none of us ever gave Uncle Audie much thought. He sat on the sidelines of my memory, serene and slightly bemused, happy, it seemed, to let her run the show. It was only when she died that we looked around and realized we'd never really known him at all.

Without Aunt Jo to guide his ship, Uncle Audie had just sailed away. He closed up the big house on Quarles Avenue and sold his share in Bruce, McKelvey and Moake only six months after she died, becoming more and more reclusive until he finally moved out as far as he could and still be on southern land. His house sat between the Carolina marshes and the Atlantic Ocean, down a long, sandy road rarely traveled by anyone save the postman who brought his few bills and the UPS man who delivered our Christmas presents, the slippers and neckties that were probably still stacked in white boxes under his bed.

Our mother never took us to visit him, and recently we'd heard from Abby that he had slipped somewhat downhill. "They say he's gone squirrelly," she'd said, in her usual descriptive way. "Don't doubt it myself, living all that far out, all by himself like that. Course, Mama always told me he was odd, so I don't know how anybody can tell he's gone off any more than he ever was. And besides, he's got to be . . . what? Eighty-something now?" I hadn't given him much thought in years, but now Uncle Audie was the only person in the world I wanted to see. It was not yet two, so if we left right away, we could be there by dawn.

Melanie was dabbing at her eyes with a handkerchief. Andrew had his hand placed over hers. The clock in the hallway could just barely be heard keeping steady rhythm to a world spinning out of control. "Henry and I are going to see Uncle Audie," I said. "You two stay here and get some sleep. We'll be back as soon as we can."

"I think I should come, too," Melanie said. Her voice sounded fragile in the night-quiet kitchen. "But I don't really want to." She started to cry in earnest now.

"You don't have to come, Melanie. You're exhausted. We all are, I know. But our uncle is the only one left that knows the answers to all this, and I have to go see him. Tonight. I promise I'll tell you everything he tells us."

"What am I going to say to my mother?" She looked up at me, confusion written all over her face.

"I don't know. Nothing right now. Just get some sleep, and we'll talk when we get back. Okay?"

Henry and I went upstairs, leaving Andrew and Melanie alone

in the kitchen. I splashed some cold water on my face, ran a brush through my hair, and changed into a clean pair of pants and a fresh shirt. When I met my own eyes in the bathroom mirror, I stared into them as though into the eyes of a stranger, nearly sick with a fearful suspicion that I hadn't known my parents at all.

WE DROVE IN silence, stopping only once to let a leathery armadillo complete his trek across the empty, moonlit road. Halfway through he turned his helmeted head to stare accusingly into our headlights, as if even he knew being out at this time of the night signaled trouble. Try as I might, I couldn't think of anything to say. The facts made apparent from the letters we'd found flew round in my head like a murder of crows, never landing long enough for me to solidly grasp their meanings.

I had lost so much the day Daddy died. I couldn't even fathom the ways I'd been changed. With each year that followed, even the faith that I'd had as a child had receded. I'd always pictured Daddy taking it with him, tucked up under his arm like a ball of light, growing dimmer and dimmer the farther away he traveled. I was still haunted by its shadow.

The moss-mantled oaks that lined the way to Uncle Audie's place laced their massive arms above us, throwing the road into the darkness of midnight. Henry drove slowly. Here and there our headlights found pairs of mirrored eyes hiding in the undergrowth of palm fronds and fern. The sand crackled like fire under our wheels.

The house appeared first as a shadow, its edges vague in the hazy dawn. It took shape the closer we came, finally revealing itself to be a rambling structure of screened porches and tall windows, serene and eccentric at once. Henry pulled the car off to the side of the drive and stopped. The barking commenced immediately as five large dogs came running, disturbed from their early-morning routine by the rarity of visitors. They jumped and bounced beneath our car windows like bubbling broth, but despite their vociferous greeting we could tell that they probably meant us no harm, so we opened the doors and got out.

The slap of a screen door brought our attention back toward the house, where on the weathered porch steps stood an old man, his milky eyes peering out over tortoiseshell glasses in an effort to determine exactly who or what had entered his domain at such an early hour. Gray-haired, lanky, and lean, his long-sleeved cotton shirt buttoned up to the neck, he stood with one hand on the porch rail, the other holding a china cup. The canine greeting committee immediately left us and rushed toward the old man, who patted the head of the largest one absent-mindedly.

"Uncle Audie?" Henry spoke softly, and stepped forward into a bright brushstroke of sunlight. "That you?"

He stared hard at Henry, confusion turning slowly to astonishment. Then his face split into a wide grin. "Why, I never," he said. "Penn, it is just like you to show up here without telling me you were coming. I can't believe it. I knew you'd come one day. I told Dot you would. And who's this you've brought with you?"

Henry froze where he stood, looking back for my help. I moved forward. "Uncle Audie? It's me, Lila. We've just come to see you and bring you back to Wesleyan with us. . . . If . . . you would like to come up for a visit." I stopped short of mentioning Mama's death.

"Lila? Well, I swan. Look at you. Why, you're as tall as your daddy. Tell you what, I can't see any reason to go all the way up to Wesleyan when everybody's here now. No, I can't. Y'all come on in." Still grinning, he turned to go back up the steps, the five dogs following behind him, meek as kittens. "I was just starting to make breakfast. I'll throw some more bacon in the skillet."

As we climbed the four steps to the back door, Henry bent and whispered in my ear, "He thinks I'm Daddy, doesn't he?"

"Looks like it."

He gave a heavy sigh and motioned for me to go ahead of him as he held open the screen door.

The intoxicating smell of a real southern breakfast washed over us—coffee, bacon, butter, sorghum syrup—all mingling with the sweet bouquet broadcast from a vase of blowsy garden roses sitting in the middle of a small round table in the corner of the room. The kitchen was spotless. Five Jadeite bowls full of clean water were lined up against one wall, and each dog assumed his place in front of one to noisily take a drink.

"Now, Penn," Audie began. "What'll it be? I remember how you like your breakfast. Eggs over easy, right? And Miss Lila, would you like some pancakes?"

"Oh, please don't go to any trouble on our account, Uncle Audie," I said.

"Trouble? Child, it's not any trouble. I've been waiting for this visit for so long, it's the least I can do. You-all take a seat now and tell me what you've been up to this whole time."

"Actually, Uncle Audie, I was wondering if I could freshen up a bit. We haven't slept much, and that car ride was long. Could I maybe use your bathroom?"

"Sure. It's just through that door and down the hall." He pointed to his right. "Second door on the left." Henry threw me a withering look, which I ignored, as I went out of the room. I hated to abandon him but wanted the chance to collect myself a bit.

Beyond the kitchen was a sitting room with tall, bare windows that showcased a clear view of the greenly waving marsh. A well-loved chair sat with its back to the rest of the furniture, a comfortable perch for enjoying the view. Books lined the walls in horizontal rows of color, their spines dusted and neat, and a large brown jug sat on a low rattan table holding a cluster of glossy magnolia leaves that reflected the early-morning sun like velvet-lined mirrors. The entire room was much like Uncle Audie appeared himself: well cared for and tidy.

I found the bathroom to be much the same, with towels hanging so evenly they could have been measured and little pink soaps in a bowl on the sink. Coming back out into the hallway, I stuck my head into what was obviously the old man's bedroom and found the high double bed neatly made, a Bible on the night table, a pair of leather slippers by the door.

On the long polished dresser sat two framed photographs. One was of a laughing Aunt Jo taken on a snowy day in the mountains when she was young, and the other was of my father. It was a picture I had never seen, and the resemblance to Henry was stunning. Daddy must have been in his thirties. He was sitting on a low stone wall, his hair as black as a crow's wing in the sunshine, and he was smiling up at the photographer with an unabashed joy. The land behind him was foreign to my eyes, certainly unlike anything in the vicinity of Wesleyan, and it fell away sharply to a faint silver line of sea. Behind him I could make out a corrugation of mountains rising up like the shadows of unimaginable things. I turned the frame over and gently pried my thumbnail under the metal stays that held the photo in place. Carefully I removed the cardboard backing. The underside of the picture bore the handwritten words "Scotland, 1969."

A canine chorus jolted me back to the present. I heard the screen door slam, and the sound of booming laughter rose up above the barking. I considered, only briefly, sticking the photograph into my pocket but thought better of it and secured it once again in its frame, placing it back exactly where I'd found it. Uncle Audie's confusion was somewhat clearer to me now. If he'd spent the last decades seeing that photograph every single day, it was no wonder he thought Henry might just be his long-lost brother. They looked practically identical.

TWENTY-ONE

She was a large woman, and I heard her before I saw her. Her voice was loud, pitched at the booming volume of one whose hearing has begun to go. I stepped into the kitchen and was gathered up into a bone-bending hug before I could speak. It was one of those hugs that your body resists at first but which, the longer it lasts, awakens a comfort inside you normally left behind in childhood. My shoulders relaxed for the first time in days, maybe months.

Her smile was wide and impossible not to return. Tight gray-blue curls covered her head like flowers on a swim cap. It was a hairstyle destined for extinction but one still popular, even expected, among a certain stratum of elderly white women in this part of the South, those who held weekly standing appointments at local hair salons proficient in its creation. She was dressed in a navy plaid skirt and a crisp white blouse, and a string of pearls shone at her neck. It was almost the uniform of a schoolgirl, but despite her age and ample frame the look seemed to suit her perfectly. I liked her instantly.

"Well, my goodness!" she bellowed, one arm still clamped tight around my shoulders. "I feel like I know you already. I'm very happy to meet you both."

Henry's bewildered expression almost made me want to laugh out loud. He was, like myself, exhausted and confused, waiting for the next chapter in this strange journey we were on, totally out of his depth. This woman was clearly not someone he, nor I, had expected. Uncle Audie was setting the table, a grin on his face. It was clear he had no intention of introducing us. No doubt he thought we knew each other already.

"I'm Lila. And this is my brother, Henry. Audie is our uncle. We're his brother's kids."

"Oh, yes, hon. I know who you are. Your uncle has told me about you. He's very proud of you both. And I've spoken to your mother, once. My name is Dorothy. Dorothy Wright. Audie here calls me Dot. He's the only person alive who's ever called me that, but considering he started out calling me Dotty, I see it as an improvement. No woman my age wants to be labeled 'dotty,' I can tell you." She pulled out a chair and put a heavy hand on my shoulder to sit me down. "Now then, let's all eat some of this grand-looking breakfast Audie's cooked up for us, and later on I'll take you two down and show you the view from the dock. It's wonderful out there." She said these words in a thick Carolina accent that managed to shove a few extra syllables into the word "wonderful." Her blue eyes shone with a fierce intelligence, and when she gave me a wink, I understood we would be able to speak more freely on that post-breakfast walk. So I did as I was told, sat down and picked up my fork.

Whenever I chanced to make them, Franklin would always tell me southern biscuits were essentially the equivalent of schoolroom paste. "Same ingredients, think about it," he'd say through a mouthful of hot biscuit slathered in butter and jelly. He'd been right, of course. As I looked over the spread laid out before me, I knew that fewer and fewer people set a breakfast table like this anymore and might just live longer as a result, though Uncle Audie wasn't doing too badly at all.

Pancakes, dripping in butter. Cathead biscuits, a moniker earned for their shape and size. Muscadine jelly. Sorghum syrup. Golden, creamy eggs. A platter full of crispy, curly bacon. Hot coffee. Grits, with more butter. Four tiny glasses, decorated with red tulips, held the only fruit on the table—a child-size portion of fresh-squeezed orange juice, one for each of us.

Over the next half hour, between first and second helpings, my uncle shared the biographies of his five dogs, often prompted by Dot. "Tell them about Scooter there, Audie. Remember that time he hopped in my car for a nap and I didn't find him until I got home? He slept the whole way there. I just kept him at my house that night. A little pajama party for the both of us. Fed him cheese and carrots. He loved it."

Uncle Audie's grin never faded. Henry ate the last biscuit, and Dot began to stack the plates. I stood up to help clear the table, but Audie held out his hand. "No. Now, you were going to let Dot show you around the place. Let me do this. I've got a system. And I get to listen to my program while I work. It's just about to come on."

Dot smiled at my questioning look. "It's the garden show. *Pickles and Pines.* Comes on the radio every morning at seven. Audie never misses it, even though he doesn't grow anything except tomatoes these days. But they're good tomatoes, aren't they, Audie? Come on now, he's serious, he doesn't want any help, and I think we three need a little get-to-know-you talk, don't you?"

TWENTY-TWO

The dewy air outside hung wetly on every palm and palmetto. The sand stuck to the soles of our shoes like damp salt. Henry and I followed along in Dot's great plaid wake till we emerged from the sticky cloud of pine trees into the unfiltered glare of the sun. It shone on the emerald-green marsh grass like unmeltable ice, almost painful to the eye. Trails of dark water snaked through the marsh, old roadways well traveled by sea trout and alligator. They call this land the Low Country, a region that sits serenely in the palm of the earth's hand, so close to the sea that grasses and salt water intertwine like tapestry threads.

"This is really a beautiful place," I said, my voice no louder than a whisper.

"Yes, nowhere on earth quite like it," Dot said. "I was born here, and I tell you, when I'm away from this place, it feels like my heart won't beat properly. These marshes get into your bloodstream. I wouldn't live anywhere else. I kind of think your uncle feels the same way now."

"He must," I said. "He's been down here a long, long time."

"I suppose it's you we have to thank for how well he's doing," Henry said. I felt the shame of irresponsibility creeping up my spine and could hear the same in his voice. "We should have checked on him more often."

"No, now, don't you two beat yourselves up about that. He's been just fine. It's only recently that his memory's been a bit sketchy. Like I said, I've talked to your mother about it. And I know you two live a good ways off. Of course, Audie would have a fit if he knew I'd ever called her. The only time I've seen that man lose his temper was when I mentioned her name. And if you'll forgive my candor, your mother wasn't a great deal of help. She didn't seem to want to talk about him at all herself." The old lady stood facing the water, but I could see her eyes blazing in profile.

Henry was staring out to the blue-green line where the marsh melted into the sky. Almost to himself he whispered, "He thinks I'm his brother. He thinks I'm Daddy."

"Yes, I noticed that." Dot spoke softly and motioned to a swath of thick grass that carpeted this side of the house. "Come on, there's some shade over here." We followed her to a cluster of lawn chairs that were grouped beneath the spreading limbs of a gargantuan live oak. Slightly nauseous from the rich breakfast I was so unused to eating, I sat down gratefully with my back to the kitchen window beyond which my uncle was washing the dishes. A salt-flavored breeze brushed my cheek.

"So," said Dot as she eased herself into her chair. "Tell me what's happened."

Henry rubbed his forehead with the palm of his hand. "Our mother's died," he said. "A few days ago. And we found some letters that she'd kept hidden for years. Well, buried. Literally. In the backyard, if you can believe that."

Dot nodded, saying nothing.

"And . . . well, the thing is . . . we think . . . we think now that maybe. . . ." Henry looked over to me for help.

"We think there's a real possibility our father might still be alive." I looked at Dot, hungry for her reaction.

"I see." She nodded calmly, her eyes still on the sparkling marsh. "Well, I always knew it was something."

"What do you mean?"

She sighed, folding her hands in her lap. "You see, I got to know Audie at church. My late husband was the priest at St. Anne's Episcopal, about three miles from here, in Seabrook. I still help out there on Sundays. It's a small church, and we do a lunch every week after the service. I'm often in the church kitchen instead of a pew. Well, a few years ago, I started noticing this dignified older man hanging around outside under the trees during services. I'd watch him from the kitchen window most Sundays. He never went in, just sat on one of the benches in the shade, listening to the music. He'd usually leave before the sermon started.

"So one Sunday I went out and joined him. Took him a cup of coffee. We sat there together, the two of us, just listening, and when the music was over, he thanked me and walked off. But he was back the next Sunday, and the next. We finally got to talking. He was articulate and wise, and we had far-reaching conversations on a wide variety of things. But I could never persuade him to go inside that church.

"Now, there's two reasons people behave like that. Either they're afraid of people, which Audie certainly didn't seem to be, or they're afraid of God. And if they like church music as much as Audie did but still won't go inside a church, then I figure they think God's mad at them about something. Or maybe they're a little mad at him.

"I think that's the case with your uncle, kids. He's had a secret. He's never told me what it is, and I've been knowing him for over five years. Do either of you have a clue? Was he close with your father?"

Together Henry and I outlined the plot of our childhood. The old woman listened silently, her broad brow furrowed with concern. When we got to the part about Daddy and Charlie, we faltered.

"I mean, we don't know for certain that it's true. But from the letters and the picture we found, it seems to be. . . ." Henry's voice trailed off into nothing.

Dot sat up straighter in her chair. "Oh, my good Lord. So much hurt in the world, and for so many years. All over who people love." She shook her head. "It's not easy now, I'm sure you know. But back then it was impossible. You can imagine. And your daddy a Baptist preacher? Well, the whole town would have blown up over that, I suspect. It would have been a lot easier for your mother to become the respected widow than the preacher's wife whose husband left her for another man, believe you me."

"Yes, that's probably true. But to tell everybody, to tell her own children, that he was *dead*? And to hold to that secret till the day she died? How could she do that?" I could hear the edge in my voice, sharp and accusatory.

"People do some crazy things, Lila. I've lived long enough to know they can justify almost anything. And religious people seem to be the best at this. See, it's a dangerous thing to let people grow up believing they have all the answers. They close their minds and stop questioning. Nothing's a mystery anymore. Nobody's right but them. They begin to confuse God's will with their own. I've seen people manage to convince themselves all sorts of lies are true, especially if they're trying to explain away something they can't, or won't, understand.

"Your mother probably saw it as an easy way out at first. Then the lie got so big she couldn't have escaped it if she'd tried. Like I said, she probably began to believe it herself. I know you may not be able to understand, or forgive her. And you certainly don't have to. At least not today. But there will come a time when you'll need to try. For yourself, not for her. And of course you'll be doing it for that old man in the kitchen. He knows about all this. I'm sure he does. And it's been eating his insides out for years."

"Do you think he knows where Daddy is? We found this letter he wrote to our mother, and it says that Daddy wrote him, at least once. We want to find him if we can." Henry's voice shook a little.

"Of course you do." Dot heaved herself up from the low-slung chair. "The only thing to do is to go and talk to him about it. His memory is a bit unreliable about some things, but I think he's been wanting to tell this story for a long, long time. So we have to try. For him, and for you." She began to head back down the sandy trail that bordered the marsh at a drum major's pace, Henry and I at her heels.

"So you take care of him? I mean, his house is as neat as a pin," I said, trying to keep up.

"Oh, well, after I found out his name and where he lived, I just popped in with some fresh okra from the garden one day. I could tell he needed a bit of help around the house, so I got some of the ladies to take turns with me. There's about six of us, I guess, and we alternate weeks. We just stop in and do whatever needs to be done. We don't make a big thing of it, just keep up a conversation while we do a bit of cleaning. We get him to help, and we're done in an hour or so. Audie just thinks it was a visit with a nosy woman." She laughed. "There's always a way to get old men to do what you need them to do. Just takes a bit of practice." I heard Henry cough.

"And the cooking?" I asked. "Do you all take care of that, too?"

"We just stop in with meals or groceries a couple of times a week." Dot held back a large palmetto frond to let us pass through. "We tell him we made too much, or bought too much, and it'd help us out if he'd take some. As you can see, he still knows his way around a kitchen pretty well, so we just make sure there's plenty in the pantry for him to cook." She marched up the stairs, opened the screened door, and we reentered the cool kitchen, now completely spotless once again. The house was quiet save for the whirl of a ceiling fan in the sitting room beyond.

Dot strode straight through from the kitchen, and we followed. The dogs were napping, scattered around the room like furry throw rugs. Audie sat with his back to us, facing the marshes in his big leather chair.

"Audie, these kids need to talk to you." She turned a chair around and pulled it up alongside him. "They need to know about their daddy. About Penn. I think if you try, you can remember what I'm talking about. Can't you?"

It took Audie a long minute before he turned his head to look at her. From where I stood, I could see that his eyes were bright with unshed tears. He stared at Dot. She nodded at him and patted his knee. "It's time, Audie," she said. "Past time." Slowly, with effort, he stood and turned to face us. In his hands was a long blue tackle box, its edges rusted orange with dampness and age. The old man lowered himself onto the sofa that faced the cold fireplace and held the box in his lap. Henry and I sat down in the chairs across from him, waiting.

"You're Henry, aren't you? And you're Lila." His voice was low and measured.

We nodded.

"So she's told you? I wondered if she ever would." His voice was a whisper, and he sat up straight, almost formally. Both gnarled hands gripped the handle of the tackle box like it was the back of a pew. "I never knew what to do, you see. All the time we were growing up, I never knew what to do. How to help him. It was all my fault he married your mama. She was crazy about him, and I thought it would fix things. Make him forget about Charlie. And for a while it did. At least I thought it did. Both he and Charlie got married, to nice girls. He had you two, and everything seemed all right. He was the preacher, and everybody loved him.

"Then I stopped hearing from him regularly. Your sister was born, and he didn't even call to let me know. Then, not long after that, Charlie went and hung himself, and I knew. And then Penn joined up, just left everything and went over to that war. He called me before he left. Said he wanted to do something brave for a change, something that would get his mind off himself. Said he couldn't stay with Geneva, not anymore. I knew he meant after what had happened to Charlie. I thought maybe this would help him, he felt so strongly about it. But he never wrote me. And then Geneva called and said he'd been killed."

Audie's voice broke, and he stared down at the box in his lap. With one bony finger, he lifted the latch and opened it. "It was seven years later that I got this letter. I thought it was some kind of joke at first, couldn't quite believe what I was seeing. But then I knew Penn's handwriting as well as I knew my own. He told me what Geneva had done, told everybody he'd died over there. Nobody even questioned her. She just said she'd gotten a telegram, and that was that. She handed Reverend Weaver an urn and said Penn was in it, and of course nobody batted an eye. At the funeral Jo told me she thought Geneva was in shock, that that was why she wasn't crying or anything. It was the shock that made her look so angry. I figured she was right. I know better now."

The room was so quiet that even the dogs seemed to be listening. Audie reached into the blue box and took out a letter. It was thin, the writing on the envelope nearly rubbed into transparency from years of being read, again and again. With one cleansing sigh, he handed it over to Henry.

"Please don't feel hard at me," he said, looking up at us for the first time. "I just never knew what to do. By the time I got this, Jo had gone and I couldn't talk to her about it. She might have told me to tell you kids the whole story. But I just couldn't. I didn't know how. Your mother wouldn't talk to me about it at all. I wrote her, but she never wrote back." He took off his glasses and rubbed his eyes. "I just didn't know what to do."

Henry and I stared down at the letter. Once again, as it had done in the kitchen in Wesleyan, the handwriting across the front of the envelope tickled a sleeping part of my brain, awaking a forgotten memory that swam before my eyes like smoke. I saw images of childhood birthday cards, school permission slips, letters to summer camps when I was homesick. There in front of me was the same old way he looped his *r*'s, the way the *L* of my first name continued on to underline the rest of the word. There before me was my father, almost tangible and all too alive.

The letter was well over thirty years old. A foreign stamp, ghostly with age, still clung to the upper right corner. The postmark was almost invisible, but we could just make out a familiar word.

"He went home," whispered Henry. "He went home to Scotland. Just like he used to tell us he would when we were little."

It happened without warning, like lightning traveling from the tips of my toes up through my body with the rapidity of a thought. A crop of icy sweat broke across my forehead, and the walls of the room turned liquid. I could feel the blood draining from my face.

"Excuse me just a minute. I'm so sorry." I got up and left the room, trying my best to appear as though nothing was wrong.

The cool air of the kitchen turned to steam the moment I stepped outside, making me feel even sicker. I hurried into the pine thicket at the side of the house, put my hands on my knees, and threw up.

A hand pulled my hair back from my face. My head still bent toward the pine-needled earth, I saw a pair of oxfords and the hem of a navy plaid skirt. "Here, now. Take this." Dorothy Wright handed me an icy washcloth, which I placed over my eyes, holding it tightly across them till kaleidoscopic patterns of orange and white sparkled inside my lids like summer fireworks. The old woman stood there quietly beside me, and when I finally looked up at her, I could see the genuine concern written on her round face.

"Lila, I am so sorry you and your brother have to go through all this. Sorry for your father and his brother, too."

The tears came then. Like a great wave that rose up and broke across the flimsy dunes of pride and composure behind which I'd been sheltering, they flooded my brain, erasing all thought, all control; they ran like a river whose source was the loss of my father, a

river that coursed through the shadows of my childhood, past the
loss of my husband, and alongside a mother I'd never really known.
I wept the tears of shock, of betrayal, of anger. I wept because my
life had been built on lies, and I didn't know if I had what it was
going to take to rebuild a new one on the foundation I'd just been
given. And I wept on the shoulder of a woman I barely knew.

She patted my head and gave my shoulders a squeeze. "Let's get
you something cold to drink and you'll feel better." I stood looking
at her, my arms hanging like limp rags at my sides. She smiled.
"Lord, for such a pretty girl, you do look awful," she said, and I
laughed weakly. "Don't worry, now," she continued. "You'll get
through this. This is just one of life's curveballs. We all get them if
we live long enough. Trust me. I've had a few of my own."

She steered me out into the sunshine and over to the back
porch stairs. I climbed them slowly, feeling like I'd aged a decade
in the last twenty-four hours. Inside the cool kitchen once more,
I sat down dumbly at the table and watched Dot as she put ice in
a glass, opened a green bottle of Coca-Cola, and poured it slowly
in, the chocolate-colored liquid foaming up to the rim of the glass
but never quite spilling over. It was like I'd never seen anyone do
this before. She set it down in front of me. "Sip it. Don't gulp," she
said.

I could hear the low voices of Henry and Audie still talking
from the other room, but my curiosity had been defeated by too
much information. I sat with both feet flat on the floor, sipping my
Coke like a three-year-old.

"You need some sleep," said Dot.

My laugh sounded fake and unfamiliar, like laughter from
someone in an old black-and-white movie who'd never quite
learned how to act. "Sleep?" My voice came out higher than I
could remember ever hearing it. "I've got to go home and host a
party for my dead mother who didn't want a funeral. And I've got
to figure out how to tell my baby sister, who, incidentally, has kind
of gone nuts since yesterday, that her dead father might just be

alive. And oh, by the way, it looks like he's not her real father either. We don't know who that man might be." I stared into Dot's
open face with defiance. *Just try to tell me everything's going to be all
right,* I thought. *Just try it.*

"Well, you still need some sleep." She smiled at me, her eyes
soft. "And your mama might have felt too guilty to have a funeral.
Ever think about that? All those people in the pulpit saying how
wonderful she was like they always do about the dead? She knew
her secrets even if nobody else did. Don't tell me they didn't keep
her up at night. Especially if she knew she didn't have long on this
earth. But come on now, you two need to get back on the road if
you've got all that to deal with today." She left me sitting at the
kitchen table and went into the sitting room. The rumble of male
conversation came to a stop. I got up and followed her, the icy glass
held tightly in my hand.

"Audie, we need to let these kids get going. They've got some
miles ahead of them and a lot on their plates today."

My uncle looked up at me, his face lighter than it had been
when I'd last left the room. He smiled. Reaching down, he picked
up the letter and the framed photograph of Daddy I'd seen in his
bedroom and placed them both in my brother's hands. "You promise me, now?" he said.

Henry smiled back at him. "I promise," he said.

TWENTY-THREE

The way back seemed shorter than the way down. Impatience, fueled by anxiety, no longer had the power to slow the clock. All the sights had already been seen, the billboards already read. The car flew down the road unhindered by distraction of any kind.

While a dense cloud of shock and confusion had filled our car on the trip over, rendering us both mute with disbelief, words now tumbled over and on top of each other like wrecked train cars. The impossible had really happened. The unbelievable was true.

From Henry's long conversation with Audie, we'd pieced together a whole new version of our parents' lives, one we'd been wholly ignorant of and one that ended with the numbing conclusion that our father, once dead, could now, very possibly, still be alive. Like Mama's so long ago, his first death had never happened at all. I'd been so sure of both at the time. And I'd been so wrong.

Audie had given us the letter along with the photograph and in doing so had secured from Henry the promise to try to find his brother. With no more to go on than a thirty-year-old postmark, Henry knew it was a shallow promise to make, but he did it anyway. The letter had been brief. The faded date on the postmark corresponded with Uncle Audie's fiftieth birthday, but if that milestone had prompted Daddy to finally let his big brother know he was still alive, he didn't say. It seemed apparent our father never expected to be found. He'd made his love for the three of us clear, and a major part of his decision. *"I'd ruin their lives if I came back. It's better this way, Audie. You know it is."*

Dot had walked us out to the car as we left. She radiated the sort of kindness and strength that reminded me of Maureen, and like Maureen she almost made me feel I could tackle whatever I had to in order to navigate this shiny new map of my life. I wished we could take her with us.

She'd pushed a torn piece of yellow paper into my hand. On it was scrawled her name and number in purple ink. "You call me if you need to talk or if you think I can help in any way. Okay? And remember, you are not responsible for any of this. None of it is your fault, and you couldn't have done anything to change it. And it doesn't matter one bit what anybody says or thinks if and when they find out. So you two hang tight to each other, you hear?" We'd nodded and hugged her back, feeling as if we'd known her much longer than the few short hours that were in fact the reality. Her sweet reassurances had covered us both in confidence and determination for miles, but they were now beginning to dissolve, leaving us feeling unmoored.

"What on earth are we going to tell Abby?" I wondered aloud, staring out the window as another clay field surrounding yet another two-pump gas station flew past in a swirl of bleached color.

"Not one damn thing," Henry shot back. "Not with her behaving the way she is right now. I mean, what? We're supposed to tell her that the man she thought was her father really wasn't. And oh, yeah, that man didn't die when we were told he did and might actually still be alive? Come on, Lila. When we find out the whole story—*if* we find Daddy—then we'll tell her. *Maybe* then we'll tell her."

"You're right. I know you are. It just seems weird, us knowing all this and her not. You know?"

"I'm telling you, better weird than crazy." Henry stared at the road ahead, drumming his fingers on the steering wheel, the miles clicking by. After about ten minutes, he asked, "He'd have to be blond, wouldn't he? This Loren guy. I mean, Abigail's white as cotton. Always has been."

"Not necessarily. Mama was blond too, remember?"

"Well, yeah, but Mama was a dyed blonde for most of her life. And she was never as fair as Abby. You know, Lila, it makes sense now if you think about it. I could never figure out why Mama sort of held you and me at arm's length. I used to think it was because she suspected I wasn't the man she hoped I would be, if you know what I mean. But then she treated you pretty much the same way, didn't she? And she doted on Abby like a spaniel. Now I think it was because we reminded her of Daddy."

"That's funny. That's what Melanie told me just yesterday morning. I can't believe she was right. Of course, she could never have known all the reasons. God, what Melanie must be going through right now. She always thought Mama missed Daddy so much and we looked so much like him that we were a constant reminder of his death." After a few minutes, I added, "Boy, was she way off."

"Hmmmm. Instead we were a constant reminder of his life. Poor Daddy, he never realized how much I took after him." Henry gave a short, wry laugh. "We would have had a lot to discuss."

"Dot was right, though. Things were so different then."

"Not all that much different, sis. I expect the very same thing would have happened today. What did Dot say? 'The whole town would have blown up over it'? You're telling me that wouldn't happen now if the pastor of Second Avenue Baptist Church came out as gay? Please. Even poor Audie, who's been living with this for decades, couldn't bring himself to say the word 'gay.' He just said 'different.' Lord, what a mess."

I looked over at Henry, seeing him, as I could never help but do, as the little brother I'd been assigned to protect in lieu of my father. "Henry?"

"Hmmmm?"

"Why do you think it was easier for you? You've never seemed uncomfortable being who you are. Ever. Why didn't you have the kind of emotional issues I've read about?"

Henry gave a great whooping laugh and stared over at me. "Who's saying I didn't? Let's just say that I survived as well as I did because of you, you idiot! I always knew you were in my corner, no matter what. That's all it takes sometimes. Just one person who really knows you and who's got your back. But I mean, think about it, I still left town the very minute I could. I knew I'd never be able to be myself in Wesleyan. I was smart enough to know that even if some people in our circles might have suspected I was gay, they would only accept me if they didn't know for *sure*. I'd seen it happen in the church before. You remember Drew? That tall guy with the big Adam's apple who used to sing in the choir? Well, tell me he wasn't gay. And the sweetest guy that ever walked. Everybody loved him at Second Avenue.

"I watched him become the pet of all the old women in the church. They shared recipes with him, took his fashion advice, just thought he was 'the sweetest thing.' He was their gay best friend. The men always kept him at a distance, while the women adored him. But I knew if they knew who he really was, they'd be morally obliged to let him know that he was not one of them. And that, quite frankly, he was on the road to hell. You don't think I watched? And learned?

"There are men like that in every church, the ones known as 'confirmed bachelors' or some other equally acceptable euphemism. You do know that Drew died, back in the late eighties? Of AIDS. When he found out he had it, he told everybody he'd taken a new job out in California and he moved away. Died out there, in the home of some friends the people in Wesleyan knew nothing about.

"So I left, and I've had a really happy life. But don't be too hasty to declare me free of . . . what'd you call it, 'emotional issues'? I've got plenty of those, I can assure you. As do you, I'd bet my shoes on it. And you know how I love these shoes."

His voice betrayed not even the slightest hint of resentment as he told me all this, and not for the first time I marveled at his ability to forgive. In that moment the love I felt for my brother draped itself around me like an angel's wings. No matter what knots we were going to have to unravel in this journey we were on, I would be forever grateful he was traveling with me.

"About what you told Audie back there. Are you really going to try to find Daddy?" I asked.

"Yes. *We* are," replied Henry, with a tone in his voice that told me not to argue, not that I had any intention of doing so.

TWENTY-FOUR

When we got back to Wesleyan, it was shimmering in the glare of a cloudless afternoon. The town wore the heat like a fever, each sharp line and corner of the city square softened and blurred, as if any minute the old buildings might just melt into great torrid puddles of mortared lava and noisily flow away. Released for lunch, people who worked at the courthouse stood waiting for the light to change, men in suits pulling at their damp shirt collars, women in heels twisting their hair up off their necks in all manner of haphazard styles. Pigeons sat still in the fountain, their feathers iridescent in the water and the sun.

We turned off the square onto a wide street where gray Gothic shadows from the spires of St. Patrick's lay across the road like medieval etchings. Mama always told us there weren't many Catholics in Wesleyan, in spite of this redbrick cathedral that rose up like a vision amid the sea of maple trees here on Meridian Street, but then when it came to religion, we Baptists tended to trust only our own kind. The Catholics, with their rituals and rites, were a mystery best left ignored.

Of course, the truth was there were a lot of Catholics in our town (which was the reason Tillman Elementary School always served fish on Fridays), and as I grew older, I secretly envied them their easily mapped-out pathways to God. A lifelong Catholic himself, Franklin tried his best to disabuse me of the notion, but I still saw the liturgy, the confession, the rosary beads (not to mention the Virgin Mary, who was so kind, so understanding, and so unlike the God of Leviticus we Baptists revered even as we cherry-picked which of his orders to follow) as a much clearer route to heaven than the one we'd been handed over at Second Avenue.

Looking back, I remember hearing Daddy talk a lot about grace from the pulpit when I was a little girl, but the concept seemed alien once he left us. The preachers we got after him seemed much more focused on sin. Guilt is the bit in the mouth of a Baptist congregation, and when the reins are handled by an expert, he can lead them right off the pages of the Holy Scriptures and into thickets of judgment and fear, and these men were experts. Society had pivoted onto an unrecognizable road by the seventies, and Second Avenue Baptist Church responded by digging in, refusing to budge an inch from what was familiar, believing that the only way to be truly safe from the clutches of an evolving society was to retreat to a place where we alone owned the monopoly on truth. Faith might very well have built the structure we sheltered beneath, but that structure couldn't stand without the unwavering certainty that our blueprint was the only true one. Opening our minds to other points of view could very well deliver a kick to the foundation, a kick that could lead to a crack that could splinter and spread till it brought the whole thing crashing down on our heads. It didn't take having a gay brother for me to realize the importance of keeping the lion's share of yourself out of the hands of the holy, lest they reshape it into something that could eat you alive. For the memory of my father, I played along as best as I could for as long as I could, but by the time I left for college, I'd already left the church.

Now as we drove through the articulated shadows of St. Patrick's, I could feel a germinal anger in the center of my soul. As much as I tried to ignore it, a rope had been snapped when I saw Daddy's handwriting on the back of that letter—postmarked a month from the day that I thought he'd died—and it was sending waves of hurt straight toward me. They were as unavoidable as time, and I knew that when they hit, I might very well be knocked off my feet. My father had been my touchstone; everything began and ended with him. The very notion that he'd actually played a leading role in such a severe alteration of our lives, that he'd willingly left us, felt like ice settling in the marrow of my bones. Gripping the seat beneath me, I took a deep breath. I had to get ready to face what was waiting for me in the coming hours, and anger was not my friend right now, however tempting his whispers might be.

We pulled into the shade of the cedars at the side of the house, both of us grateful to find no other cars in the drive. "I guess it's too early for the hordes," said Henry. "I'm heading straight up for a shower and a nap."

I followed him along the breezeway, my feet feeling like lead, and gasped when he opened the door. Flowers festooned every surface of the kitchen, from counter to table and back again. A monstrous fern squatted in the sink, its emerald tendrils spilling over the rim as though it had a mind to escape. A dragon wing begonia perched atop the refrigerator like a great pink, slightly embarrassed, gargoyle. Beribboned baskets of white lilies lined the way to the garden door, each one looking for all the world like it had been dropped there by Little Bo-Peep herself. Taken individually, each of these arrangements might possibly be considered pleasing, but crowded all together they made the bright, open kitchen feel like a claustrophobic closetful of perfume-drenched, loudmouthed old ladies. I wanted out of there, fast.

"No wonder people often request no flowers." Henry kicked a basket of lilies out of his way as he headed for the stairs. "Leave it to our mother to request *only* flowers. God, what are we going to do with these things?"

"Don't use all the hot water, Henry," I called after him. "I'm right behind you."

I squeezed past a thigh-high schefflera and opened the refrigerator door to grab a cold sparkling water. Heading back into the sitting room, I glanced through the window and saw the back of Andrew's blond head peeking up over a garden chair. I opened the door and went outside.

Andrew was seated at the table, fanning himself with this week's *New Yorker* and chewing on the end of a pencil. The morning paper was spread out before him, and a half-completed crossword stared up expectantly. He jumped when he heard the door shut behind me.

"Whooo. Oh, Lila! It's you. You two just get back?" With a slippered foot, he pushed a chair out and motioned for me to sit. "What's a three-letter word for regret?" He looked over to me as I sat with a thud. He laid his pencil down on the table. "I hope I can say this, Lila, what with us being family and all, but, girl, you look dreadful. Was it that awful?"

"I threw up." This was more reportage than confession. I regarded him, sitting there impeccable in his crisp linen shirt, the fresh smell of soap and hot coffee still clinging to the silk paisley threads of his tie, and I began to laugh. Once I started, I couldn't stop. My laughter squeezed tears from my tired eyes and wrenched up a stitch in my side, but still I continued. Andrew, for whom laughter was as contagious as pox, joined in helplessly.

"Stop it! Stop it, Lila. What in God's name is so funny? Tell me!"

I took a couple of deep breaths and wiped my eyes on the hem of my wrinkled shirt. "Nothing, Andrew. Absolutely nothing is funny. That's why I'm laughing."

"Oh, Lord. It's one of those laughs where you're going to start crying hysterically any minute, isn't it? Well, please don't, darling. I want to know what's happened, and you have to tell me. I don't know if you remember, but we've got a few people dropping by here in a little while, and we've all got to have our game faces on. I need to hear every last thing about your adventure, and I need to hear about it now while there's still time. And then, trust me, you've got to go and get cleaned up. Now, here, drink some of this."

Andrew picked up the cold bottle of water I'd brought out with me and placed it in my hands. I took a long drink and let my eyes wander around the garden. I blinked. The transformation laid out before me was stunning.

The six lichen-covered stone urns stood sentry around the swimming pool, each now holding a white hydrangea in bountiful bloom. Like garlands of giant pearls, white paper lanterns were draped along every low-hanging tree limb, and here and there sat small round tables in white linen dress with baskets of ivory roses in the center of each. The effect seemed to erase at least ten degrees from the thermometer. Tears stung my eyes once more.

"Pretty great, huh?" Andrew said, noticing the look of surprise on my face. "Those lanterns are strung up on little white Christmas lights. And we hid tiny speakers in the bushes so we can have music playing. Don't thank me, it was all Melanie's idea. Did you know she has a warehouse full of this kind of stuff? For clients' parties and magazine shoots, that sort of thing. She took me there early this morning, and I swear I felt like Howard Carter at Tut's tomb when she opened the door. I saw 'wonderful things'! I never had so much fun. We tried to arrange all those blasted flowers in there as best we could. In the end we brought most of them out here. Took for goddamned ever, and there's still some more to move. But as long as it doesn't come one of those big-assed thunderstorms, we'll be all right. I'd hate to have to try and haul all this stuff inside. You know, now that I think about it, I did work my butt off in this god-awful heat, so yes, you can thank me if you want."

"You two are amazing. You really are. It looks beautiful, Andrew. I don't know what to say."

"Oh, please." He held up a hand. "I told you I had fun. We both did. Plus, it helped to keep Melanie's mind off all the strangeness we found in that scary old snowman tin."

"Did she talk about it at all?"

"Not a peep. And *I* didn't bring it up. But the more I've thought about it, it seems pretty clear to me that your two daddies were, shall we say, 'like-minded'? Did you see your uncle? Am I right?"

"Yes, I believe you are." I rested my face on my hand and looked up at him. "And that's not the half of it." I proceeded to tell Andrew all we'd learned on our trip to the coast, including the very real possibility that our father could be, as hard as it was to believe, still alive and living in Scotland. "So," I said, finally finishing the story, "like I said. I threw up."

"Well, I just bet you did." He had listened without moving a muscle, his stillness only occasionally punctuated by a whispered "Holy crap" or "Are you kidding me?" Now Andrew placed his hand over mine and stared down at the treetops reflected in the motionless blue waters of the pool.

"How is Henry taking all this?" The concern in his voice was evident.

"Pretty well, I think. You know Henry, he rolls with things better than anybody. But we're both still fairly numb. It does help explain our mother a bit, though. Why she was always different with us than she was with Abigail, I mean."

"Any clues about Abigail's father? This 'Loren' fellow?"

"Not one. Audie told Henry he didn't remember the name, and neither one of us has ever heard of him."

"So what are we telling Abby?" Andrew raised his eyebrows and looked over at me.

"Not a thing. Not today anyway. Which reminds me, has she been by yet?"

"Haven't seen hide nor red hair of her. She hasn't called either. All the more reason for you to get ready. She could show up here any minute, along with a bunch of other people I do not know and should not be expected to entertain on my own."

He stood up, and I followed suit. He put both hands on my shoulders and turned me toward the back door. "Go on now, sister. Time's a-wastin'."

With my hand on the doorknob I called back to him over my shoulder, "It's 'rue,' by the way."

"What?"

"The word you're looking for in the crossword. The three-letter word for regret. It's 'rue.'"

"Ah. So it is."

TWENTY-FIVE

Seeing my bed still neatly made from yesterday was a sharp reminder of my total lack of sleep and one that my face reinforced when I stared into the bathroom mirror. Any makeup that I'd put on the day before had been erased by the hours, leaving me looking melted and waxen. The semicircles of darkness beneath my eyes seemed almost comical, like clown paint, and in full rebellion against any attempt at dignity my hair was half up and half down, adding an unsettling air of insanity to my already unfortunate appearance. I had never looked worse.

I barely resisted the notion of stuffing the clothes I was wearing into the extravagantly flowered trash can that sat beneath the pedestal sink and instead kicked them behind the bathroom door as I shed them piece by piece. These clothes were tainted now, I knew.

There are perhaps a handful of occasions in life momentous enough to thread their memories through the very warp and weft of the garment you were wearing when they happened. Some of these clothes we keep. We hold them close, like textile talismans, unfolding them on rainy afternoons when we're alone, running our aging fingers along their weave, remembering. Wedding dresses, of course. That certain first date. The little hand-knitted jacket the baby wore on her very first journey home. A green cashmere sweater is still neatly folded in the back of my wardrobe in Maine, the same green sweater I was wearing when Franklin asked me to marry him. I've held it to my heart more than once.

I'd worn a dark blue dress to my father's funeral. It had a Peter Pan collar of lace, and I loved it. But as soon as everybody was gone that afternoon, I took it off, balled it up, and threw it into the garbage can out back. It had seen the worst day of my life and was forever changed for me. In the same way, I knew now I'd always associate the white linen shirt and beige cotton trousers I'd just kicked behind the bathroom door with this day in July when I found out about Daddy, and at the moment I didn't know if this memory was one I'd want to preserve quite so tangibly. I wasn't yet sure how the story would end.

After a hot shower, I lay naked across the unwrinkled bed, letting the slow circular breeze from the ceiling fan dry my wet hair. Within seconds I was lulled into a sleep I could ill afford. I fell like a stone into baroque dreams of dark forests where unopened letters fluttered down through the trees like snow. I ran to catch them, but the gnarled green fingers of menacing vines chased me away, ever multiplying, leaf by leaf, as they clutched at my ankles, threatening to wrap themselves round my legs with paralyzing strength if I stopped running even for a moment. And all the while the letters kept falling around me, forever just out of my reach. I awoke frantic and freezing, my heart beating like a rabbit. Looking at the bedside clock, I knew I'd been asleep for two hours. It felt much longer.

Deciding what to wear was easier than it should have been. The sleeveless black dress I'd brought down with me was my only choice. The length hit right in that sweet spot of the knee, and best of all, the thing was comfortable. I took a little time with my

makeup in an effort to ease the dark circles and add a creamy veneer of serenity and calm. I left my hair down.

Closing the door behind me, I turned to look down the long
hallway. It was time to do something I'd avoided for two days. My
mother's room sat at the opposite end, closest to Abigail's and as far
away from Henry's and mine as the architecture of the house would
allow. I couldn't remember the last time I'd been inside it alone
and headed toward the door now with reluctance, fearing a fate
like Pandora's.

Mama had slept in this room for decades, so I expected to feel
her all around me the moment I opened the door but was unprepared for her almost corporeal presence; it permeated every inch
of the room from the July issue of *Victoria* magazine lying open on
the chintz-covered chaise longue to the unmade bed. The west-
facing room was squash-casserole yellow, and in the late-afternoon
sun its glow was both unexpected and Olympian. Dust motes rode
inside clear, straight lines of light now slicing through the tall windows, and a plush wall-to-wall carpet, the color of hay, covered the
floor. The air was swollen with the combined smells of Fracas,
Bengay, and Lemon Pledge.

I stared down at the bed. My mother's pillow lay there, the in-
dentation of her head scooped out of its center. That pillow had
been privy to her thoughts, her plans, her secrets—secrets I now
knew were legion. She'd been an enigma to me the whole of my
life, and now that I knew some of her reasons, I felt as hollowed
out as that pillow. Had Dot been right? Had the lie Mama told us
eventually become something she believed herself? She'd certainly
played her part as the stoic widow for the rest of her days. Daddy's
gold-framed photograph was still sitting atop the living-room
mantel for all to see.

But I'd always known there was another person behind the face
she wore for others. The first time I'd seen it was the afternoon I
was told that Daddy had died. The principal drove me home from

school that day, something that underscored the frightening gravity of the event in a way only a child could fully appreciate. The house was too quiet when I opened the door; it seemed even the walls were in shock. Through the kitchen window, I could see Mama sitting alone in a chair by the pool, her face unreadable, her eyes dry. I remember I went out to join her. I placed my small hand over hers. Searching for something to say, I landed upon the phrase I'd heard time and again in church, certain of its power and truth. "God never gives us more than we can bear," I said in a small voice, looking to find comfort as well as give it.

"Don't tell me that nonsense!" she'd snapped, each word like a bite from an angry dog. She regained her composure almost immediately, putting an arm around my already shaking shoulders just as my best friend burst through the garden door in tears. Melanie had grabbed me in a hug, and together the three of us walked back into the house, where we were engulfed by the women of Second Avenue already assembling in the kitchen, ready to be of help in the ways they knew best.

From that day on, I was certain there was more to my mother than what she was willing to show me. For that one brief moment, I had glimpsed the other side of the mirror and never forgotten the sight. Maybe it would be different in time, but today this room did not welcome my presence. I left and shut the door.

TWENTY-SIX

When I was growing up, Jungle Gardenia was the favorite perfume of every older southern woman I knew. In the mistaken belief that they became a floating replica of that glorious flower every time they wore it, they spritzed and slathered and powder-puffed it all over themselves every chance they got, until their senses were so dulled they were blissfully unaware of the overly saccharine scent that covered them like a second skin. Once it came into contact with a dress or a jacket, this athletic aroma was impossible to eradicate. Consequently Jungle Gardenia seemed to become an intrinsic part of the women who wore it, seeping into their personalities as well as their clothing and setting them apart, for good or for ill. Even today I can tell the difference between the lovely white flower and its bottled pretender at fifty paces, so I recognized it the moment I came downstairs. It told me Abigail was back.

I found her in the library with a sweating glass of something iced balancing on the leather arm of her chair. From the hallway I watched as she stared down at her hands, laying one atop the other on her fuchsia-colored lap. The new red hair clashed shockingly with the just-purchased suit. When she reached for her glass and took a long drink, I squared my shoulders and entered the room. My sister looked up.

"Oh. It's you. I wondered where you were. It's almost four. People should be getting here by six." Her voice was calm. Too calm.

"You okay, Abby?"

"Huh? Me? Yes, I'm fine. Why?"

"Why? Well, you just seem a little . . . tired, I guess."

"Tired? Yeah, well, I didn't sleep much. What do you think about the dress?" She stood up and put the glass down on Daddy's desk, smoothing out her skirt and turning around.

"You'll be the star of the show." There was no such thing as helpful criticism now. It was too late for her to change; the best I could do was try to keep her as happy as possible. But I knew instantly I'd said the wrong thing. Wound as tightly as she'd been, one little word of kindness was all it took to split the floodgates. Abigail burst into tears.

"Abby, don't. You'll ruin your face." I put my arm around her shoulders, which only made her cry all the harder.

"I don't want to do this, Lila. I don't want all these people coming over here and us acting like we're putting on some kind of shindig and Mama just dead. It's not right. She's already been burned up, you know." She raised her tearstained face to mine. "It happened this afternoon. I asked. Wendell's supposed to bring her by any minute . . . well, her 'urn' or whatever. Can you imagine? What are we supposed to *do* with her? Stick her on the buffet table with the green beans?"

"We don't have to do anything with her, Abby. We can just put the urn in here. In the library. People won't come in here, and nobody has to know anything about it. And this isn't a shindig. This is just a gathering of people who knew Mama and want to pay their respects. Mama would've loved it, you know that. Think of it as a wake. Like they have in Ireland, you know."

"Yeah, well. We're not Irish." Abby picked up her glass and downed it. Only then did I detect the scent of whiskey underneath the heady top note of ersatz gardenias.

"Abby, you're not drinking, are you?"

"And what if I am?"

To my knowledge the last time my sister had consumed any excessive quantity of alcohol, she'd been brought home in a police car wearing nothing under the policeman's jacket but her tiny cheerleading skirt and a lei, the origin and significance of the latter being something she never could recall. It had been during the summer break from her first year at college, and I'd been the one to open the front door for my sister to stumble through. Mama, though mortified, not only had managed to keep knowledge of the event from everyone else—even Henry didn't know—but had also successfully convinced Abigail of the dire consequences should she be tempted in that direction on any future occasion. As far as I knew, Abby had not only never indulged again but was, till this very day, an ardent critic of those who did.

"I just didn't know you drank."

"Well, I don't. Not usually. But I'm shook up, okay? Can't I be shook up?"

Her voice was rising, and I could feel the eggshells beneath my feet beginning to crack. I kept my tone gentle. "Of course you can. I just want you to take care of yourself, Abby, that's all. You've had a shock. You're grieving."

"Well, this sure doesn't feel like grief. This feels like I'm mad. I'm just really mad, Lila. And I don't even know why." She began walking the length of the room, back and forth. "I mean, it was a shock and all that Mama didn't want a funeral, but the main thing is she didn't tell me. She was so sick, and she didn't tell me. I thought we were best friends, you know? That's what she always told everybody: 'I don't know what I'd do without my Abigail. She's my best friend.'" At this, Abby transformed her voice into a remarkable imitation of our mother's primly imperious drawl.

"She always had to know every little detail of my life, and I always told her, 'cause that's what best friends do, right? Well, it wasn't a friendship, not really, Lila. She knew she was *dying* and she didn't even tell me, and I realized, when you get right down to it, I was just a character in her story. That's what I've always been. To you and Henry, to everybody, all my life. Just a character in somebody else's story. My story just went a little ways, then stopped. I always thought it was going to be so good, and then it just stopped. And you know what else? It stopped the day Mama made me give up Jackson. He didn't fit into *her* story, so she just yanked him out of mine."

I didn't know what to say. I reached for her, but she stepped back. "I can't do this now, Lila," she said. I watched her walk across the room and pull a bottle of whiskey from her large black purse. She poured some into her glass, downed it in one go, then slammed the glass on the desk and spun around to leave. "Let's get this show on the road," she said, and left the room, wobbling ever so slightly atop her four-inch heels.

I sat down like I'd been pushed. Running my fingers through my hair, I tried to collate all my concerns in order of priority. At the top of the list was obviously my need to get through this evening with myself and everyone else basically intact. The rest . . . well, I couldn't worry about that right now. I'd just have to worry about that tomorrow. I rested my head on the back of the tall-backed chair and closed my eyes.

TWENTY-SEVEN

The sounds ringing out from the kitchen entered my brain as though from a long distance away. The opening and closing of cabinet doors, the clink of silverware against china, the sharp clack of heels on hardwood floors. In my solitary perch in the library, responsibility gave me a pointed poke in the ribs, and I sat up straight. The clock on the mantelpiece showed nearly six. Why hadn't anyone woken me?

I sprang up from my chair, and the room swam before me like a reflection in a wet mirror. I placed two hands on the desk to steady myself. When was the last time I'd eaten? Breakfast hadn't stayed with me long enough to count. I took a deep breath and headed for the kitchen.

The room was a kaleidoscope of women in their Sunday clothes, all moving harmoniously in an age-old domestic dance. Some were placing iced cakes on cake stands, others were emptying plastic containers of homemade food onto china platters, while still others were going to and fro transporting heavily laden trays from the house to the garden. The soundtrack was a familiar one of tinkling glass, rattling silver, and the soft companionable murmur of feminine voices. I stood in the doorway, unnoticed, and was immediately spirited back to the years when this was a common sight.

I knew all of these women, though each one had changed. The whims of time had etched every face but left their secrets hidden; it was impossible to tell if the lines around the eyes had been drawn by the cold hand of loss or the warm touch of laughter. Aging is very egalitarian in that way.

Standing over by the sink in a Thatcheresque suit of royal blue, her once-brunette hair now dyed ash blond, the more acceptable alternative to gray, was Honoria Wood, my mother's oldest friend and the lady who'd organized everything I saw going on before me. With all the pleasured focus of an artist, she was placing, one by one, a clutch of deviled eggs onto a daisy-patterned plate designed for just that purpose. I moved into the room and stood by her side. She looked over and stared into my face for longer than she might have done if she'd seen me even once in the past twenty years.

"Oh, my goodness! Lila!" Setting down the Tupperware container of eggs, she wrapped her arms around me in a motherly hug. Then, standing back with her hands on my cheeks, she searched my face. "How are you, honey? You look a little peaked. Have you eaten?" I shook my head like the child I suddenly felt I was. "No? Well, come over here and let us fix you a plate. Everybody?" The room stopped like a cakewalk. "You-all remember Lila. Just as pretty as she ever was!" She gave me a squeeze, and every woman in the room looked at me kindly. "Let's get her fixed up with a plate before we do anything else. Come on, honey. Why don't you sit in there in the dining room where it's quiet and eat you something."

Feeling a bit like a character in an old tale, I watched as a rainbow of women bustled around the room like good fairies, filling a large dinner plate with fried chicken, candied sweet potatoes, fresh

garden beans, sliced red tomatoes, and several varieties of trembling, fruit-filled Jell-O's. Mrs. Wood pushed open the door to the
dining room, a lace place mat under her arm, and gently nudged
me inside.

"Here now, you just sit. I don't want you doing anything or
talking to anybody till you eat something."

I did as I was told, taking a starched white napkin from her
hand and placing it in my lap. "Mrs. Wood, I really don't know
how to thank you for all you've done. Mama would be so touched."

She held up a hand, palm out. "Now, I do not want to hear a
word of that. You know there's nothing I'd rather be doing." She
pulled out a chair for herself, sat down, and folded her perfectly
manicured hands on the table in front of her. "It was such a shock,
Lila. For all of us. I mean, I talked to Geneva just two days before
she died, and I swear she said she was feeling just fine. Only a little
back pain that she said the doctors couldn't do anything about
anyway. Said if she could get that cleared up, she'd be fit as a fiddle.
Not one word about being sick. And poor Abigail, having to take
care of her all by herself like that. We could have helped the child
if we'd known."

"Abby didn't know herself. Mama didn't tell any of us she was
sick."

"What? Oh, good Lord. Well, that just beats all. You mean to
tell me that Abby just found her out there? Collapsed like that, and
she didn't even know she'd been sick? Bless that child's heart. No
wonder she's taking this hard. None of us have even talked to her.
Her phone's been off for two days."

"Abby's not herself right now, Mrs. Wood." I thought—selfishly,
I suppose—that laying the groundwork for the unveiling of Abigail's new look, as well as whatever behavior she chose to exhibit
this evening, might be a good idea. Better pity than outrage.

As I ate, Mrs. Wood's eyes wandered up to rest on the waving
figure of Charlotte on the wall in front of her. "Goodness, I've
always loved that painting. Closest I ever got to an art museum was

coming over here to look at it. Just beautiful. I suppose that'll be going home with you now, Lila. You being the eldest and all."

A spoonful of potato salad stuck in my throat like glue. I'd been so preoccupied with all I'd learned in the past couple of days that I'd given no thought about this house or its many roomfuls of furniture. "I, uh . . . I don't know exactly."

"Oh, well, there's plenty of time for all that. It's such a beautiful house. I don't suppose you've thought about moving back home and living here yourself?" She raised her eyebrows at me. "I know your mama always wondered why you didn't. It gets awfully cold up there in Maine, doesn't it?"

First reactions are always telling, and mine in the face of this question spoke volumes. An involuntary, and I hoped invisible, shudder came over me like a rush of cold water. I put down my fork. "No, ma'am. That's not something I think I'll do. I've been away far too long to come back now."

Honoria Wood, who apparently hadn't noticed anything, placed her hands flat on the polished dining table and stood up. "Yes, well, I figured. You've got a whole new life up there, I know. I saw that magazine article about you. We were all so proud. Yes, Maine's your home now, I guess. Well, like I said there's plenty of time to work all this kind of stuff out. And you're lucky—you've got Henry and Abigail to help you. You finish that plate, now. I'll leave you alone. We'll see you outside when you're ready." She left the room with one last look at the Wyeth.

I took a sip of tea and let my eyes wander over the room. The sheer accumulation of treasures in here alone was remarkable. Sets of exquisite china, delicate as flower petals and passed down through generations, silver fish forks, crystal goblets, candlesticks and vases of formidable value, and all totally unneeded by me. My cabinets in Maine fairly groaned with this exact sort of familial fruit that had once hung from the branches of Franklin's family tree, beautiful things I hardly ever used. No, this should all go to Abigail. I was sure that Henry, whose cottage in Rhode Island was chockablock with his own highly personal collections as well as those of Andrew, would agree.

Sitting there in the fading light finishing my dinner, I heard Henry's footsteps on the stairs. He paused in the hall. "Pssst," I whispered. He stuck his head around the corner. "Oh, there you are," he said. "I hoped I'd find you before I had to make an entrance. Hey, that looks good. Where'd you find all that?"

I tilted my head toward the door. "In there. The ladies are getting everything set up, and there's plenty if you'd like a plate."

He heaved a theatrical sigh. "I'm not sure it's worth it. They'll be all over me like ants on sugar."

I laughed. "Yep. That's the price you'll have to pay. You just shouldn't be so doggone cute."

Henry pulled out the chair Mrs. Wood had just vacated and grabbed a fat biscuit from my plate. I saw his eyes drift up to Charlotte, and my own followed, turning slightly in my chair to look at the familiar painting. "Honoria Wood was just asking me what we were planning to do with all this stuff. I haven't even thought about it. I don't need anything, and I doubt you do either. Do you think Abby would want to . . . I don't know, move in here or something? Of course, she might just want to sell it all. I'd hate to sell the painting, but it would bring a lot, I know, so the three of us will have to decide together. Maybe Abby would rather have the money. I just don't know."

Reaching behind me for my iced tea, I saw Henry staring at me, the look on his face a mixture of surprise, amusement, and concern. "What?" I asked.

"It's not real. You do know that, Lila."

"What's not real?" I stared back at him in complete confusion.

"The painting. It's not a real Wyeth. It's just a copy. A really good one, but a copy nonetheless."

I wheeled around to face the painting. "No. That's not right. You're wrong. I remember when we got it, remember the morning we unpacked it. We inherited it from Uncle what's-his-name, you know. Rufus somebody. You're too young to remember, probably. But I do. Mama told me. 'It's a genuine Wyeth,' she said. "'N. C. Wyeth.' I remember, Henry."

"No, honey. It's not. Like I said, it's a copy. An excellent copy."

"What makes you so sure?" Frustration was rising inside me, mixing with my indistinct anger and sharpening my words to a biting edge. I felt an overwhelming need to defend this friend of a painting against the slander being leveled at her by my obviously deluded baby brother.

"Now, don't go getting pissed at me. I thought for sure you knew. You forget, I'm an art-history major. I've known since my sophomore year. See, look here." He got up and walked around the table to stand directly in front of the painting. "See how that *N* is written? The way it slants a little to the left? And the way the whole signature looks a bit fancy? Well, Wyeth's signature was nothing like that. It looked like rudimentary printing. This isn't even close, almost like the artist wanted everyone to know he'd done a copy." He leaned in till he was nose to nose with the canvas. "Art students are famous for this kind of thing. Trying your hand at a famous artist's work is very instructional." Standing up, he turned back to me. "And this is a fabulous copy. Hey, now . . . don't get so upset. It's just a painting."

Tears were running down my carefully made-up face, and I wanted to throttle Henry within an inch of his life. "It's not just a painting! Not to me it isn't. God, isn't there anything in our lives that's true?" I stood up and left the room with Henry's bewildered stare following me as I went.

TWENTY-EIGHT

People were starting to arrive. There were car doors slamming and voices in the hall. I stood by the window in the quiet retreat of the library, my clenched fist holding aside the tartan wool curtain in a way that left me invisible, and watched as one by one, couple by couple, guests began entering the back garden. These were familiar faces but owners of names I couldn't recall. They were extras in the movie of my life—a cameo here, a walk-on there—people who'd populated the scenes of my childhood but who'd lacked the dramatic flair to be remembered. I saw them greet each other, saw the hugs and the handshakes, and felt as removed from the scene as an audience member in the cheap seats. Moreover, I didn't welcome the sight of any of them. As Abigail had said, this was not grief, this was anger, and it was roiling like lava in the pit of my stomach.

My life was no longer recognizable to me, the immutable facts of my own biography now seeming as flimsy as a wish. My father hadn't died when I was a child. No, my father had been in love with my best friend's father. My sister's father was someone I'd never even heard of before yesterday. Like darkness itself, all the lies I'd been told seemed now to unite to cast a weighty shadow over one of the things I loved best: the painting of Charlotte.

Henry was right. It shouldn't bother me so much, particularly in light of everything else I'd found out in the past twenty-four hours. But it did bother me. A lot. I'd seen that painting—so rare and so valuable—as a benevolent guardian in my life, a silent witness to my joys and griefs, a symbol of everything good. But Charlotte had known the secrets all along. She'd known it had all been a lie. She'd been a lie herself.

My personal history was like the beach sand on which Charlotte's feet had stood—unstable, unsupported, and susceptible to erosion in the first strong wave of reality. Faith was wrestling fact, and when they were done, I feared I would lose the one thing I'd always counted on: the unsullied memory of my father. The man who'd held me high on his shoulders so I could see the floats in the Fourth of July parade, who'd dried my tears when I'd skinned my knee and taught me how to whistle, the father with the booming laugh and warm bear hugs whom I'd trusted to keep the monsters away—already that man was dissolving like the misty edges of a dream. In his place a dark shape was forming, the image of a father I'd never known at all, a man who on a long-ago September day had chosen to leave me for good. I understood now that it's possible to be living a lie even if you're not the one who told it.

I wanted to leave, to go back upstairs, pack my bag, and head for the airport without a backward glance. My life in Maine, so peaceful and complete, now seemed very far away, and I missed it. What did I owe anyone here? I'd called up this reception for a mother who'd told me when I was eight years old that my father was dead when he wasn't and for a sister who'd just told me she didn't even want to be here. A torrent of resentment was flooding my senses, its hot waters washing away every good intention.

The garden was filling up now. Through the window I could see Henry greeting people, affable and gregarious as the captain of a cruise ship. I could hear music playing. Frank Sinatra. Tony Bennett. The door creaked open behind me, and I turned just as Andrew's blond head poked around.

"There you are. God, I thought you'd fled the scene." He held up both hands in mock surrender. "Hey, it wasn't me! I didn't do it, whatever it is you're mad about. I'm on your side, remember?"

"Let's go," I said. "Let's get this damn thing over with." I let the curtain fall.

Andrew followed at my heels, and we headed for the side door to the garden. "We thought we'd play music from when your mama was young," he said. "Seemed a better idea than Henry's collection of Blondie records." He held the door open for me, and I stepped outside. The fairy lights freckled the grass with tiny shadows, and the white paper lanterns illuminated the garden like dozens of miniature moons. I crossed the lawn and took my place beside Henry, one hand gripping the arm of Andrew's pink linen sport coat. One thing I knew for certain: there weren't going to be any lies told tonight.

Smiling as I was raised to do, I introduced Andrew to everyone who came through the receiving line. "And this is Henry's partner, Andrew Gant. Andrew's an artist, and they've lived up in Rhode Island for about fifteen years now." I was watchful as a cat, ready to pounce if I saw the slightest sign of judgment or discomfort. Henry finally leaned in to whisper in my ear, "Tone it down a little there, sis. We're not running for office or anything. You don't have to sell us to anybody, you know."

I turned to look at Henry, and he winked. Holding his gaze, I took a deep breath and felt my defensiveness slacken, its grip further loosening when Andrew stuck his head around Henry and made a face. I grinned in spite of myself. If I'd been afraid of an impolite reception to them as a couple, those fears were proving unfounded; in fact, everyone appeared gracious and kind. It was true that Dr. Peters's timidly pretty wife, Marjorie, didn't really look up to meet anyone's eye, but as Andrew observed when she'd moved along, it could have just been the enormous weight of the hideous brooch pinned to her dress making it difficult for her to lift her head.

About a third of the guests had come through the line when I saw a flash of fuchsia cross the garden. Abigail. She was teetering dangerously, her stiletto heels skewering into the grass with every step she took. I could feel the eyes of the crowd follow her as she made her way over and hear the sizzle of whispers when she reached our side. There was now a distinct whiff of whiskey mingled with the Jungle Gardenia, a scented concoction that was as revealing as a confession. I grabbed her hand and squeezed it as I said a silent prayer that she'd behave, but it took only seconds to know my prayer had gone unheard. She leaped on the next person in the receiving line like a terrier on a chipmunk.

"Miss Hester! Oh. My. *God!* Look at you! You remember Miss Hester, Lila. You, too, Henry." Abby put her arm around each of us, grinning. There was lipstick on her teeth. "She taught all three of us in second grade, didn't you?"

To an eight-year-old, Miss Hester had been a totemic figure of authority, but she now appeared strangely dwindled down, as though the weighty hands of time had placed themselves on her shoulders and pushed. Standing before us today was a rather gnomic, rotund lady in a heavy black suit, her upper lip sweating in protest of both the humidity and her unseasonable choice of clothing. Miss Hester flinched at the loudness of Abigail's voice, obviously neither keen on nor accustomed to calling attention to herself.

"Do you know . . ." Abby leaned toward Miss Hester in a conspiratorial fashion, looking side to side as she did so, "that none of us knew our mother was sick?" She stood up straight and grinned. "That's right. Not a one of us knew! Mama didn't tell us one thing. Guess she didn't want to spoil the surprise, did she? And goddamn it, was I surprised!" She let out a whoop of sarcastic laughter. "I found her, did they tell you that? Turns out the joke was on me! Well, I guess we should all be grateful it wasn't cancer, shouldn't we? I mean, she could've been like poor old Miss Lockwood. Remember her, Lila? Henry? Remember when she got all sick with lung cancer and that wiener dog of hers . . . what was that dog's name? Squirt, that was it—yeah, Squirt! And Squirt wouldn't have a thing to do with her? Left the house and went to live with the neighbors. Wouldn't put a paw through Old Lady Lockwood's door till she died. Lord knows, old Squirt would've been smarter than me. He'd have seen all this coming, I bet you anything."

"Abby, I really don't think—"

"Miss Hester. Miss *Hester*!" Abigail looked at the embarrassed elderly woman as though seeing her for the first time. "Yeah, Lord, I used to be scared of you! You were *mean*, you know that? You yelled at me all the fuckin' time!" Abby threw back her head and laughed. I saw the color drain from the faces of both Henry and my second-grade teacher. Andrew let out a choking cough.

"Abby!" I took her arm.

"What? Ow! Don't pinch me like that! What's the matter with you?" She was shouting properly now. "You always said she was mean. You did, too, Henry. Don't go acting all high and mighty with me. You think you got your picture in some fancy magazine and now you're all better than me, don't you? Well, guess what? You're not!" She swatted my hand away and grinned down at Miss Hester as though the woman was in on a joke that no one found funny.

"I'm so sorry, Miss Hester." I leaned forward to speak in the old lady's ear. "Abigail's been taking all this pretty hard." Miss Hester nodded and gave Abby a sidelong glance.

"What are you whispering about? If you're gonna talk about *me*, speak up! I want to hear. Hell, I want *everybody* to hear!" Abigail waved her arms expansively.

I turned to my brother. "Henry, get her out of here. Now!"

Henry took one of Abby's arms while Andrew took the other,

and together they frog-marched her across the garden and through the throng of gawking guests who parted like Red Sea waves to let them pass. All the while Abigail's blue cloudburst of profanity continued unabated, its top notes ebbing into nothingness when the back door finally slammed behind her.

The crowd turned as one in my direction; the faces wore expressions that ranged from pity and shock all the way out to the shoals of anger and fear. Most inappropriately, I felt a wave of laughter breaking somewhere in the vicinity of my stomach and directed all my energy toward stemming it as fast as I could. Just then I heard a chuckle from somewhere over by the pool and turned to see a large man in a tan suit seated at one of the white tables.

Someone turned the music up, and the insouciant strains of "Come Fly with Me" filled the air. People slowly began talking again, turning their attention elsewhere but no doubt filing away the scene they'd just witnessed for future, fervent discussion. I looked over to see Melanie standing by the speakers, nodded at her gratefully, and turned back to the man seated by the pool. There was a tracing of another face still visible beneath the one I saw now, and the longer I looked at him, the clearer it became.

TWENTY-NINE

The last time I'd seen Jackson Woolf had been through the window of my sister's bedroom. I'd been home for a visit and had spent that Friday afternoon helping Abigail get ready for her high-school prom. She'd been too excited to put her lipstick on straight. I'd watched Jackson come up the walk and knock on the front door, watched as he nervously ran his fingers through his hair and fiddled with the orchid corsage he held in his hand. I'd grinned when they both came back out and got into his car to leave. Like most first loves, theirs was undeniable, their smiles so bright, so genuine that I was warmed by the peripheral rays of their light where I stood. By the time of my next visit, Jackson Woolf was no more, and some essential sparkle that had shone in my sister's eyes was never to be seen there again.

Now here he sat, looking at me with a quizzical, almost amused expression on his face. I pulled out the chair across from him and sat down. "Jackson Woolf. It's been a long time."

"Yes, ma'am, it has. It sure has." He stared at the door through which my brother had just ushered Abigail. "I was afraid this would happen to her. Gotta confess, I didn't even recognize her at first. It was the voice that told me it was her."

"Well, you probably would've known her better a couple of days ago. The red hair is new. Brand-new. And the demeanor is, too, I can tell you. I'm sorry you had to see her behave that way, Jackson. She's just not been herself since this happened."

"Hey, don't apologize. Not to me. I'm of the opinion she should have started misbehaving a whole lot sooner. Maybe if she'd ever been able to step out of line a little bit, she'd be a lot happier now. But better late than never, I guess." He took a drink of bright pink punch, then looked me in the eyes. "You know, I wanted to marry her, I really did. And I flatter myself that I could have made her happy. Happier than she appears to have been at least. But your mother . . ."

"Yes. I know. Mama was a hard woman to go up against. Abby couldn't do it. I'm sorry, Jackson. Sorry for both of you. Though I gather you've done really well up in Memphis."

"Oh, yeah. I've made a packet of money. Got a couple of real decent boys. One's up at Vanderbilt, wants to be in the music business. Don't know what's going to happen to him, exactly, but you never can tell. The other one's off in Costa Rica working on building a hospital for kids. He's taking a year off before he goes to college. Says he wants to be a doctor. We'll see. I'm just happy they're doing what they want to do. My business is always there if they want to take it over someday, but selling sporting goods is not the most exciting work on the planet, so I'd just as soon they do what they like."

"That's very wise."

"Well, I learned early it's best to follow your heart. Learned the hard way, too. See, like Abby, I ended up marrying somebody who was perfect for me on paper. Same education, same politics, same religion. Our parents wholeheartedly approved. And you know what? We were flat-out miserable. For twenty years. So last summer when James, that's our younger boy, got on that plane to Costa Rica, I turned to Alice and said, 'So now what?' And she told me exactly what I wanted to hear. We divorced three months later. Crazy that it took three months. We would've gone to an office at the airport right then and there and signed some papers and been done with it if we could have. We're still friends, which is good. She's living out in Santa Fe now, teaching yoga. She sent me a picture of her and her new boyfriend last month."

"And you?"

"Me? Oh, well. I've not bought my ticket to the dating circus just yet. Been doing some traveling. Seeing all those parts of the world I've always read about and seeing my own country from other perspectives while I'm at it. That's an eye-opener, I can tell you. Turns out we're not the only country that thinks we're the best in the world. Everybody else thinks *they* are."

I laughed a real laugh for the first time all day. "Yes, I know what you mean."

"When I got Abby's note about this thing, whatever it is . . . a wake, I guess?" He drew out an envelope and turned it over in his hands. I recognized my sister's handwriting. "Well, I couldn't be-lieve it. I hadn't heard from your sister since that last time I pulled out of this driveway when she gave me back my ring. Lord knows she was always in the back of my mind. But I never dreamed I'd see her again. I walked around with the invitation in my hand for two hours. But then I just threw a bag in the car and left. And here I am."

"Has Abigail seen you?"

"No. I've just been sitting over here watching everything. Don't think anybody's recognized who I am. Not that they would. I didn't know too many of these people when I lived here. I do want to see Abby, though. But I think right now might not be the best time. You agree?"

"Lord yes. I do agree." I knew if she was sober, my sister would cringe with embarrassment at the thought that Jackson Woolf had witnessed her performance. "Is there any way you could come back tomorrow? After she's had a decent night's sleep and something to eat, I'm sure she'll be so thrilled to see you, Jackson."

"You think?"

"I know."

There were footsteps on the concrete behind us, and I turned to see Henry reach across to shake Jackson's hand. "Jackson, it's good of you to come. I'm sorry Abby's a little unwell at the moment, or she'd be down to see you."

"How is she?" I asked, and seeing the look on Henry's face, added, "It's all right. Jackson witnessed the whole thing. I've explained that she's not dealing with this as well as we'd hoped."

"Well, that's an understatement." Henry pulled out a chair and sat down with a groan. "I knew we were in for trouble when I saw her come out the door in that baboon-butt-red dress. And where'd she get that scotch? Abby's never taken a drink in her life as far as I know. There's a half-empty bottle of Glenmorangie up in her room. That's the real stuff."

"I know." I shook my head. "I have no idea where she got it, Henry. I guess she bought it herself." I saw a worried look on Jackson's face. "Come on, let's go get you something to eat. There's so much food here we'll never eat it all." I reached across the small table and took his hand. Together we walked across the lawn toward the buffet.

The poplar trees at the edge of the wood had swallowed the last of the sun. I noticed now that these were starting to sway gently in a wind that, though refreshing, was beginning to cause a bit of chaos. White paper napkins were blowing off the tables like dandelion seeds, and Mrs. Wood was making a valiant effort to secure the tablecloths that had begun to flap like flags, threatening disastrous ends for the filled goblets lined above. It was impossible to tell if the skies were darkened by the arrival of night or if a thunderstorm was brewing.

"Looks like the weatherman might have been right for a change," Jackson said, staring into the black velvet sky.

"Really? I hadn't heard. What was the forecast?"

"Oh, you know. Same as yesterday and every other day of summer in the South. Thunderstorms, some possibly severe."

A vague concern was written on the faces of some of the guests as the wind began to grow stronger. Somewhere off in the woods, I heard the sharp crack of a pine limb breaking off in a gust. All at once, without preamble, there came a detonation of thunder like the sound of a mountain breaking in half, and a swirling curtain of rain burst out from the woods, crossing the garden as fast as a finger snap. Vacant white chairs lifted into the air like cotton balls. Above the sudden screams, I heard the sound of glass shattering and felt Jackson's hand grip my arm, steering me straight for the house.

An arsenal of hail was peppering the windows as we burst through the door to the kitchen. Andrew was ushering people inside. There were shouts of "Get into the hall!" as people tried to figure out the safest place to be. Henry appeared at my side and pushed me around the corner and into the powder room beneath the stairs just as Jackson sprinted past us into the front entry. In seconds I heard his footfalls on the hallway above and knew he was going to Abby. We shut the narrow door and waited, staring at each other in disbelief.

"What the hell?" said Henry. "I mean, what the hell else can happen?"

"Shhhh." I was listening for the sound I expected, the sound I'd heard once before. With a percussive pop, the lights went out, leaving Henry and me alone in the dark. I heard some loud crashes, some cracks, and some thuds, but no freight train seemed to be charging down the street. The wind continued to prowl around the house like an angry lion; I could hear lashings of rain whip the windows. Five minutes passed.

Then, like a loudly whistling teakettle suddenly removed from the heat, everything began to rapidly settle back down. We started to hear voices out in the hall and then, from somewhere up above, a scream.

Henry threw open the door, and we ran from the tiny powder room. There was water on the marble floor of the front hall, and the air wore an oppressive black cloak of humidity. Looking up in the darkness, I saw that the stairway was open to the rolling night sky. Where the ceiling had been, clouds now raced one another across a full moon, and a fistful of tossed stars stared down at us as we bolted up the stairs. We ran down the hallway to Abigail's room and found her huddled on the floor in Jackson's arms, shivering and strangely quiet, starlight shining on her scarlet hair.

THIRTY

We made the news the next day. Camera crews filled the driveway to film the damage, and Mama got a televised obituary to boot. A tornado at a wake was newsworthy, so naturally the general angle of the story was the tragic timing and our perceived bad luck. But privately I pondered darker causes, like judgment and retribution. Mere luck seemed far too random for our family just now.

They said it hadn't been a tornado, only something called "wind shear," but Andrew refused to believe it. "If it walks like a duck," he said with a hint of sarcasm as he taped off the door to the living room. "Besides, what's the damn difference? The roof's gone either way."

One half of the roof was indeed missing, its shingles and sheathing gone with the wind, leaving the bedrooms on that end of the house open to the trees and soggy. Curtains still hung at the windows, fitfully dancing in straight-line breezes that blew in from a blue sky above. We'd spent the rest of the night moving what we could to the safety of drier rooms while the wool of the rain-soaked rugs squished unpleasantly beneath our bare feet.

At first light Jackson had bundled Abigail into his car and driven her back to her place on Rumson Road. He was still with her when Dr. Peters called at nine to tell us he'd stopped by to see her. I answered the phone in the kitchen.

"She worried me last night, Lila. I don't mind saying so. She wasn't herself, and Lord knows that load of whiskey she had didn't help matters any. I've given her something to help her sleep, but what she needs is a good long rest. She doesn't need to go back to that house while it's all torn up like it is either. And she doesn't need to be by herself. Can you think of anybody she could stay with for a while? We may need to talk about some therapy or medication for her later, but right this minute she just needs to get away from here." I told him I'd work out something for my sister as soon as I could, hung up the phone, and placed my head in my hands.

Melanie slipped into the room and sat down beside me. Without lifting my head, I asked, "Do you feel as bad as I do?"

"Probably not." Her voice sounded weary, and I raised my eyes to hers. I hadn't had a chance to talk to her since Henry and I had returned from our uncle's.

"Melanie, we need to talk about all this. Do you want to do it now?"

She rubbed the back of her neck and sighed. There was a pine needle still stuck in her hair from the storm, and I reached over to remove it. She smiled and turned toward the window, the morning light glowing in her blue eyes. When she finally spoke, she kept her gaze on the trees outside.

"You know, when somebody you love kills themselves, the first thing they tell you is it isn't your fault. I know this because Mother sent me to see a psychologist the week after Dad died. I never told you because I was ashamed. That's the way it is with suicide. Everybody feels ashamed. So they tell you you weren't to blame, but the mere fact that they lead off with that seems to indicate that maybe you should feel you were. Was it something I said? Or something I did? Or didn't say, or didn't do? At the very least, shouldn't I have seen it coming? But like I've told you, there was never a reason, never a clue. Not until now." She got up and went to stand by the window, resting her forehead against the glass.

"You don't have to tell me the details. I could see from his face in that photograph, the one in your uncle's letter. There's not a picture I have of my dad where he's grinning like that. But I don't want to know all about it. Not now. If I know, I'll have to decide whether or not to tell Mother, and I don't want to be in that position. I remember what it was like for her when he died. I can't reopen that wound, not like this. She doesn't deserve it."

She turned around to look at me. "I'm not as brave as you are, Lila. I never have been. Don't argue, you know it's true." She smiled, the same smile I remembered from childhood. "I know you say I helped pull you back together after Franklin died, and maybe I did, a little. But you want to know the truth? I never had any doubt you'd come through that time, sad as it was, even stronger than you'd been before. I'd seen you do it when your daddy died. I swear, it was almost like you grew an inch taller in the minute it took to lower that urn into the ground. You stood beside Henry at that grave site looking like those drawings of guardian angels we used to have in our Sunday-school books, all white light and golden sword, and I knew—everybody knew—that you'd make sure he was all right, no matter what. You always had more courage than you realized, Lila.

"So I know you're going to find out all you can, and if it's possible Penn's still alive, you'll find him. I have no doubt about that. And there may come a day when I'll want to know everything. If that day comes, I'll tell you. But I just don't have anyplace to put it all right now. Not with Neely about to have the baby in a few weeks."

I walked over to stand behind her, slipped my arms around her waist, and put my chin on her shoulder. "I understand," I said. "Believe me, I totally understand."

"I'll be back later this afternoon," she said. "But right now I'm going to go get me some sleep."

"Thank you for everything, Melanie." She picked up her keys off the counter, gave me a slight smile, and brushed my thanks away with a wave of her hand as she went out the back door.

Henry and Andrew were arguing upstairs, their tiredness and frustration evident in the jagged notes of their voices. The power was still off in the house, and relentlessly cheerful sunlight streamed through the open windows, innocently blind to the damage done by the storm. I knew I needed some sleep, but fresh air and sunshine seemed like things I needed much more. I had to get out of this house. Putting on my dark glasses, I made for the door.

As invaluable as ever, Melanie had been on the phone before sunrise to move her builders from their current jobs on a renovation project across town over to Greenwoods to tackle the immediate problem of our roof. Crayon-blue tarps were now being stretched across its gaping holes like architectural bandages. In testament to the storm, tree limbs were toy-tossed in the grass, and the driveway was hidden beneath a carpet of bright green pine needles. But the breeze was singing a different song. Washed clean, flower fresh, it entered my lungs like a tonic, the sort of analgesic only nature can provide. I breathed it in as deeply as I could.

At the end of the driveway next door, a peach tree had split down the middle. The creamy flesh of its trunk was now exposed to the greed of a July sun already busily drying its edges dark, like the pages of an old book. The jagged limb of a sweet gum tree now stuck out like a fracture from the sunroom of the house across the street. The air was scraped by the sound of chain saws.

All down Davenport Drive, people were out circling their houses, cataloging the damage and disorder. As I walked along, snippets of conversation jumped over the hedges to land at my feet: "What do you mean they can't come till Saturday?" . . . "See the way that limb's twisted? Don't tell me that wasn't a tornado, damn it!" . . . "The power's not supposed to be back on till when?" . . . "I guess it could have been worse."

Though this was a street that knew my footsteps well, there was much I didn't recognize. Familiar houses had either been enlarged or replaced altogether, effectively erasing all individuality in the process. No longer did a Tudor sit next to a Colonial or a Cape Cod snuggle up to a ranch. Prosaically perfect, these new homes sat side by side on perpetually green lawns, each one a carbon copy of the last. I knew without question the day we sold Greenwoods it would meet the same fate; no modern-day owner would choose to embrace its quirky old bathrooms and oddly placed nooks. What I remembered as charm would now be considered irredeemably passé, and the rooms where my memories lived would be erased from the earth with a clinical efficiency no tornado could achieve. Somehow, on this particular morning, that thought didn't bother me much.

The last of the Confederate jasmine was blooming somewhere near me. Its delicious scent, as recognizable as my own reflection, conjured up a gnawing longing to be back home on Wigeon Island. I felt none of the bravery that Melanie was so certain I possessed. Whatever battle I'd come down here to fight, Wesleyan seemed to be winning. I wanted out of here, wanted only to listen to the sea from my bedroom window, to feel the peace of the silence, to have nothing more on my mind than the way the colors danced in the soft wool beneath my fingers as I sat at my loom. I pulled out my phone to call Maureen and felt the sting of unshed tears when she answered.

"Hello?" I could hear the wind racing down through the phone and knew she was outside on the hills. In an attempt to organize my own thoughts, I told her everything: Abigail, my uncle, the scratched snowman on the Christmas tin and all the secrets he'd kept hidden for so many years. I hardly stopped for breath. To her credit she listened with only the occasional gasp. When I finally finished, I heard her sigh.

"Oh, Lila. You poor thing. I mean, I knew you weren't looking forward to going back home again, but I certainly didn't expect all this to come out. 'Come out'—great choice of words. You know what I mean. If only your father could have." She sounded embarrassed.

I laughed in spite of myself. "Daddy was a Baptist preacher, I've told you that. Telling people he was gay would have been, well . . . impossible, really. It would have been suicide."

"Turns out it kind of was."

"Yeah." I stopped to stand in the shade of an undamaged oak and gave her a wry laugh. "I'm still trying to decide if it was suicide or murder. Mama created his death and stuck by the story till she died. But of course Daddy let her do it. So I don't know who to be mad at." I rubbed my forehead. "I don't know who to blame. Or what to think." My mind felt in as much disarray as the storm-littered street on which I stood.

"Trust me, looking for someone to blame's going to get you nowhere fast. I tried that for years, and it doesn't help. Even if you find a worthy candidate, it won't make you feel any better. And you have to think your mother was getting ready to tell you about it. I mean, why else would she have been out in that arbor? Sounds to me like she was trying to make this right before she died, especially if she knew how serious her heart problem was. But what do you plan to do now?"

The sheer simplicity of her question cleaved my indecision right in two, filling me with a clarity I'd not felt since I'd been here. "I'm going to find him," I said, the conviction in my voice astonishing, even to me. "Henry and I are going to Scotland, Maureen, and if he's alive, we're going to find our father. I have got to try."

"Well, of course you do. I wouldn't expect you to do anything else."

I began pacing back and forth on the sidewalk while an almost frightening excitement was rising up through my veins. Speaking quickly, I formulated plans while Maureen made sounds of approval on the other end of the line. "Andrew has always wanted to come up to my place and paint, so he can just move in there and look after the dogs while we're gone. And Henry's got people to run the gallery whenever he's away, so that won't be a problem. I just need to figure out something to do with my sister. We don't plan to tell her anything about this until she's better, but the doctor thinks, and I'm sure he's right, that she's got to get away from here for a while, and I . . . I mean, I . . ."

All of a sudden, a smiling face framed by gray-blue curls popped into my head, and I could clearly see, stuck down into the left pocket of the wrinkled linen trousers I'd kicked behind my bathroom door, the small scrap of yellow paper with Dorothy Wright's phone number written across it in bright purple ink. In my mind's eye, I saw my uncle in his kitchen making biscuits for company, and without great effort I could imagine Abigail seated at his table, eating those biscuits with a smile on her face.

PART TWO

THIRTY-ONE

The guidebooks warned us it would rain in the Highlands. But there was no way we could possibly have comprehended the myriad Scottish variations on that one simple word. In the ten days we'd been here, we'd discovered that, far from being unwelcome, the clouds that hung low over Scotland—those clouds that misted and drizzled and poured—were actually responsible for the creation of an atmosphere that was, to Henry and me, at once romantic, mysterious, and utterly beautiful. Those rains beckoned us along mountain trails and coastal pathways, and we followed them gladly, with our hat brims pulled down low and our rain boots pulled up high.

But there was another kind of rain, a rain that seemed to burst from somewhere beyond the normal curtain of clouds, as though called forth by a minor god with time on his hands and an urgent need for amusement. It came without warning, galloping in behind great gales of wind that grabbed up fistfuls of still air and wrung them into whipping sheets of white. This kind of rain seemed to fall and rise at once. It came at you sideways; it rose up from the ground to hit you square in the face. Umbrellas were use-less, and hats were a joke. The ordinary clouds ran off to perform more elementary duties over other parts of the country whenever this type of rain came to call.

Seasoned Scots knew the signs. Looking out across a glassy sea, beneath a cheerful sunny sky, their light eyes would stare off into the middle distance and narrow with portent as they warned, "Weather's changing. I doubt you'll make that ferry tomorrow."

This particular pronouncement had just come from our inn-keeper, Ian, during afternoon tea, a deliciously civilized ritual we'd indulged in every day for a week despite the calories involved. Henry, who'd gained three pounds, slathered another spoonful of cream on his currant-filled scone and looked out across the water. "Seriously?" he said. "It's a beautiful day. Not one single cloud."

"Aye. But you're off to the islands tomorrow." Ian replaced our almost empty teapot with a full one. "Better ring the ferry tonight. See if they've changed the time. I'll get the number for you."

We stared out the spotless window at the view. A brilliantly green pasture, dotted with sheep, unfurled like a bolt of rare fabric before us, rising and falling in emerald hillocks until pulling up sharply at the edge of a cliff. Far down below was the sea, at pres-ent calm and waveless. I had never seen a sight so lovely.

To be honest, it was impossible to claim only one Scottish pan-orama as the best I had seen in a week. The whole of the High-lands was stunning. Views Americans would drive for miles to see—with picnic baskets fully stocked and cameras round their necks—were completely quotidian here. The local co-op sat on a loch where the water was as sharp and still as a new mirror, where each bordering fir tree was reflected on its surface so clearly you could look down into the dark water and spot the owls that came to roost in the branches at twilight. Laundromats lay in the shade of great mountains. The windows of the post office opened onto the sea.

After nights spent trying to decipher the faded postmark on

Uncle Audie's letter, we'd finally decided it most resembled one from the smaller islands off the northwest Scottish coast. We'd dug through what photographs we could find—there was a box under Mama's bed neither of us had known was there—but of course no photo of our father was anywhere even close to current. "Still, somebody might recognize him," Henry had said. It was an awfully long shot, we both knew, but one we felt destined to take.

In the end we decided our quick trip to see our uncle had been providential in more ways than one, for that was where Abigail was now. I'd called Dot the very hour I'd remembered I had her number in my pocket and was relieved to find that her kindness had not been a pretense. She'd explained things to Audie, and he was thrilled to welcome Abby for as long as she wanted to stay. Jackson had driven her down that very afternoon and was still staying at Uncle Audie's with her; apparently the three of them were getting along famously. Abigail was cooking as much as Audie would let her, and he and Jackson were out in the boat every day. Dot told me she'd never seen him so happy. We didn't tell our sister about our plans. She just thought Henry and Andrew were having an extended vacation with me in Maine, a not-so-white lie I'd successfully maintained through several lengthy phone calls already.

For a week the three of us had sat with Maureen around my dining-room table after dinner to plan our journey, Henry being the one most delighted at the prospect of traveling to Scotland. "Finally. I can go to Barbour and buy anything I want with no fear of looking pretentious." Andrew had set up a makeshift studio in Franklin's old office and declared that the light in that room was "stupendous." And Maureen assured me I wouldn't be missed in the few weeks I planned to be gone. "Think of all the ideas you'll get over there! It's the land of wool and weaving. I'll expect fabulous new designs from you this fall. Take your sketch pad."

Maureen had been right, as usual. The article in *Town & Country* had indeed raised the profile of our little company significantly. Orders were flying in. We would need lots of new designs, I reasoned, thereby assuaging any guilt I might have felt about leaving again so soon. Besides, Maureen had now turned her eye onto Andrew, and I had no doubt both his paintings and his photo would be above the fold on the *New York Times* Sunday Arts page before we got back. She was already trying to talk him into a retrospective of his work he swore he had no time to do.

Everything was packed and in order the night before we left, but I still lay in my bed with a knot in my stomach, flipping and flopping, turning over my pillow, trying to quiet my mind. Sleep was refusing to come. In final admission of defeat, I threw back the sheet and padded over to the fat armchair that sat beside the open window. Desmond the sheepdog heaved himself up from his bed and staggered, half asleep, to curl up on my feet.

From far beneath the tops of the fir trees that framed my view, I could hear the cadenced sighs of the ocean as it lapped back and forth across the rocks. The soft glow from a thin blond eyelash of a moon washed the room, and from its spot on the wall across from me Franklin's portrait seemed illuminated from somewhere deep within. The desire to touch his hand, hear his voice, rest my head on his chest as we dozed in our bed—it was almost like pain. I longed to examine my thoughts with Franklin, to hear his calm voice as he assured me all would be well. Instead I sat by myself, fighting feelings I neither welcomed nor controlled.

Unlike Henry, who seemed to view this journey as an adventure both unique and fated, I was queasy just thinking about it. I didn't mention my feelings to him; voicing them would make dealing with them imperative, and I just wasn't ready for that yet. Working out all the details for the trip kept my worries at bay during the daytime, but they increasingly troubled my sleep. Maureen had been right, I knew, when she'd told me not to look for someone to blame. But my father had left without a word. He'd never tried to contact us in all the years he'd been gone. How was I supposed to forgive him for that? If there was the remotest possibility

I might look into his eyes again, I knew it would be his job to explain himself to me.

Of course, there was also the undeniable fact that it had been decades since we'd seen Daddy, and between all the time that had passed and the secrets he'd kept, I knew he'd be greatly changed. He was a stranger to us, we had to admit it. But perhaps more important, we were strangers to him. If we could somehow manage to find him, would he even want us to do so? This could all go so horribly wrong.

But now here we were in Scotland, and try as I might, I couldn't help feeling Daddy's presence everywhere around me. I didn't know what I'd do with the disappointment if we had to give up. It would feel like losing him all over again. Strangely, though, this fear only served to make me more determined than ever to find him.

We'd diligently shown the photo we'd gotten at Uncle Audie's to everyone we met, the result being many picturesque side trips down one-track roads that wound round sea lochs and up hillsides, never yielding an exact replica of the view we were seeking. But a few days ago, we'd placed the picture in the hands of an elderly man who'd sat down beside us in a pub in Glencoe, and our hopes had been elevated to plans.

THIRTY-TWO

The road that threads its way through Glencoe twists and turns past mountains that make you feel small. Even on the drizzly afternoon we drove it, when those mountains wore a silver brume of mist as thick as morning porridge, we were stunned into silence at their scale. I pulled the car over to the side of the road, and the two of us reverently stood at the base of the Three Sisters till the mist soaked us wet as rainfall and chilled us to the bone. When we were once again on our way, we were sober with awe and in serious need of someplace warm.

As though reluctant to call attention to itself, the little white pub sat quietly beneath the arms of viridian trees, its windows flickering with an orange light that spoke to us immediately of comfort. Henry looked over at me and grinned. I turned into the car park without a word.

When we pulled open the heavy wooden door and went inside, our senses were immediately cheered by the smells of woodsmoke, fresh bread, and hot soup. Henry ordered for us at the bar while I went to grab a table nearest the fire. He soon returned with two tall glasses of pear cider in his hands and a clear expression of excitement on his face.

"Look at this!" He pulled a colorful postcard from his coat pocket and slapped it down with a flourish on the table. "Our dear ancestor, Robert the Bruce himself, is buried less than an hour from here. Well, not all of him. Just a bit of a bone or something. But still."

I picked up the postcard to see a carved wooden effigy of a crowned figure, his alabaster face translucent in the cool light that streamed through the windows behind him. His white hands were folded across his wood-robed chest, and he appeared to be sleeping the sleep of the dead. The postcard declared this to indeed be an image of Robert the Bruce, the first king of a united Scotland. A sliver of his bone was encased in an ossuary beneath the effigy in a church called St. Conan's Kirk. We stared at the picture.

"Do you really think we're related to him?" I asked Henry.

"You know, I'll tell you what . . ." Henry said, setting his glass of cider down on the table, "I wouldn't have cared a week ago. But now that I've been here for a few days, I want to be. Know what I mean? There's something about this place that makes me feel like I belong here or something. Is it just me? I mean, it's what Daddy used to tell us, isn't it? This is where we came from? This is our starting place? This is our home?"

I hadn't defined the feeling even to myself, but I knew what my brother meant. "They call it ancestral memory. Franklin said the only time he'd felt it was on a trip to Africa, and I guess, when you think about it, we all come from Africa if you go back far enough. I can't say I thought much about the concept when he told me, but yes, I've been feeling the same way. Everything here is . . . I don't know, familiar somehow. It's weird."

"So it's not just me. Good to know. Well then, to your question, yes, I'm going to think we're related to him. Grandpa, it's good to meet you!" Henry gave the postcard an enthusiastic salute, and we heard a chuckle from the table right beside us.

An old man leaned back in his chair, one hand on the head of a white terrier sitting serenely in his lap. He wore the tweed cap like a native, and when he spoke, his brogue bounced toward us like music. The lines on his face told us nothing; he could have been hopelessly ancient or eternally young; the twinkle in his eye as he looked over at Henry said wisdom and whimsy in equal measure.

"So, you think you're related to the man himself there, do you?"

Henry reddened slightly but recovered in an instant. "Well, sir, that's what we've been told. Our last name—our surname, that is—is Bruce." He stuck out his hand. "I'm Henry, and this is my sister Lila."

The old man pulled a hand from his raincoat pocket and shook Henry's. He tipped his cap to me. "Kenneth. Kenneth MacLeod. And this here's Tommy." The terrier wiggled a little before comfortably resettling himself. "Well, that surname counts for you, I reckon. You two on holiday?"

"A bit of a holiday, I guess," Henry said. "Our dad always told us our people came from around here, so we're doing a bit of family research. In a very unofficial way."

"Aye, well, we get a lot of that around here. A healthy number of Scots ended up in the States through the years. And a lot of 'em come through the glen here." He nodded toward the window at the mountains beyond. "Can't say I blame them. Come here myself almost every single day. Have since I was a boy. Well, these mountains here? They are just my place. I've always felt like they know me. Like God really does live here and likes me to visit as much as I can."

His dark blue eyes were bright in the firelight. He looked into mine, and I could almost feel what he meant. "It's good to have a place all your own," I said. "A place where you feel at home above all others."

"Aye, lass. 'Tis at that."

"Mr. MacLeod?" Henry pulled the picture of Daddy from his

shirt pocket and held it out. "I wonder if perhaps you might take a look at this and see if you recognize the place in this photograph. It's a bit faded. But does anything about the landscape look familiar to you? Anything at all? We've been trying to locate exactly where this is, and we've not been having much luck."

Kenneth MacLeod held out his hand and took the photo, with his other hand reaching into his shirt pocket for his glasses as he did so. Tommy the terrier jumped down from his lap and curled up in a ball by the fire. Mr. MacLeod turned in his seat to better catch the light.

"We have a postmark on an old letter. Just part of a postmark, really," I said. "It's pretty worn, but from what we were able to make out, it looks like it might come from one of the Western Isles. It's kind of a long word, too. Looks like it might start with an E. But we can't be sure. We—"

"Eynhallow," he said, quick and certain. "Yes, no doubt in my mind. It's the Isle of Eynhallow. The mountain in the back there?" He pointed down at the photo, and we leaned over to get a closer view. "See how it stretches out into the sea? What does that look like to you?"

"What does it look like? Uh, well. Just looks like a mountain to me." Henry stared at the photo and shrugged, raising his eyebrows at me. "Does it look like something to you?"

I took the photo from the old man's hands and held it up to the light. "I don't think I see . . . Hold on . . . It's a . . . it looks like a bear! Like a big sleeping bear." Glancing up, I saw Mr. MacLeod grinning at me, and I felt as if I'd passed some sort of essential test. I could feel my heart begin to beat faster.

"Well done, lass. That's exactly what it looks like. That's Ben Mathan, that is. Supposed to have been summoned up by the mer-folk of Eynhallow to protect the island from sea monsters, thousands of years ago. That is, if you believe in that sort of thing. Though, if it happened true, it doesn't really matter what you believe."

"Where?" Henry snatched the photo from my hands. "I don't see any bear."

"Look here." I traced the bear's rocky outline with my finger. "See? The ridge here is his back and . . . you just follow that down his head to his—"

"His nose! There's his head! I see it now. Wow, once you see it, you can't see anything else."

Kenneth MacLeod laughed. "Aye. That's Ben Mathan. At the very top of the Isle of Eynhallow. Couldn't be anyplace else. My dad took me there when I was just a boy. Prettiest island in the Hebrides. Better plan ahead, though. They used to run only one ferry a week, and it can be a real rough sailing in the fairest of weather, so best keep a watch on the tides." He took off his glasses and returned them to his pocket, smiling at our obvious astonishment.

"Eynhallow." As we stared at the photograph with new eyes, Henry repeated the unfamiliar name in a whisper, like a conjurer trying out a new incantation, unsure of the power of his own words. The circle was closing. Our journey had brought us one step closer to our past.

THIRTY-THREE

Ben Mathan stands guard over the north end of Eynhallow like the great bear for which it is named. Since I'd seen it for the first time, looming behind my father in the photograph I'd found at Uncle Audie's, the mountain had become almost allegorical to me. And now that I knew its name, I imbued its ursine formation with all the qualities of magic. It was hard not to expect it to shelter an enchanted portal deep in the clefts of its rocky face—a way back to my father and home.

The ferry had doubled its schedule. Now it sailed twice a week to the island, a raucous four-hour journey that had the reputation of rendering the novice sailor a bit green around the gills. We booked our place on the next boat out, leaving in three days, and as those days counted down, I knew that reality could be something far different from what I'd imagined. Magic rarely happened. Ben Mathan wasn't the gold at the end of the rainbow; no wizard lived there to guarantee a happy ending. Although I kept telling myself this over and over, hope still fluttered around somewhere in the vicinity of my heart as we spent the time remaining exploring the Highlands in all their late-summer glory.

With the crest of Clan Bruce looking down from the wall of his library, Daddy had told us the stories of Scotland, a land made even more bewitching because he swore the tales were true. Throughout the seasons of our childhood, we would listen—curled up together like puppies in one of his old leather chairs by a crackling fire or stretched out beside a wide-open window while the sound of crickets scratched the humid air—lost in the land of our ancestors. He said Scotland was a place where mountains are draped with ribbons of rainbows, like highways for fairies to tread, where white clouds of swans ride turquoise blue waves all the way to the shoreline and long-whiskered seals wave hello from slippery wet rocks as you pass.

I had years ago placed those stories on the shelves of my memory alongside the many myths of my youth, but now as we drove along each sea loch and mountain, I knew all he'd told us was true. In the full bloom of August, heather really did cover the hillsides like blankets of amethysts and the night skies truly were white with stars. It was as though we'd stepped right into the stories he'd told us. I could almost hear his voice on the wind.

True to my promise to Maureen, I dragged Henry behind me as I visited every tiny farm shop we passed, turning sharply into each long, rutted drive that bore a handprinted sign reading WOOL. I scooped up armloads of grass-flecked skeins still smelling of the sheep who stood in the green fields outside, soberly watching us leave. Henry, even more susceptible than I, especially when it came to sartorial temptations, bought a tweed cap. It was three wonderful days. But as the day of our sailing grew closer, the knot in my stomach tightened. I wanted to share my feelings with Henry, but he seemed so carefree, I knew I'd need to do so carefully.

We'd been working our way closer and closer to the Isle of Skye and the small port town of Uig from which we'd sail off to Eynhallow, staying at B and B's and tiny tartan-clad hotels along the coast.

One night on our way back to our inn after dinner, Henry pulled the car over and we got out to climb onto the hood and look up at the stars. With our heads resting side by side on the windshield, we stared heavenward. The Milky Way split the sky; it hung so close we felt we could touch it.

After several long minutes, Henry whispered, "Can you imagine how free Daddy must have felt, coming here with Charlie on that first trip after high school? I'm surprised that they ever came back."

I said nothing for a minute, and when I spoke, the words came out in a rush. "Henry?" I kept my eyes straight ahead. "Have you thought about what we're going to say to Daddy when we find him? I mean, *if* we find him? Can you honestly tell me you're not the least bit angry with him? Truly? Because I have to tell you, I sure am."

There was a long pause in which nothing could be heard but the sound of the wind strumming the tall grasses at the edge of the road. "Yeah, I've thought about it," Henry said quietly. "Of course I've thought about it. To tell you the truth, Lila, I don't really expect to find him. Not really. I mean, let's face it, the chances are slim."

"And if we do?"

"Well, if we do, I guess I just want to let him off the hook. Let him know I don't hold it against him. None of it. I know you don't feel the same way. I can tell you're mad, and you have every right to be. But you forget, I know some of what he must have felt at the time, Lila. I can't begin to imagine the pain he was in back then, and I think, what if he and Charlie were me and Andrew, you know? We're talking life-and-death stuff here. Trying to be something he wasn't killed Charlie, and I'm pretty sure that about killed Daddy. I think he was probably scared to death that he'd end up doing the same thing. He had to be. So he let Mama do what she did. Some would say it was a coward's way out, but I don't see it like that. I guess that's what I'd tell him. But if we could just see the place where he's spent all these years, just look at the things he looked at, well, I think I'll be happy. I feel closer to him just being here. Closer than I've felt since we lost him."

"But don't you resent him, even a little, for leaving us? Leaving you in particular? I mean, he had a gay son, for Pete's sake. A gay son who had to grow up in the same town that Daddy couldn't even bring himself to come home to."

Henry sighed and clasped his hands behind his head. "Well, he never knew he had a gay son, though, did he?"

"No. But I mean . . . well, he could have been such a help to you. He'd have known how you felt. Made it easier."

"Look, one of the first things I remember Daddy telling me was that God loved me. That stayed with me like nothing else, so in a way he did make it easier. I always knew in my heart I hadn't done anything wrong. I was just who God made me. Sure, I still remember old Mrs. Reed telling our Sunday-school class that AIDS was the homosexual's punishment for sin and all that, but I just never felt in my bones she was right.

"I guess that's why I've always been able somehow to separate God from religion. See, you were never able to do that, I know. I've always thought it was because you felt you had to protect me, to stand between me and the people who might make me think I was messed up. You always had such a hard time believing that some people—even church people, even people we know, even *family*—are wrong. That just because they claim to speak for God doesn't mean that they do. Just because they're in the majority doesn't mean they're right. Once you realize that, you can hear your own soul a whole lot better. You don't have to fight so much. And you're a whole lot happier to boot. I guess letting go of what other people might believe and living true to myself has felt like a form of forgiveness."

I smiled up at the star-strewn sky, feeling calmer than I had in weeks. "You really are something special, you know that?"

"Not hardly. I just decided a long time ago that love can never be evil."

"Like I said, something special."

As we lay back with our eyes fixed on the wide expanse of night above us, a star shot across the sky in an arc of yellow fire, and I shivered, wrapping my arms around myself. Henry continued, his voice almost a whisper. "You know what? I wanted to hate Mama when I read those letters, I really did. But now I think, how can I, really? How can you hate somebody you don't even know? And that's what I realized, reading them. We didn't know her, Lila. I've just got to accept that the lie she lived, all the secrets she kept, they held her away from us. And it's too late to fix that now. I haven't even given myself time yet to think about how sad that is. It'll probably take years, and a good therapist, to get past it.

"We were so little when we lost him. It was like he just . . . just disappeared, you know? We didn't see him get sick, there wasn't a car wreck or anything as evidence that he'd died. He just left and never came back. I swear, I think I've thought of him every day of my life. And if there's any chance at all that he's alive, if there's the smallest chance I might still have some sort of relationship with my father, even at this late date . . . well, it'd be worth it to me. No matter what. I realize that what he did—what they did—was awful. But I'd be willing to forget it all if I thought I could know my dad again. If there's the slightest possibility we could find him, I'd like Daddy back a whole lot more than I'd like to be angry with him."

I felt my throat tighten, and I leaned over and gave him a kiss on the cheek. "I'm so glad you're my brother," I said. Henry just looked up at me and grinned.

ON THE AFTERNOON before our sailing, we sat in our whitewashed inn perched high on a hillside overlooking the sea. The day was sun-drenched, its edges ruffled only by the slightest of breezes, and on such a day it was difficult for either of us to believe the weather was destined to change as drastically as Ian, our innkeeper, had just said. But he spoke with an authority that was hard to ignore, so when he returned from the kitchen with the number of the ferry company in his hand, I took it and immediately pulled out my phone.

"Oh, aye." The woman's voice on the other end sounded almost amused. "We'll nae be leaving on the usual schedule. We're sailing at eight to beat the storm. Best be here forty-five minutes early. And take your seasickness pills."

THIRTY-FOUR

Sometime in the night, rain topped the hill and charged down upon the inn like a cavalry, attacking my window with such noisy resolve that I woke up long before my alarm was set to go off. Too nervous to just lie there, I went ahead, got up, and dressed. I entered the dim, flagstoned dining room before anyone else, and took a seat at a corner table. By the time Henry joined me, the rain was blowing parallel to the ground.

"Do you think we'll sail? In this?" Henry put the question to Ian as soon as he emerged from the kitchen, balancing a tray full of coffee cups and toast.

Ian bent over our table to better peer out the window. "This isn't too bad yet. You'll be going. Just be glad you're not planning on returning today. It's going to get worse as the day goes on." He grinned as he set our food down before us. "Don't look so worried. The ferry crews know their way around a storm, you can count on that. They won't sail if they don't think they can make it. Eggs and bacon are on the way, and I'm packing you a wee something to take with you. Today's Sunday, so nothing will be open on the island when you get there."

They told us at the tiny terminal that ours was the last ferry out, something that did nothing to assuage our trepidation. The weather seemed to be deteriorating with each passing minute. "Shouldn't we wait till tomorrow to sail?" Henry asked the bundled-up man who took our tickets as we waited in the car.

"This? Ah, people'll pay good money at a fun fair for a ride like this one's gonna be," came the laughing reply as water cascaded in on Henry through the barely cracked window. He hurriedly put it back up, and we sat in the boarding lane looking out at a storm so fierce the large ferry bobbed like a top in its waves.

"Well, this is just nuts." Henry rubbed the windshield with a gloved hand. "I mean, I can barely see a thing. I wonder how bad it has to be for them to cancel?"

"Worse than this, obviously."

At a quarter to eight, the tall green loading ramp of the ferry creaked open, slowly lowering till it banged down on the dock with a thud. A yellow-gloved man began waving us forward, and Henry started the car. We inched along behind several other brave souls and pulled into the brightly lit hull of the boat. Leaving our bags in the car, we joined the other passengers as they climbed the narrow steps onto the upper deck, where Henry made straight for the concessions. I found a small table by the long row of windows, sat down, and waited, knowing full well that the unsettled feeling in the pit of my stomach had nothing to do with the waves.

The boat swayed and dipped on the churning sea, and I noticed that all the tables and chairs were bolted to the floor, which, oddly enough, gave me a sense of reassurance. If they were so accustomed to bad weather that they bolted down the furniture . . . well, then they must really know what they're doing. I shared this observation with Henry when he returned, bearing shortbread, pastries, and tea.

"If you say so. Personally, I am not looking forward to this one little bit. Look how we're pitching around on this thing, and we haven't even left port yet." He leaned across me to look out the window and shook his head. "I sure wish you'd learned to swim. If we turn over, it's going to be my job to haul you out of the water."

"Damn straight," I replied with a shaky grin.

It was a long four hours. We took our cues from our fellow passengers, who barely looked up from their conversations when the boat tilted so far to the right that my uneaten shortbread slid off the table and landed at the feet of a bemused black Labrador who was leading his owner to the observation deck. Their behavior told us nothing about this journey was unusual, and I could feel Henry begin to relax.

The rocking of the boat became rhythmic the farther out we sailed, swaying deeply left and right in an oversize imitation of a cradle. Full of shortbread, muffins, and tea, Henry finally succumbed, sinking down in his seat and falling sound asleep with his recently purchased tweed cap pulled low over his eyes. In an attempt to steady my nerves, I took my sketchbook from my bag and peered out the rain-streaked window at the watercolored sea. So many shades of gray and blue. I was just beginning to visualize a beautiful version of the view outside replicated in a woven shawl when a woman sitting behind me leaned forward and tapped me on the shoulder.

"Excuse me, I couldn't help but notice what you're drawing there. Are you a weaver?" After almost two weeks of listening to the lyrical lilt of the Scots, I found that her American accent sounded flattened and bland. I turned halfway round in my seat to answer her.

"Yes, I am."

"Oh, and you're American, too! Well, I wasn't expecting that! So I guess you'll know all about Eynhallow, then. I've read a little about the weavers there. You know, how they all have weaving sheds out in the back of their yards where they make all those beautiful tweeds? And that they just let you come by and watch them at it? At least I hope that's true. I'm just dying to scoop up some of those tweeds for my house. I'm Sarah, by the way. Sarah Coffee. From Rolla, Missouri. I'm over here on vacation with my husband, Len. He's in the 'loo,' as they say. Gets sick as a dog on every boat we board. Can I see what you're working on?"

Unable to think of an adequate excuse, I held up my sketchbook so she could see the rough outline. "It's just an idea, really. I'm trying to capture the colors."

"Well, that's so pretty. Just beautiful. I wish I could do something like that, but I swear I'm all thumbs when it comes to anything creative. I cross-stitch a little. You know, sayings and stuff. I just finished one for my daughter—she's expecting again. It said 'God Couldn't Be Everywhere So He Made Mothers.' I thought that was so sweet. But how in the world do you do something as complicated as weaving or knitting? With those patterns that look like hieroglyphics? I could never. So that's why you're going over here, too? To visit the weavers?"

Sarah Coffee was one of those women who'd never seen the need for conversational boundaries. Her chatter was constant and agile; she swiveled and swerved through a Gordian knot of subjects, nimble as a noodle, completely oblivious to my tepid responses and overblown sighs. In fifteen minutes I heard the outline of her biography, from the length of her (happy) marriage (forty-two years) to the way she takes her tea (two sugars and lots of cream). I learned that her two daughters were both blond like her ("though I do have a bit of help these days!") and that her husband had made a "fortune" in commercial real estate and was finally retired. "So now we can go to all the places we've wanted to and stay longer than one week! We've been in the UK two weeks already. This is our last stop before going back to London and heading home. But that's enough about me now. I want to hear all about you. If I'm not mistaken, I hear a little bit of a southern accent there, am I right? How did you find yourself all the way up in Maine?"

I hesitated, racking my brain for a way to convey to a woman unencumbered by tact that her familiarity was unwelcome. Her enthusiasm, though exhausting, seemed genuine, and I didn't want to hurt her feelings. But there was nothing I wanted to do less right now than share with this stranger my reasons for moving to Maine or, more important, my real reason for sailing to the Isle of Eynhallow.

I had just taken a breath when I looked over her shoulder and saw a lanky man in a navy corduroy coat coming toward us. Thin as a broomstick with a shock of white hair, he was clearly struggling to maintain an elemental dignity as he made slow progress across the boat, holding on to the back of each seat to steady himself as he went. His pallid face was glutinous with cold sweat. Sarah Coffee followed my eyes with her own, and when they came to rest on her husband, she said, "Len, you look awful. Here, sit. Put your head back."

"Don't talk to me. Just don't talk to me." Len Coffee slowly sank down next to his wife, closed his eyes, and laid his head on the back of his seat, looking like a greener version of Henry, who continued to sleep peacefully beside me. Sarah gave me a "what can you do?" shrug, and I hastily grabbed the opportunity to turn back around and resume my stare out the window.

The low-hanging storm clouds still sat right on top of the sea, blotting out any hope of a satisfying view, but just as I was turning away, I noticed that off in the distance they seemed to solidify into immense gray shadows. I wiped away a crescent of fog from the window with the back of my hand. Mountains were rising up out of the waves on either side of the boat, mountains that bore no kinship with any I'd ever seen before. As much a part of the sea as the land, they towered above us like giants of stone, sentinels of the Isle of Eynhallow. I nudged Henry with my elbow.

"I think we're almost there." My voice came out in a whisper.

"Huh?" Henry sat up straight and stretched.

"Look." I pointed out the window, rubbing it free of condensation once again.

"Sheesh." Henry leaned over me and looked out. "Well, that's not impressive at all, is it?"

The coastline of Eynhallow was visible now, its tiny port a mere dot of white on the steel-gray horizon. As the boat made its way ever nearer to shore, I could see cottages scattered on the hillside, their lighted windows glowing like tiny flames in the gloom. I had tried to keep this thought at bay for days, but now it broke through my brain with as much force as the waves I could see biting at the rocks of the harbor: my father might be behind one of those windows, staring out at the very same sea on which my eyes now rested, totally unaware of my presence. I shivered and pulled my raincoat tight around my shoulders, nearly dizzy at the thought.

The ferry rocked and lurched so much in the turbulent water that an easy landing seemed impossible, but with only the merest of bumps and thumps we were suddenly stationary. "Thank the good God," I heard Len Coffee mutter from his seat behind us. Sarah helped him to his feet and gave me an apologetic little wave as they shuffled up the aisle to the stairwell. Henry turned to follow close behind, but I grabbed his arm and held him back.

"Wait a minute," I said. "I want them to go on ahead."

"Who? That couple?" He nodded toward the Coffees' receding figures.

"Yeah." I watched as Len and Sarah Coffee disappeared into the group of people moving away. "She's just a bit too much for me right this minute. Too familiar. Too many questions."

"When did you become so unsociable?" he said, grinning.

"I'm not unsociable, I'm . . . well, I'm nervous. And I've been getting more and more nervous the closer we've come to this place. My heart's beating like a rabbit's. And I just can't talk about the reason we're here in a casual way, to strangers." I slung my bag up over my shoulder. "Look, can't we just tell people we're here to work on designs for my business? I don't want to broadcast to everybody that we're looking for Daddy. It just feels . . . I don't know, too personal. Too private."

"Well, okay." Henry looked at me quizzically. "You do realize, though, we're going to have to ask some questions. Show his picture to some people. We can't just stand on the pavement and watch who goes by."

"I know that, Henry. And believe me, if he's here, I intend to find him. I just need some time to take this place in. I'm sorry."

He tucked my arm under his. "It's all right. We'll take it slow. C'mon, let's go. That nosy old woman's gone now." He laughed, and together we made our way up the empty aisle and down the stairs to the car.

THIRTY-FIVE

To reach the Isle of Eynhallow, we had crossed several islands as though they were rocks in a pond, increasingly struck by the dissimilarity and uniqueness of each. Like members of the same family so distantly related they bore almost no resemblance to one another, each island had carved out its individuality through centuries of battering sea and brutal winds. Where one was greenly bucolic, the next could appear eerily prehistoric, offering up landscapes so imposing they seemed supernatural. But nothing had prepared us for the sight of the island now unfolding itself just outside our car windows.

Huge warped and twisted rocks lay tossed on the hills like the remains from an ancient battle of giants. As far as the eye could see, the ground rolled and tumbled away from the road like a serrated carpet of gray, its jagged surface pierced here and there by sharp whiskers of olive-green grass. The scene seemed more lunar than earthly, its effect more curious than bleak. I had never felt so far from home.

"Where did you say we were staying?" Henry sounded doubtful as he shifted into lower gear while the windshield wipers flapped futilely in the horizontal rain.

"It's an inn across from the beach. And from what I can tell, it's the only inn around."

"*Beach?* There's a beach? You've got to be kidding." He sat up closer to the window to better see the road, his knuckles white on the steering wheel.

I fumbled in my bag for the reservation confirmation I'd been sent before we left. Finding it, I unfolded the letter and read aloud, " 'Situated on one of the most magnificent beaches in the United Kingdom, Clement House evokes the spirit of another age, one in which hospitality ruled and comfort was king. Come unwind in our breathtaking surroundings. Sleep in one of our four-poster beds where the windows open out to the sea. Dine by the fire in candlelit splendor. We guarantee you'll never want to leave.' "

"Hyperbole if I ever heard it." Henry grabbed the letter and held it up before him, snatching quick glances at the tiny map printed on the bottom as he negotiated the curving road, now almost invisible in the rain. " 'Never want to leave,' my ass. I just hope we *get* there. I'm starving."

Remembering Ian's gift of a lunch, I swiveled in my seat and found the brown paper sack he'd pushed into my hands as we left. Opening it, I was happy to see a couple of grated-cheese sandwiches, two apples, two bottles of sparkling water, and a large Kit Kat bar. I unwrapped a sandwich for Henry and handed it to him. He took one big bite, and little orange slivers of cheese fell out all over his lap.

"Damn it. Exploding cheese sandwiches again. Why can't they just use sliced cheese like everybody else?" He handed the letter back over to me. "Look at this thing and make sure we're on the right road, would you?"

"Henry, I don't think I'm going to spot a lot of road signs out here, do you? Just keep driving. We can't have taken the wrong road. There was only one going east, and we're on it." I broke the Kit Kat bar in half and stuffed it into his mouth.

We crested another rocky hill and felt a gust of wind push against the car as though trying to rid the road of our presence. The road fell forward in front of us, corkscrewing down the mountainside until there, wedged between the pewter grays of the rocks and sky, as unexpected as a peacock in a rook's nest, lay the sea. Bright turquoise waves ran toward the cupped white hand of the shore almost playfully. The startling beauty was both a mockery to the blowing gale and a rebuke to the hubris of first impressions.

"Good Lord," Henry exclaimed as he slowed the car to a stop. We sat in silence for a full minute, staring down at the shining blue-green water. He leaned back in his seat and sighed. "That's worthy of the Caribbean. Seriously. What kind of place *is* this?"

"An unusual one, obviously. Look down, over there. I bet that's our inn." I pointed to a cluster of lights shining across the road from dead center of the sandy beach. The outline of a whitewashed building was just discernible on the darkened hillside.

"Well," said Henry, putting his foot on the gas pedal and shifting into gear, "they weren't lying after all. It is on a 'magnificent' beach. Now I want to . . . what was it? 'Dine in candlelit splendor' and go straight to bed."

THIRTY-SIX

The hand-painted sign to Clement House swung back and forth like a laughing man as we pulled into the graveled drive. Bent double against the winds of a gale that had only seemed to gather strength the closer we came to our destination, we unloaded our bags with comic difficulty and were thrown toward the blue front door like rag dolls. Any hope of a dignified entrance was gone.

Henry turned the doorknob and pushed forcefully. We struggled into the tiny vestibule, and the door slammed behind us like a gavel, sending a neatly stacked pile of scenic brochures flying into the air like a flock of angry birds. The room was very small and oddly silent, the howl of the wind smothered by its thick stone walls. We looked at each other. Henry was breathing hard. His hair was twisted, and his cheeks were bright red. I could tell by the smirk on his face that my appearance had not fared any better, and together we began to snicker, each of us shushing the other as we did.

"Don't laugh. Don't laugh! You'll get me going, and we already look like idiots. Here, help me pick these up." Henry was on the floor with his head under a gateleg table as he spoke, his voice a loud whisper.

This only made me laugh the harder as together we scooped up the rest of the fallen brochures and returned them to the table from which they'd flown. I stuck my hair behind my ears in an attempt to make myself more presentable. Henry put on his tweed cap and cautiously opened the door.

The hall we entered exuded warmth. It wasn't merely that the temperature was more comfortable in here than outside, though it certainly was, but coziness just seemed to encircle this room like a muff. The walls were the color of honey. Splendid in their Highland dress, Scottish chiefs and lairds eyeballed our entrance from inside heavy wooden frames that hung from carved moldings by long golden chains. Red tartan rugs were thrown here and there across an uneven stone floor, and a thick tartan runner was fastened to a steep staircase that rose straight up before us.

Henry set his bag down on the stone floor and took a few steps forward. He was just about to reach for the bell standing on a lamp-lit table when the door directly to my left creaked open. A sweet aroma flowed into the room, and we turned to see a small man enter the hall, his head bent in concentration over an empty silver tea tray.

The hair on his head was wispy, like the down of a newly hatched bird, and little round glasses were perched on the bridge of his nose. He couldn't have been more than five feet tall, and all his features seemed smaller than normal; he looked almost abbreviated somehow, as though he'd gotten impatient and jumped off the human assembly line before he was fully completed. Sensing our presence, he looked up at us over his glasses.

If we were tempted to wonder whether his stature placed him at any disadvantage, his self-assured greeting told us otherwise in a flash. "Oh, hello there! I guess I didn't hear you come in. Sorry. Did you ring?" He placed the empty tray on the table and nodded toward the bell. His slightly formal manner told us he was English even before his clipped accent confirmed it.

"We were just about to." Henry stuck out his hand. "I'm surprised you couldn't hear us, though. A herd of wild elephants would have made less noise than we did. I'm Henry Bruce, and this is my sister, Lila Breedlove. I believe we have reservations."

"Yes, yes. These old rooms are pretty soundproof, you know. Walls are at least a foot thick. Now, if you'll just follow me, I'll get my book. I'm Russell. Russell Winskill. My wife, Gemma, and I run the place here. Unfortunately, Gemma's had to leave rather quickly this afternoon, hence my sadly unprofessional attire." He gave a nod to the noticeable moth hole in the arm of his camel-brown sweater. "I do apologize. Her mother's been in hospital. Nothing serious, but, you know, she's got to go. Only child and all that. She caught the ferry across this morning. Back Wednesday if the weather clears up. Pretty fresh out there today, right? I hope the drive gave you no trouble."

Mr. Winskill talked as he walked, and he walked at a brisk pace, a man for whom the word "scurry" could easily have been invented. Together Henry and I followed him into a small, cluttered room that was obviously the office. Stacks of file folders were precariously balanced atop a desk whose surface had disappeared years ago beneath a chaos of envelopes and papers, some yellowed with age. Standing on tiptoe, the little man dove headfirst into this ocean of disorganization, shuffling and rifling through the various piles, apparently more than able to distinguish between what was vital and what was not. Within thirty seconds he popped back up with a crisp white letter held aloft in his hand.

"Here we go. Breedlove and Bruce. Sounds like a law office, doesn't it? Ha!" He blushed at his own joke and handed Henry a pen. "Now, if you'll just sign here. Staying three nights with us? Good. Good. Weather's supposed to be better tomorrow, you'll be happy to hear. How was the crossing?"

We shared the account of the ferry trip over and listened politely in turn as he gave us some information about the inn and the island. "Dinner's at eight. And you're still in time for tea, which is currently being served in the sitting room. Door to your left as you entered. There should still be some other guests in there now. Americans, like yourselves. Breakfast is between seven and nine thirty, and there's a menu in each of your rooms so you can let us know what you like before you retire. Just hang it on the outside of your door when you turn in. Now, if you'll come with me, I'll take you up."

We followed along behind him, leaving our cases in the main hall. "I'll get one of the lads to bring those up for you," he said as we started up the stairs. "You're both on the front of the house, facing the sea. Good views there, but your windows might rattle a bit tonight in this wind. Hope that'll be okay. They're old."

Outside the landing window, I saw a couple of cottages clustered behind the inn as if they were sheltering from the storm. "Those are our long-term rentals," Mr. Winskill said, noticing where I was looking. "We've got a couple of students here this summer. It's their last week, though. Been studying weaving, I believe. Color theory and all that. Well, most do. It's a pretty big deal here on the island. Either of you interested in that?"

"My sister's a weaver." Henry grinned over at me, anxious to show he'd remembered what I'd told him. "That's why we're here this week, so she can have a look around and get some new design ideas."

"That so? Well, if you'd like to meet any of the artists here, just let me know. Most are more than happy to give you a little tour. Not all, mind you. Some are pretty standoffish when it comes to interacting with the public. But most of those live so far out you'd have a difficult time finding them anyway, so it's just as well. Now, here we go, Mrs. Breedlove. Here's your room." We had reached a door just to the right of the top of the stairs. Mr. Winskill placed an old-fashioned key into the lock and turned it with a click.

The first thing I saw was the sea, framed like a Turner in the large sash window on the opposite side of the room, its slash of bright water splitting the gray air outside in two. Facing the window, draped in copious yardage of a Jacobean linen embroidered with flowers of pale blue and beige, stood a massive four-poster bed, a fluffy meringue of white sheets and down coverlets. The room wore the fragrance of the fresh apples that sat in an etched glass bowl on the wide windowsill.

"This is beautiful, Mr. Winskill," I said as I set my handbag down on the bench and walked to the window. It shook slightly in a gust of strong wind.

"'Tis, isn't it? Well, I can take no credit. It's all Gemma's doing. This inn was her dream. She used to holiday up here with her family when she was a little girl. Took us three years to restore it." He went around the bed, smoothing out a wrinkle on the white duvet as he walked, and opened the door to the bathroom. "Here's the bath. I think there's everything you'll need in here. Just be careful, the water can get quite hot." Then, turning to Henry, he said, "Now, Mr. Bruce. I'll take you down the hall to your room. The same view, just slightly different colors in there." Looking over his shoulder as he went past Henry, he said, "Remember, tea downstairs, Mrs. Breedlove. We clear it up at six." Henry stepped out into the hall behind him, and Mr. Winskill closed the door, leaving me alone in the silence.

I took off my coat, hung it up on a peg behind the dark wooden door, and bent over to look inside the dressing-table mirror. Fishing around in my bag for my hairbrush and lipstick, I managed to tidy myself up a bit, pleased to notice that the effects of the wind had alleviated any need for makeup. My cheeks were rosy.

I had made myself call Abby every few days since we'd left, careful not to tell her where I was. The subterfuge made me feel a bit terrible, but I knew that, as Henry had so concisely phrased it, she'd go "batshit crazy" if she were to learn the truth. I told myself that my sister was happier than she'd been in a long while, and to puncture that happiness with this particular pin of truth would be nothing but cruel. This was certainly not a conversation to be had over the phone, that much was sure. Abigail answered before the third ring. Her voice sounded cheerful; it carried in its tone a hint of recent laughter.

"Lila! I thought it might be you. I was out on the porch with Audie. He's churning ice cream, can you believe that? We haven't done that since we were little. I told Jackson we could just go down to the Piggly Wiggly and get a couple of cartons of Mayfield's—that stuff's almost like homemade—but then he asked me how long it had been since I'd tasted homemade, and that shut me up real quick. I can't even remember how long it's been. Besides, as far as Uncle Audie's concerned, ice cream isn't real unless you churn it yourself. They're out there laughing right now, I bet you can hear them. I'll hold the phone up."

There was a pause in which nothing could be heard but the slight rattle of the window in my island room, but once again I saw no harm in a white lie. "Yes, I think I can hear somebody laughing," I said.

"Yeah, I bet you can. I tell you, Lila, I have never seen a couple of men who get along better than these two do. You know what Jackson told me yesterday? He said that Audie's like the father he never had. Said his dad was always about business and money, too busy to throw the ball with him or take him fishing or anything like that. And then he died before Jackson was thirty, so he never got to see Jackson's kids grow up or anything. But now, with Audie, I swear, they're like two big kids themselves. They've been teaching me to clean fish 'cause they've been catching so many. To tell the truth, I'm not too good at that. Creeps me out. But Audie taught me to make hush puppies, and that's something I *can* do. We had a fish fry Saturday. Whole bunch of people came over . . . well, mostly Dot and her friends, but they're all so sweet and nice. Oh, and, Lila? I've lost ten pounds! Didn't even realize it till I got on Audie's scale the other night. Well, my pants were fitting better, so

I had a clue it might not be bad news if I stepped up on one this time, and I was right! I feel as though I'm eating like a pig down here—Uncle Audie believes in three meals a day, you know—but I guess I'm running around a lot more. Oh, and Dot took me to her hairdresser. Well, actually it was this lady who does hair out of her kitchen—can you believe people still do that? Anyway, she took me over there, and that lady put my hair back the right color. Don't know what I was thinking. Well, I was upset. I guess everybody knows that, don't they? I mean, I went kinda squirrelly that night." She gave a little laugh that ended in a sigh.

"Don't worry about that, Abby. Everybody understands, I'm sure they do. You were under a lot of stress, and besides, you know what? It really doesn't—"

"'Doesn't matter what those old crows think.' Yeah, I know that's what you're about to say. Well, it's easier down here, that's for sure. I don't know, I feel like I'm wearing new skin or something. Oh, and I didn't tell you, did I? Here's the big news. I called Dr. Pitt last Tuesday and gave him my notice! I mean, he'd given me some time off anyway, what with Mama and all, so I figured that now, since he's starting to get used to me not being there, it was a good time to just tell him I wouldn't be coming back. I talked it all over with Jackson, and he said I deserved to be happy in what I did, and to be honest with you, Lila, I got to thinking after sixteen years if I had to go to that place one more morning to just sit there all day and act like getting your teeth cleaned was the most impor-tant thing in the world, I'd spit up, I swear to God I would. So I quit. Jackson says we'll figure it all out later and for me not to worry about it now. So I'm just not. Worrying, that is. You're shocked, aren't you?" I heard a little scared defiance in her voice.

"No, of course I'm not shocked, Abby. I think Jackson's right. You do deserve to be happy. I want you to be happy. Henry and I both do."

I could hear the snuffly sound of tears. "Oh, Lila. You are so sweet. You really are. You're just the best sister. Here I am not letting you talk at all. How's Henry? And Andrew? Y'all having a good time up there?" I heard her blow her nose.

"Yes, we're having a great time. Henry bought a new hat." So far all true.

"Oh, I want to see! Henry always did look good in a hat. Send me a picture!"

There was a soft knock on my door, and Henry stuck his head inside. "I will," I said, holding the phone up for Henry to see and placing my index finger against my lips in warning. "But I'd better go now. You take care of yourself and rest up. I'll call you in a few days."

"That Abby?" Henry asked as I turned off my phone and plugged it into the charger on the wall.

"Yeah. She sounds like she's doing really well, believe it or not. She's quit her job, lost ten pounds, and learned how to make hush puppies. She's also put her hair back to a more human color."

"She's in love. Has to be." Henry shook his head. "You know, of all the crazy things we've found out about our family this past month, the one that makes the most sense to me is that we're only halfway related to that girl. I mean, don't get me wrong, she's my sister and I love her. But for God's sake, I have never understood her." He held open the door. "Now, let's go get us some cake. I'm starving, and I'll never make it till dinner. Oh, and by the way, I phoned Andrew, and everybody's fine. Maureen's talked him into doing a big show in Toronto in December. He can't believe he agreed to it. Oh, and Fidget caught a squirrel."

THIRTY-SEVEN

The small room was brimming with the sweet smell of a peat fire softly burning in the wide stone fireplace. Crowded bookshelves lined three of the walls, and on the fourth a row of casement windows could just be seen hiding behind thick formal curtains already drawn against the cold rage of the wind. Several squashy armchairs had been pulled up close to the fire, their downy seats still flattened by the weight of recent occupants, and a low wooden table full of teacups and cakes formed a friendly boundary between two tapestried sofas that faced each other in the middle of the room. A couple were cozily sitting on one of these now, their two gray heads bent low over a very large book. My heart sank to my knees when I recognized them.

Sarah Coffee turned as we entered; there was no time to beat a retreat. "Oh, my soul. Would you look at this!" she cried. "Len! Turn around, Len. It's that nice lady I told you about. The one from the boat. The weaver!"

Len Coffee wore the expression of a man who'd spent most of his life in tacit apology, and this made him impossible to dislike. He put his hands on his knees, pushed himself up from his place next to his wife, and stuck out his hand to Henry. Henry shook it warmly, introducing us both as he did so.

From her spot on the sofa, Sarah spoke up just as words of reciprocation were leaving her husband's mouth. "Brother! Oh, he's your *brother*! Well, I wondered. I mean, I've heard of married couples growing to look alike, but I've got to say, you two are almost identical. I told Len—didn't I, Len?—that it was odd to see a couple look so much alike. But you're brother and sister! That all makes sense now. Here, Lila, come over and sit by me. Tea's still hot and everything." She patted the seat beside her enthusiastically.

Being interrupted in midsentence was obviously a common occurrence in Len Coffee's life. But as he turned to look at his wife, his expression softened to one of affectionate amusement, and I could see, in that one tiny moment, the simple reason their marriage had lasted for forty-two years. He loved her. And as nearly always happens when you see someone look at a person with love, I saw Sarah Coffee in a different light.

Henry crossed the room to one of the armchairs, fluffing up the seat cushion before he sat down. Len held out his hand and led me, gratefully, not to the seat right beside his wife but to the one directly opposite. He sat back down next to her and smiled at me in genuine warmth. When finally allowed to speak, he had a voice that was low and pleasant.

"I'm sorry you had to see me looking so unwell on the ferry. I've never had a problem with seasickness before, but as Sarah keeps telling me, over and over, I've never been on these particular seas before."

"Well, I warned you, didn't I?" She patted her husband's knee before reaching out to pour the tea. "Let's see here, now, there's some Earl Grey left, and I believe this is . . . oh, what did he say this was? Do you remember, Len?"

"I'm pretty sure it's Darjeeling." Then, looking over at me, he said, "Whatever it is, it's quite good. I recommend it. And that

Victoria sponge cake. Definitely take a piece of that. Don't re-member when I've tasted a cake that good."

"I'm going to ask Russell for the recipe, but I bet our sugar is different in the States, don't you, Lila? Everything's different over here. And God knows you can't make a decent scone in Missouri, because you can't get any of that good double cream like they have down in Devon." She had sliced pieces of cake for Henry and me and held them out for us before cutting one more for herself. "So best enjoy it while we can, right?"

Henry nodded enthusiastically, his mouth full of Victoria sponge. As the gale slashed the windows outside, the four of us slipped into an easy conversation that wound around our recent travels in the Highlands and through the Coffees' upcoming trip to London before ebbing away in a reflective sigh from Len.

"Boy, we've had some wonderful times in London over the years," he said. "I'm really looking forward to being back. And I'm glad to see you share in our love of that city. Did you two start off there this time?"

"No," said Henry. "Lila and I flew straight into Inverness. The Highlands were our primary focus this trip. She has a knitwear business back at her place in Maine, and she wanted to come up here for some fresh inspiration and perhaps some sourcing for a new line." I grinned at my brother.

Soon the talk split in two, and I found myself giving Sarah a greatly condensed primer on my passion for weaving.

"So you look at a particular view and take those colors and weave or knit them into something?" she asked. "How can you remember everything correctly?"

"Well, I generally have some colored pencils with me and a notebook of some kind, and of course it helps to keep a camera close. But my designs don't have to be exact. I use color to convey what that landscape makes me feel. If that makes any sense."

"It does. I'm going straight to your website when we get home and snapping up a few of those shawls. Just imagine wearing some-

thing designed by someone I actually know! Or then again . . .
maybe I should wait and get one from the new collection you create after being here. And I can tell everybody I saw the very same
views that inspired it. What do you think?"

I laughed. With my guard lowered, I had to admit that Sarah
Coffee had the ability to make you feel as though you'd known her
for years. "Well, I have no idea how long it'll take me to make the
leap from idea to finished product. I'll just have to let the beauty
sink in and see what blooms after I get back."

She gave me a smile. "You really need to take a look at this.
Here." She lifted the large book she and Len had been looking
through when Henry and I walked in and handed it over to me,
saying, "Watch it, it weighs a ton. You sound just like some of the
people in it, though. Take it up to your room with you tonight.
I'm sure nobody will mind."

I reached out and took the book with both hands. It had a
bright red cover and the words EILEAN GLAS written across it in
spruce green. "Eilean Glas?" I asked. "Gaelic, I suppose."

"Yes. It means 'Gray-Green Island.' And no, I didn't already
know that. It's right there on the first page. All the photos are from
Eynhallow. Beautiful pictures. But there's also some interviews
with some of the weavers here, and to read what they say . . . well,
they just sound an awful lot like you. I think you'll enjoy it. I'm
serious, take it upstairs with you tonight. You'll be inspired, I
know you will."

I had no sooner settled the book onto my lap when the flames
in the fireplace flickered as the door opened. Russell Winskill
stuck his head around the corner. Now dressed in a maroon suede
jacket and crisp white shirt, he spoke quickly and with authority.

"Mrs. Breedlove, Mr. and Mrs. Coffee, Mr. Bruce, I just wanted
you to know we'll begin our dinner seating in about an hour.
Here's a wine list if you'd like to take a look." He placed a long
leather booklet on the tea table and hurried over to stir the fire,
which had begun to doze down to a simmer. From a basket at the

side of the hearth, he pulled a couple of thick peat logs, which he tossed onto the grate. Immediately the flames rose up, filling the room with a sweet aroma so unlike the fires I knew at home.

"Russell? You don't mind if Lila here takes this book up to her room tonight, do you?" Sarah gave me a wink.

Mr. Winskill turned around, his face registering only the slightest twitch at the uninvited use of his first name. "*Eilean Glas?* No, no, of course not. That's why we have it here. In fact, I believe there's another copy in the upstairs sitting room. Very popular, that book. It's a wonderful record of the island."

I lifted the heavy book in my arms and followed Henry and the Coffees out into the hall. As I climbed the stairs back up to my room, I heard nothing but the howl of the sea wind as it raced past the landing window. There was not a whispered hint that the heavy book I now carried held the answer to a thousand questions. No inkling that inside it was hidden the proof of a newly born, barely imagined hope.

THIRTY-EIGHT

Candlelight danced within the inky blackness of three uncovered windows that faced the invisible sea in the dining room of Clement House, setting the mood for an enjoyable dinner. By the time Henry and I had finished off the generous servings of panna cotta that crowned our meal, we were both feeling sleepy and dull. We declined Russell Winskill's offer of a whiskey in the sitting room, and I saw the disappointment in Sarah Coffee's eyes as we left, both of us longing for bed.

The wind got louder as we headed upstairs, and tiny blades of rain etched the landing window as we passed. We said good night, and I opened the door to my room. Someone had been inside to turn down the feathery bed. The curtains were drawn, the lamps switched on, and a tall decanter of whiskey and one solitary glass had been placed on the night table. Tomorrow our search would begin in earnest, but tonight I wanted to forget everything and just lie back in that cream puff of a bed with a good dram of whiskey and a book.

★   ★   ★

FRESHLY CLEAN AND utterly relaxed after a hot bath, I headed to bed a half hour later. As I passed the chair by the window, I saw the big red book that Sarah Coffee had pressed into my hands at tea. I picked it up and tossed it over onto the bed, where it sank into the white down like an apple in snow. Pouring myself a generous glass of whiskey, I crawled up into the overstuffed bed, and my bare toes found a hot-water bottle, a touch that was enormously welcome.

The windows were rattling like Jacob Marley's chains as I took a sip of my drink and laid the book across my lap. The warm liquid fell down my throat like melted amber as I slowly opened the shining red cover.

It took me only a minute to realize that Sarah Coffee had been correct in her assumption that I would relate to this book in a special way. My brain sparked with the turn of each page. The photographs were stunning, each one obviously taken by someone in possession of the eye of an artist. In chapter after chapter, I saw colors and patterns I'd only dreamed of, scenery that seemed more unreal than actual.

I read of weavers who'd learned their art from ancestors long departed as well as those whose love for it was only newly found. Stories of people who had stumbled onto this tiny, strange spot on the globe and felt such a pull of home they'd chosen to stay, some at great cost. In reverence to the unbroken thread of the Eynhallow tradition, they'd taught themselves to weave in the old ways, pedaling Hacksaw looms in tiny sheds outside their simple homes. Their soul connection to this island had not been guaranteed by birth, yet they'd recognized from the first moment they stepped out onto its rocks that they felt more at home here than anywhere else in the world.

I felt the old longing rise up within me, the same longing I'd experienced on the damp afternoon I'd sat beside Kenneth Mac-

Leod in that pub in Glencoe and watched his seasoned face soften with gratitude as he spoke of his attachment to that one particular place. His roots there ran deep. It was both painful and perplexing to know that nothing grew on that patch of my soul where home should be. If my father had indeed been one of these people for whom the Isle of Eynhallow had become a refuge, I could no more blame him than I could blame myself for never having found such a place of my own.

As I continued to slowly flip through the colorful chapters of *Eilean Glas*, the pictures and stories of the Isle of Eynhallow took on a quality of myth. Near midnight I read of an incomer named Seamus Charles who'd landed on the island more than thirty years before and who had, through trial and error, taught himself to weave in the old style. Following no family tradition, his designs were original and intricate, and they showcased a masterful eye for color. Though he only occasionally sold his cloth in a small weekly market in town, it was photographed by some vacationers attracted by the uniqueness of its design. Those photographs eventually landed upon the desk of a fashion designer in Edinburgh, who'd commissioned his cloth for a range of women's wear. His colorful woven fabrics now could be seen in magazines and on runways all over the world.

It was a marvelous story, and I quickly turned the page to the accompanying picture, anxious to see this man who'd achieved such success, almost by accident. The photograph covered two full pages. It was bisected by a rocky wall that separated land and sky like a long, gnarled finger pointing out to the sea. The man sat on this wall, his face turned away from the camera lens, two black-and-white dogs following his gaze across the stony field to the water.

None of us are prepared for a shock. There is nothing we can do—no practice, no rehearsal, no test. We stand on an open plain, as sure a target as a bull's-eye.

THIRTY-NINE

There was no doubt it was him. I required no corroboration from Henry asleep down the hall. I had always sat in the seat behind my father as he drove our family wherever we'd gone. Trips to and from school, to and from church, the long eight-hour drive to our favorite beach in summer—all these had been done with the back of my father's head right in front of me. I remembered the way his hair grazed the horizontal line of his collar, the way one ear slightly cocked to the right. I could still draw the silhouette of his shoulders with my eyes tightly closed. And though the hair was white and the shoulders slightly stooped, it was him. I knew it without question.

With shaking fingers I flipped to the front of the book. The publication date seemed to rise off the page and waver in midair before my eyes. June 2009. Two short years ago.

Suddenly unable to sit still, I let the book slide from my lap, got up, and walked to the window. The view had changed. The waves of gray clouds had vanished, and in their place hung the stars, so many stars it seemed as though the world had been tipped upside down, flipping a field of white flowers over my head and the old stormy sky into the sea.

I paced the room for a good ten minutes, unsure exactly what to do next. The beat of my heart was more like a quiver, and for a second I thought I might faint. Then, without actually deciding to, I grabbed up the book, opened the door, and turned toward Henry's room. I was running, my bare feet cold on the polished wood floor, and before I could formulate a cohesive thought, I was knocking on his door.

I knocked again in impatience. Finally I heard a loud thump followed by a string of expletives, and the door was thrown open to perfectly frame my pajama-clad brother, who looked half asleep and murderous as he vigorously rubbed his right toe.

"Henry, I've found him. I've found Daddy." I pushed past him into the room. Opening the book to the page with our father's photo, I held it out to him like a supplicant.

Henry closed the door and walked toward me, his eyes drifting down to the book in a short journey from disbelief to shock. His face lost all color, and he reached for the edge of the bed, never taking his eyes from the two-page photograph. Sitting slowly, he cradled the book in his hands like a fragile pane of glass.

He stared at the picture for a long minute before lifting his face to mine. "We can't know for sure this is him. He's got his back to the camera. And this says his name is Seamus Charles. I guess . . . I guess he could have changed it. But there's no way to tell. Not really. To find him in a book you just happen to be looking at? That's a hundred-to-one shot, Lila. A hundred to one. You're just letting your imagination run away with you." His chin was slightly raised in a posture of feigned assurance. I recognized it from child-hood.

"Are you kidding me?" I grabbed the book from his hands, forcefully pointing at the photo with my finger. "Look at it, Henry! I mean, just look at it. That's Daddy. No question. I don't have a doubt in my mind." Henry tried to roll his eyes, but I could see his heart wasn't in it. "Look, damn it!" I snapped. Obediently, he stared back down at the photo. "That's his back. That's his profile. That's his hair. That's his hand on the head of that dog. Look! This book was published two years ago. He's here, Henry! I know he is."

Henry stared down, his face tight, his jaw set. When he finally looked up at me, his eyes were shining. "What do we do now?"

I stared at him in disbelief. "What do you mean, 'What do we do now?' We've talked about this. *You* were the one who told Audie we'd try to find him. Are you telling me you never really even seriously considered what we'd do when we did?"

Henry got up and began to walk around the room, talking with his hands as he always did when he was upset. "Well, I just never . . . I mean, it's been over forty years. We weren't even sure this was where he'd gone. That postmark could have been from some vacation he was taking or something, I don't know. I really didn't think . . ."

"No, apparently you really *didn't* think. Lord, Henry. I've been lying in bed at night for weeks worrying about what I'd say to him, what *you'd* say to him, trying to swallow the anger that kept rising up whenever I thought how he'd left us. And you mean to tell me you haven't? What's this been? Just a holiday for you?"

"No! No. Not that. I told you, I just wanted to see for myself where he and Charlie had gone, see where he'd been so happy." He rubbed his forehead with the palm of his hand. "God, Lila. What are we going to do?"

I couldn't help but look into my brother's eyes and see the little boy who had so often asked me that very same question. I sat down on his bed with a flop, all the adrenaline evaporating from my body like fog in the sunshine. It was a long minute before I spoke.

"If there's one thing I've come to realize, it's that, try as you might, you can't change the past, Henry. All these things that happened? You or I couldn't have stopped them with an army. We couldn't have changed Daddy, or Mama, and what they did. But now that we're here, now that we've seen this picture, the next decisions are up to us. Just us. And I'll tell you what we're going to do. Right now we're going to get some sleep. And then, first thing in the morning, we're going to take this book and ask everybody we can about the man in this picture. Then we're going to get into that little rental car that's parked outside and we're going to drive wherever we have to and find him. That's what we're going to do.

"Now, I'm exhausted. And I don't want to be by myself. So if you don't mind, I'm going to crawl into your bed, and we're both going to try to sleep. Crack that window. I want to hear the sea." I stuck my feet beneath the sheets and pulled the puffy white coverlet up under my chin.

Henry opened the window, and the sound of the waves rode into the room on a ribbon of salt-sprinkled air. Wordlessly, he crawled into the bed beside me and folded his arms across his chest, once again in a pose well remembered. Either from the whiskey or the emotion, I felt drained of all fear. Windows were opening in my soul, windows too long closed too tight. Tiny shafts of light were combing through the cloudiness that had filled my life since the death of my father, perforating the gray in much the same way that rays of sunlight had pierced the leaves of the muscadine vine when I was a child, sitting there all alone in the cool green darkness of the arbor. One way or the other, things would be different after tomorrow. Of that I was finally certain.

FORTY

Just before dawn I tiptoed back to my room to get ready for the day. The moon gave me all the light I needed to dress. I took longer than usual. The magnitude of my nervousness was unsettling; my fingers shook as I brushed my hair. I purposely chose the chocolate-brown sweater that matched my eyes and tied one of my bright red shawls in a loose knot at my throat, wanting—no, needing—to look my best today.

An hour later a soft knock at my door pulled me away from the mirror. I heard Henry whisper, "Lila? You ready?" I crossed the room and opened the door to my brother.

Apparently having dressed with as much care as I had, Henry looked like a page torn from a catalog for sporting gentlemen. He was wearing a pair of gray tweed trousers with the black-and-green Fair Isle vest I'd knitted him a couple of Christmases ago. After our many rambles in the rain, his new Barbour coat bore the appropriately discreet mud stains that set him apart from the tourist, and he had his tweed cap on his head backward, signifying a nonchalance I knew he did not feel.

"You ready?" he asked again.

"Almost. Are we the only ones up, do you know?"

"No. I could smell breakfast as I passed the stairs. But I don't think I want anything to eat."

"Me neither." I couldn't even think of food. "We'll just show Mr. Winskill the photo and see if he recognizes Daddy. I mean . . . well, you know . . . if he knows who the man in the book is." I picked up the book and handed it over to Henry. "Here, take this."

I followed Henry out the door, shutting it softly behind me. As we came down the stairs, I could hear the clink and rattle of cutlery. The main hall was still dark, so we turned toward the voices we heard coming from the kitchen.

The room wore the flavor of the freshly baked bread a sleepy-looking young woman was removing from the oven of the large red Aga stove. All around, eggs were being cracked, porridge stirred, fresh fruit sliced into mounds of primary colors.

Russell Winskill flitted beelike from worker to worker, his words of encouragement and instruction brightening each face as he passed. Catching sight of Henry and me, he spun around in surprise. "Well, you two are up early, aren't you! I hope you both slept all right. The storm didn't keep you awake?"

"No, no. We slept really well." Not wanting to interrupt the choreography of the kitchen, I stayed where I was in the hallway. Mr. Winskill wiped his hands on a tea towel and hurried over. "If you don't mind, we just have a question for you," I said, holding up *Eilean Glas* and opening it to the photograph of Seamus Charles. "By any chance do you know this man?"

In one hurried motion he'd clearly performed many times before, Russell Winskill jerked his chin downward, sending the round glasses perched atop his tiny head flying straight to his nose. He pushed them up to their appropriate place with his index finger and bent toward the book, squinting slightly. "Oh, yes," he said. "Yes, I know him. Well, not personally, but I know *of* him. Very few people know Seamus Charles personally, from what I gather. His work is very well known, of course, but he keeps to himself. Always has, I believe. He lives far up island, near the Mathan. Not an easy place to get to. Pretty weak roads around there, too." A young woman with purple hair came toward him carrying a large glass bowl full of strawberries and green melon, and he took it from her and headed down the hallway at full speed, Henry and me on his heels.

We stood at the doorway to the shadowy dining room as the little man bustled from table to table, straightening silverware and setting out juice glasses, talking all the while. "Gemma, my wife, she's met him. Went to his house several years ago when we bought this place to see about getting some of his original tweed for the sitting room upstairs. She was tickled he sold it to her. His work is pretty exclusive—you don't just see it everywhere. That's it on the sofa up there. We liked it so much we used it in several rooms here. The cushions in your room, Mr. Bruce, those are done in Charles Tweed. Anyway, Gemma said he couldn't have been nicer, despite his reputation for being a bit of a loner. But when she invited him down here for dinner, she could tell by the way he thanked her that he'd never come. He's not unfriendly, mind you. Just keeps to himself. But people respect that around here."

I struggled to stop my voice from trembling. "I'd really love to see his studio if I could. Do you think you could tell us how to get to Ben Mathan?"

"Oh, well now, Ben Mathan's easy to find." He looked up at me with a smile. "Just hit the western coast road going north and stay on it—straight to the top of the island. The road follows the sea most of the way—really spectacular views, so even if you don't find Charles, it won't be a trip wasted—and then it turns out over the moor and ends up winding down a one-track trail into a valley, where it stops. I believe he lives out past there somewhere, not too far from the end of the road. Gemma said there's a path to his place through a little wood. Ben Mathan is off to the left of that dead-end road, I do know that. Lies right out in the sea. Gets the rough edge of the weather as a result. Today's fine . . ." He leaned over a neatly laid table and looked out the window, where a pink-dappled dawn was melting into the blue of a crisp, clear morning. "Yes, it's going to be a fine day, so you shouldn't have to deal with any of that. Wear your boots, though." He looked down at our feet and nodded approval. "You'll need them after last night's storm."

Apparently believing he'd given us all the directions we'd need, he picked up a tray and headed back up the hall to the kitchen. Already we could hear footsteps and voices coming in from the cottages behind the inn. The thought of breakfast with the Coffees seemed impossible. We looked at each other and headed for the front door, leaving *Eilean Glas* lying on the hall table, its red cover shining in the lamplight.

FORTY-ONE

As I opened the door of Clement House and stepped out into the morning light, I couldn't stop thinking that this could actually be the day I'd see my father once again. The joy I felt at this prospect was real, as real as the hurt and anger that continued to pulse in my veins whenever I thought of the years we'd spent without him. I needed answers, and the possibility I could be this close to getting them made my heart race.

The morning felt scrubbed clean by the storm, its cool air so pure it seemed almost medicinal. Henry shut the blue door behind us, and we walked out into the inn's front garden, our eyes blinking in the dazzling light of the sun reflected off the sea across the road. The change was so extreme from our arrival yesterday that we could have been at an entirely different place. There was no crayon in the box to match the color of the water. It was brighter than ordinary turquoise; the wet sand was so silver it glowed.

"Man, I can sure see why someone would want to live here." Henry lifted his hand to shield his eyes, turning around from the sea before us to take in the mountains behind. "It's like another planet. You drive, okay? I just want to look." He strode out of the garden, around to the passenger side of the car, and got in.

As I settled myself into the driver's seat, I could see Henry looking at the bright red shawl tied around my shoulders. "I'll tell you one thing," he said. "If it really is Daddy in that picture, you better send that Sarah Coffee lady as many of those things as she wants."

As we'd been instructed, I followed the road back across the petrous moorland till it met up with the western coast. In the clear light of morning, we could see the road stretched out before us for miles, hugging the blue water like a gray satin ribbon. Fulmars rode the waves like tiny white boats, their feathers tucked tightly beneath them. We rolled down the windows and breathed in the sea air. Any other day this drive would have been a carefree joy. But any other day wouldn't have the potential to change both our lives. I gripped the steering wheel tight enough that my fingers went numb.

"So what, we're just going to wing it?" Henry's arm was out the window, his fingers drumming on the side mirror.

"I haven't rehearsed anything. Have you?"

"No. No, I haven't. But I'm beginning to think we should have. I mean, what do we say? 'Hello, Dad'? Surely not." He pulled his tweed cap down lower to stop it from blowing off in the wind. "I don't like the idea of lying to him."

"We're not going to lie to him, Henry. What do you mean?"

"Well, we can't just knock on his door and say . . . I don't know . . . we can't just say, 'Hi, Dad, how's it going?' Can we? And I don't feel right about saying we're, oh . . . I don't know, Jehovah's Witnesses or anything. And what if, well . . . aren't you afraid he might have a stroke or something if he realizes it's us? He's not a young man, after all."

"Henry, it's been decades. Do you really think he'll recognize us right away? I don't. I think we'll have time to broach the subject gently."

"But what if we don't? Huh? What if he opens the door, takes one look at the two of us, and keels right over. What do we do then? What do we tell *Abby* then? 'Well, you see, we found out Daddy was alive, but then we killed him'?"

"Henry, you're dancing around what you really want to say. Just spit it out."

"Yeah, well. All right. I've been thinking. Maybe both of us shouldn't go to the door." I started to speak. "Now, Lila . . . wait. Hear me out, okay? What if . . . what if I wait in the car. Winskill said it wasn't a long walk to his place from where you have to park. What if I just wait there and let you go. That way . . . that way you could sort of check out the situation and come get me if it's all okay. That way, too, he'd be less likely to recognize us right off the bat. I mean, if we both show up, you know, looking so much alike like we do, then he might be quicker to catch on than if it's just you. Right?"

The landscape was changing. Trees were breaking through the rocky ground, their trunks contorted by the constant wind. I drove in silence for a long moment, feeling Henry's dark eyes boring a hole in the side of my face. Finally I said, "I think that's a very wise move."

"I knew you'd . . . Wait . . . what? You like the idea?"

"I do. I think you're absolutely right. He'll be much less likely to know it's us if I go alone." I omitted the fact that Henry's obvious nervousness would only make it more difficult for everybody, me in particular. "I'll go down and see if he's home . . . see if it's even him. I'll check it out and come back for you if it's all good. You sure that's okay with you, now? You won't change your mind and come squealing after me like you used to when you were little, will you?"

Even with my eyes on the road, I could tell that Henry flushed a little. But I could also hear the relief in his voice when he told me to shut the hell up.

FORTY-TWO

Travel has a way of making the calendar irrelevant. Henry and I had been in Scotland for ten days now, days that had lost both their names and significance without either one of us noticing. As I left my brother sitting in the car and entered the pathway leading into the woods, it could have been any day of the week for all I knew. And the farther I walked, it could have been any year.

Rowan trees lined both sides of the path, their plaited branches so closely clustered together they nearly blocked out the sun, but my eyes adjusted quickly to the light. I felt I had been here before. My footsteps were cushioned to silence in the wet, velvet leaves, and I breathed in the plush perfume of mossy earth like memory itself. Once again I was sheltered, alone in an arbor of green. Where once there were muscadines, now there were rowanberries. Where once I was young, not so anymore. But each sensory impression of the muscadine arbor was fixed to my soul and returned to me now, summoned by the palpable similarities all around me. I could feel apprehension thawing, then melting away.

Not far up ahead, I could see the end of the pathway dissolve into sun, forming a perfect round circle of light. Just then I heard a bark and saw a flash of black and white break through into the green. A dog, a large one by all appearances, was heading straight for me. I froze, trying to stay as calm as I could. But the closer he came, the bigger he looked, and by the time he was on me, that calmness was just a veneer.

He skidded to a stop right in front of me, his sizable paws digging into the dark earth like shovels. Then he began to dance, a leaping, jumping exercise that conveyed nothing less than pure joy. I reached down the short distance to pet him and received a chorus of seal-like barks of excitement for my trouble. Then he spun abruptly and ran back the way he'd come, turning around three times to see if I was following along.

I've always considered dogs to be the best omens—Franklin trusted their opinion far more than those of either family or friends—and as I stepped out into the sun-stippled shadows at the end of the path, I was grateful to have made the acquaintance of this one. He bounced around me, looks of welcome mixed with curiosity written boldly across his furry face. Too tall for a collie, too long for a sheepdog, he was obviously a mélange of canine ingredients staggering in variety and scope, and one who had absolutely no talent as a guard dog. With his tail wagging, he sat down at my feet as I stood there deciding what to do next. I scratched his head and looked around.

Hardy red hydrangea blooms flopped over the top of a pale stone wall that encircled the back of a house at just the right height to prevent a good look at the garden. Standing on tiptoe yielded no better view than the tops of the trees—a collection of sycamore, chestnut, and pine—their emerald arms waving in the wind coming up from the sea. The upper half of the whitewashed house was just visible, and I could see five single windows lined up like dominoes across the top floor.

As I turned and continued on up the rutted drive, the front of the house began revealing itself with every step that I took. It stood, face to the winds, in a small copse of misshapen fir trees, their tangled bodies evidence of the fury of previous storms. A curving stone walkway, lined on either side with oyster shells and yellow gorse, led up to a porch, where a muddy iron boot scraper in the shape of a dachshund stood by a cherry-red door. In what was obviously a later addition to the old house, a small conservatory bubbled out from the ground floor, its windows dark and tightly closed, all signals the owner was out.

The house sat inside a small glen, bordered on the left by a sheep-speckled mountain that just grazed the sky. On the right, out across a moorland of bracken and heather, was the wavering line of Ben Mathan, a line that would eventually fall into the shape of a great bear standing guard in the waves. Though the path that extended before me didn't yet permit a view of the sea, its presence was everywhere: in the salted air, the continuous wind, the ceaseless drone of invisible waves. I continued to let my eyes wander over the property, searching for hints of my father. The surroundings bore no resemblance to Greenwoods, and as I tried to imagine the man I'd known living here—walking along this pathway, playing with this dog, cleaning his muddy boots before pushing open that bright red door—I shivered a little in spite of the warmth falling down from the late-morning sun.

There was a small white building up ahead to the left, tucked into the foot of the gorse-covered mountain like a pearl in honey. Its red double doors looked shut tight, but I headed that way nonetheless. This must be the studio, I thought, eager to peek inside.

The windows were clean enough for me to see my reflection approaching with the big spotted dog at my heels. Confident in the belief that no one was about, I cupped my hands around a center pane of glass and looked inside. A spectrum of brightly colored bolts of tweed lined the walls, and in the center of the room stood a huge loom all threaded and ready to go. In front of the loom, facing a crystal-clear picture window, was a bicycle seat. This, I knew, was how the loom was powered. The thought of coming out here every morning, cup of tea in hand, to sit there and pedal along, all the while looking out at this beautiful view, made me feel envious and homesick at the same time. I twisted the doorknobs in an attempt to gain entrance, but they were, as I expected, locked tight.

In a desire to see the view that window afforded, I walked around the side of the building, where the yellow gorse was up to my knees. The sun turned the glass to a mirror, and I stared at myself for a long minute before detecting movement in the reflection. There in the window, I could see the big dog running away up the path, fast as a comet, toward something or someone I couldn't yet see. I waited, not turning around but staring straight into the mirrored glass as though it were magic until, there, coming down the path from the sea, was a man.

FORTY-THREE

His hair shone white in the Hebridean sun. I could tell by his movements that he'd called out to the dog, but the roar of the wind and the sea smothered his words. Stepping into shadow, I watched as he stopped and petted the big dog before continuing on toward the house. My heart was beating like storm rain.

It wasn't until that moment that I realized how prepared I'd been to be disappointed. Despite the determination I'd felt since that morning I'd spoken to Maureen—boldly vowing to come here and find my father—I hadn't really expected the dream to be realized, I knew that now, and if it were, I'd thought it could never match up to my memory; it could only be smaller and paler than what I'd held in my heart. But as I shrank against the studio wall and watched him, allowing myself the luxury of that one last moment unseen, the man coming toward me looked like a giant. It was my father. Time might have faded my memories, but it could no more disguise this man than it could move in reverse.

I could see it in the way he was walking, in the way he cocked his head just a little to the left as though listening for an answer to an unspoken question. It was there in the way he lifted his arm to shield his eyes from the sun as he watched the dog run toward him. And as he came closer, it was there in the way he suddenly stopped when he saw me frozen by the window with my red pleated shawl alive in the sun.

"Can I help you?"

An echo of the South swam through his voice; it drenched me in memories and robbed me of breath. "I, um . . . I heard about you in town." My own voice sounded threadbare, and my sentence drifted up at the end like a plea. I cleared my throat and continued, aware of his black eyes staring at me in a gaze so familiar I couldn't bear to return it. "I'm a hand weaver. From the States. I'm over here working on some new designs, and . . . and I thought, that is, if you don't mind, I'd love to see where you work. I . . . I know you don't . . . well . . . I was told you don't especially like visitors, but I thought . . ."

"You thought you'd just come out anyway?"

I couldn't tell if it was irritation or amusement I heard in that question. I moved away from the building and out into the light. "You are Seamus Charles. Is that right?"

"Yes." His hesitancy was justified; I knew I sounded idiotic. He looked at me for a long moment, his expression impossible to read, his quizzical stare burning my confidence to ash. I felt small and intrusive. Finally he said, "Yes. I'm Seamus Charles. And since you've come out all this way, I suppose I can show you where I work, if it's that important to you. Though I don't exactly see why it should be. There are lots of folks here on the island who do the exact same thing." He passed in front of me and went to unlock the studio doors. I followed a little ways behind.

The double doors swung open, and the big dog was the first one to enter. "Okay, Rex. You go lie down now. You've been out running enough this morning." After taking a drink from a bowl of water by the door, Rex went under a long cutting table and curled up on a fat, lumpy bed, turning round and round till he

flopped down with a dramatic sigh. Seamus closed the door behind us. "It's the midges. Damn things get in here and you'll never
get them out. They'll be gone completely in a couple of weeks
when the colder weather comes in. I can leave the doors wide
open then, which is the way we like it, isn't it, boy?" Rex banged
his tail against his bed in agreement.

"Well, here she is," he said, gesturing around the room. "There's
the loom, it's an old Hattersley. I finally got a Bonas Griffith a few
years ago. It's there in the back. You can weave double-widths on
that one, so some designers prefer it. But I still love the sound of
the Hattersley best. The fleeces are back there, too. I still keep a
few of my own sheep. Just a dozen or so Cheviots. I send the
fleeces out to be carded and spun. I used to do it all myself, even
the dyeing, but now I've found some folks over on Skye who do it
for me. Of course, the designs are still all my own."

He walked around to the back of the loom nodding at the hun-
dreds of warp threads racing through the heddles. "If you do this
yourself, you'll know the most tedious bit is setting everything up.
I can tie on over two thousand threads, and that's just if I'm using
the same colors as the last bolt. That can take me up to three days.
I used to do it in two, but there you go. Course, if I'm starting
with a brand-new color palette, I have to thread them all fresh, and
that takes even longer. But it's a meditative process. The real treat
is the weaving, which I'm sure you know. Just to sit there pedaling
and looking at that view. I do love it."

I ran my hands lightly over the green and orange threads already on the loom. "Let me see you take a turn," he said, patting
the bicycle seat. I climbed up and began to slowly pedal, guiding
the shuttle carefully as I went along.

"That's it. Yes, I can see you've done this before."

"Do you have anything new you could show me? Anything
you've recently finished?"

"I guess so." He reached up above him to take down a particularly vibrant bolt of green tweed. It was shot through with strands

of bright yellow and blue. "See here, see how this one perfectly matches the view outside that window today? I just finished this design. It's going to a tailor in London who makes it up into fine coats for rich men." He laughed. "But I'm really happy with the way I matched the colors to the view right outside that window in summertime. What do you think, Lila?"

"Oh, yes. It's perfect. It'll be like wearing a little bit of Ben Mathan in summer, all winter long. You couldn't have—" I stopped, noticing with surprise that my hand running along the weave of the tweed was shaking. The sound of my name reverberated through my head like the echo of a bell rung decades ago.

FORTY-FOUR

"When did you know?"

"The minute you stepped into the light. Is Henry with you?"

"Yes. He's . . ." The anger I'd felt for weeks was thawing under the gaze of the father I'd always loved, but the hurt was growing into a lump in my throat that painfully strangled my words. I was scared and embarrassed at once. Tears were not expected and, once they began, could not be controlled. I bent my head down toward the cloth on the table and watched them land one by one like dewdrops on the emerald tweed.

"Here. Here, now. Don't do that. Come on, let's go into the house. I'll make us a cup of tea."

He put his hands on my shoulders and steered me outside, pausing briefly to allow Rex to follow before he shut the doors behind us. We walked across the path to the front garden and up the steps to the door, my head bent so low all I could see were shells and yellow gorse. He held the red door open, and I walked inside.

My eyes were so bleary with tears I didn't notice much as I came into the house, just the lingering aroma of this morning's coffee and the sound of a clock in the hall. He led me into the kitchen and sat me at a long wooden table. Then he took a freshly laundered handkerchief from his coat pocket and handed it to me. "Blow your nose," he said. I obeyed, my eyes still fixed on my lap.

As he turned to fill the teakettle, I looked around me. The kitchen was a large one, with a fire burning low in the grate of a fireplace set in a stone wall at the end of the room. Rex had taken up residence in one of the two dog beds by the fire. Ensconced in the other was a shaggy white sheepdog who was gazing up at me with suspicion, a low rumble coming from the back of her throat.

"Hush, Tillie. It's all right." The dog locked eyes with Seamus for a long moment, then sighed and rested her head on her paws.

He set a cup of tea in front of me. I could smell a whiff of whiskey inside it. "Now, drink some of this. And tell me where your brother is."

I probably should have lied to save Henry the shock of his father suddenly tapping on the car window but had neither the creativity nor the nerve to make up anything believable. "He's down at the end of the path. In the car." I felt bad for selling my brother out so quickly and completely. I just hoped Henry would understand.

"Is Abigail here, too?"

"No. She's back home. She's staying with Uncle Audie. I—I mean, we—we're here because . . . well, Mama died."

"I see." He walked to the window, his hands in his pockets. For a long minute, neither of us said a word. Rex swiveled his big head from one of us to the other, finally letting out a questioning whine. Seamus turned to me and said, "So Henry's in the car? Well, he can't stay there all day. You sit here, I'm going to get him. You both need to hear this story, and I'm not sure I can tell it but once. Drink your tea. We'll be back in a few minutes."

He patted his thigh, and Rex jumped up immediately. Together the two of them went out of the room, leaving me under the vigilant eye of the sheepdog, Tillie. I heard the front door close and went to stand by the window to watch them leave.

Whenever we talked about time travel when we were little— and it was one of our favorite games—Henry always wanted to go straight to the Renaissance. He said he'd purchase art by the bush-elfuls, have long conversations with da Vinci and wear hats with feathers on them. For me it was always Tudor England, where I'd wear luscious clothes, sleep in tapestry-draped beds, wander through rose gardens, and with my beneficial knowledge of the future, steer clear of King Henry VIII. But if time travel were real, I was no longer certain I'd wish to participate in any journey it might have to offer. Sitting here alone in my father's house as the rhythmic metronome of the hall clock punctured the silence, I couldn't seem to shake the feeling that I'd gone back to the years of my childhood. It was a bewildering thought.

Seamus and Rex were down the lane and out of sight by the time I stopped crying. While Tillie the sheepdog watched me closely for any sign of unacceptable behavior, I waited, wrestling with several conflicting emotions at once, guilt being the primary one.

How could I have so cavalierly waltzed back into my father's life with no warning? Shouldn't I have at least given him the option of not seeing me if he didn't want to? And then there was Henry. I imagined him waiting at the end of the road, worriedly drumming his fingers on the side of the car, half hoping we'd find Daddy, half hoping we wouldn't, not realizing he was about to be face-to-face with the man himself. No warning. No time to pre-pare. How could I have let that happen? And of course I couldn't forget my sister, so blissfully unaware of any of this.

Then, as usually happens, anger was added to guilt, stirring up a toxic formula that caused me to stand to my feet and pace up and down the flagstoned floor. Why on earth should *I* be the one to feel guilty? None of this was my fault. How could my mother have done this to us? How could he have let her? How could he have just started a new life without ever letting us know? What kind of people were they to tell such a monstrous lie?

The bottle of whiskey sat on the counter. I poured some liberally into what was left of my tea and drank it down like cool water. Tillie continued to stare at me from her comfortable place by the fire, and I felt inexplicably self-conscious. "It's okay. I'm not going to get drunk and smash up the place." Her tail gave an equivocal wag, her eyes kind but skeptical.

A door led off the kitchen into a semicircular glass sunroom where two large armchairs sat facing the concave side of the crenellated window I'd seen from outside. I collapsed into one of these to watch for their return, more nervous than I could remember being in the whole of my life.

The wind whistled round the curve of this room with an eerie voice that was almost human. From my chair I could see the entrance to the green-tunneled pathway leading back to the car, the bright orange berries of the rowan trees still shining in the sun. I kept my eyes trained to that spot, and I waited.

Tillie heard them first. The sheepdog came into the room and stood in front of the window—ears cocked, tail wagging. My entire body went cold, and the ticking of the clock seemed to intensify until I felt it had entered my head. My eyes stayed riveted on the window. Then, stepping out into the light, there they were, walking silently side by side and resembling each other so completely they looked like two ages of the same man. Henry's eyes were red. He'd been crying.

I jumped up and went into the kitchen, sitting down, then getting right back up again, unsure what to do or where to stand. Their shadows crossed the window, and I heard the front door open, then close.

FORTY-FIVE

Henry came into the room first. His face wore an expression I'd
not seen before, and when his eyes met mine, they were shining
with tears. He sat down heavily in the same chair I'd just vacated
and placed his hands on the table in what looked like an effort to
steady himself. He looked deflated somehow, as if over the course
of thirty short minutes his clothes had gotten too big. Instinctively
I went to sit beside him, pulling my own chair up close to his as
together we watched our father refill the teakettle and set it back
on the stove. I was surprised when Henry spoke first.

"Why 'Seamus Charles'? Why did you change your name?"

Seamus turned around to look at him and unexpectedly let out
a laugh. "That's your first question? Well, let's see. I guess I figured
since I was dead, I needed a new name, didn't I? Pennington was
out of the question. Too far from the ordinary here, too apt to
cause undue attention. So since my first name is James, and as you
may or may not know, one of the Gaelic equivalents for James is
Seamus, I just took that. It wasn't too much of a stretch. As for

Charles . . . well, I think you can figure that one out for yourself, can't you? I suppose it was a small attempt to reclaim a life that was lost."

"But you weren't dead, were you?" Henry's voice sounded accusatory and sharp, both qualities rare in my brother. I shifted uncomfortably in my chair.

"What Henry *means*—" I began.

"I know what he means," Seamus interrupted, looking directly at his son. "Well, Henry, I was and I wasn't." His dark eyes traveled from one of us to the other. "I guess you should tell me how much you already know of this story." The steadiness of his gaze told me that whether it had died in holy battle or just been left by the roadside, the shame he once felt held no power over him anymore.

"We know about you and Charlie." Henry's voice was strong, but his words tumbled out in a rush. "We know you two were in love. And had been for years. We found a photograph of you, taken right here. And Audie had kept a letter. We could still see the postmark, so we thought we'd try to find you. We know Mama lied to us, lied to everybody. And we know that when you found out about it, you never got in contact with anyone to say it wasn't true. Oh, yeah, and we also know you're not Abigail's father. I almost forgot that tidbit." He sat up a little straighter after this speech, his eyes meeting Seamus's like a challenge.

Seamus sighed and walked to the window. He stared out past the bracken-covered moorland, and his eyes were bright. "I see. Well. So it's over." He turned around, and I held his gaze for the first time in more than forty years. Age had written its signature across his face, lines running like tributaries from his tear-filled eyes. "So she finally told you. About everything."

"No," I said, dropping my eyes to my lap. "No, she never said a word. Not one word. But she kept your letters. She . . . uh, she buried them. Out in the muscadine arbor. She was sick, and . . . well, she went out there in the middle of the night last month, and we think she was trying to dig them up. Anyway, she died before she could do it, but we found them. And that's . . . uh, that's how we learned the whole story."

"Are you saying she died in the arbor?"

"Yes," said Henry.

"And what do you mean, you 'found them'? You mean the two of you dug them up?"

"Yes," said Henry.

"Good Lord."

"Yeah. Good Lord." I blew my nose again.

He walked to the stove and poured out three cups of tea, placed them on a tray, and brought them to the table. He set a cup in front of each of us, then stood with his back to the window. Rex, perhaps sensing emotion, rose and came to his side.

"You know, Henry, there was a day, years ago, when you could have told me all you just said and I would have probably died from sheer humiliation. But I've lived so far past that now I can barely remember the feeling. I know there are those who would say how horrible that is, but all I can say is thank God. But you're right, of course. Right about it all. Those are the facts of the situation, and I never in a million years would hope for your forgiveness. You've lived so long without me we're practically strangers, and forgiveness for what I did would be impossible even from a friend.

"That picture you found? The one of me and Charlie? Well, it was taken right out there on the hill. It was the happiest time of my life. Of our lives. There wasn't a hint of anything improper about our trip together. No one thought anything at all of two best friends going on an adventure together the summer after high school. We were both heading off to college in the fall—me to Wheaton and Charlie to Duke—so everybody felt that we both needed the break. They were happy to see us off.

"Of course, Charlie and I . . . well, we'd known how we felt about each other since childhood. Oh, we didn't know what it *was* for years. We just knew we were never as happy, never as much ourselves, as we were in the company of each other. No girl made us feel the same way, no matter how hard we tried. And Lord knows we tried. Both of us, if you'll pardon my frankness, were blessed with the sort of looks girls seemed to admire. Prom dates, homecoming dances—we were never at a loss for a partner. But we were both miserable during each and every attempt to be like the other guys in our class.

"We never did anything about it, you understand. It was an unspeakable thing, even to us. It wasn't until we were here, on Eynhallow, right here on this very slice of coastline, that we admitted how we felt about each other. It felt like being let out of a metal cage. That month we were here was . . . well, like I said, the happiest time of my whole life.

"But there was always that word that rang in my ears. 'Abomination.' That's what the church called it. From the time I was little, I had a love for God that seemed to have been born in me. I saw myself as his child before ever being told I was. And I wanted more than anything to help other people know that same love. It was my dream to pastor the church I'd grown up in. But how could I do that and be what I was?

"Charlie tried to get me to change my mind. He said I was smart enough to come to Duke with him. I remember him reciting a list of possible careers, trying to tempt me in the direction of one I could live with. But I had convinced myself I had a calling. I remember him asking me how that could be when God himself thought I was, well . . . you know . . . an aberration. We had a big row, and in the end we went our separate ways. I was as determined as I'd ever been about anything to erase these feelings from my life.

"So we both tried to do just that. I completed graduate school just two months before old Preacher Carlton up and died and Second Baptist called me to be their pastor. I couldn't believe my luck. It was like God was rewarding me for all the hard work I'd done in separating myself from who I'd thought I'd been.

"Of course, then everybody started telling me I needed a wife. I still wasn't seeing anybody, but Audie kept trying to introduce me to this girl he'd met in his office. I'll tell you, there's this feeling you have when you're someone like me, it feels like you're being watched all the time. Like every time you're around people, they'll see it. In the way you walk. In the way you hold a coffee cup, the way you ask a question. Even in the way you laugh. In every single thing about you. It gets to where you're convinced people can hear your thoughts. I was so afraid that what I was was written all over me. To hide it became the most important thing in my life. I knew that had to change. And the best way I could figure out to change it was to get a girlfriend. So that's what I did.

"Geneva and I slept together on our second date. I knew it was a sin, but not as bad as the one I'd been living with all my life. Plus, I wanted to prove to myself I could be like everybody else. Of course she got pregnant that very night. But rather than being upset, I figured all my problems were solved. I was finally in the right lane, moving along with everyone else. Everything around me looked like proof that God finally approved.

"The wedding was a big one. All white flowers and a dozen bridesmaids. Audie was my best man. I'll never forgive myself for not telling Charlie face-to-face. But I didn't dare trust myself to do it. One of the many cowardly acts of which I am guilty. He just got the invitation like everybody else. And it wasn't six months till he'd married Catherine and we both set about trying to forget our past, I guess. Naturally, we didn't count on you and Melanie becoming best friends, Lila. We ended up being thrown together more than we would have liked. More than was comfortable. But we never talked about it. If anyone was around us, they never would have guessed.

"So a couple of years went by, and we had you, Henry. I was so proud to have a son of my own. God was rewarding me for my obedience with a beautiful family and a church who loved and supported me. I did my best to preach God's love above everything else. Like so many men before me, I tried to convince myself everything was just as it should be. Now, to do that you have to shut off certain rooms in your head, and if you're lucky, you never find out that those rooms are where your heart really lives. If you're lucky, you get so used to playing the part that your brain just forgets who you are. But I wasn't lucky.

"By the time you were about five, Henry, I was beginning to lose my grip on things. I couldn't hold a thought long enough to write a sentence. I was losing my temper over insignificant things. Your mother suggested I get away for a while, so I asked the church for a sabbatical. And of course that's when everything changed.

"You see, Charlie and I didn't just come here to Eynhallow when we were kids. We came here again not long before he died. I wrote and told him about me going away. I shouldn't have done it, I know, but it was killing me to think he was under the impression that all this was easy for me, that I'd forgotten him, forgotten us, completely. So he told Catherine he had to go to a conference in Edinburgh. We didn't travel together. I didn't even know he was coming. Though, if I'm honest, that's probably the reason I wrote, in the hopes that he might.

"He showed up the first week I was here. We pitched a tent out on this very beach and stayed here for two weeks together. We forgot everything and everybody. We just put all of Wesleyan out of our minds. Pretended it was just us. The only two people on earth. We talked about getting a little cottage—in fact, we saw this one, this very one. But it wasn't for sale. I swear, if it had been, I think we might have bought it on the spot. We'd been that determined we were going to break free and be together. Seems you're always braver the farther you are from home.

"When the time was over, we promised each other we'd own up, tell our wives and everybody that knew us, what we were and how we felt about each other. We'd take the heat, and if we had to, we'd leave town and start our lives somewhere else." His laugh sounded more like a sneer. "We had no idea how impossible that would be, how deluded we were. Or maybe we did and we just didn't want to admit it to each other.

"Anyway, that was our plan. But before we could set anything in motion after we got home, Geneva told me she was pregnant. I knew the baby wasn't mine, of course, and she knew I knew. I had a good idea who the father was. Loren Graham was the interim preacher who came in for the month I was gone. Real handsome fellow, blond, young. If I had any doubt, the moment I saw Abigail, I knew for certain. But by that time Loren had run back off to Tennessee, supposedly racked with the sort of fraudulent guilt that would allow him to commit the same sins over and over. Last I heard, he had at least three other kids spread across the South before they finally threw him out of the church.

"Geneva just pretended to everybody the baby was ours, sort of daring me to say it wasn't, and we never talked about it. I didn't feel like I could say anything. Lord knows I'd been unfaithful to her. Marrying someone you don't love is probably the ultimate betrayal. I know Geneva would agree. She knew I had my secrets, even if she could never have guessed what they were. I think the baby was her way of paying me back for not being the sort of husband she'd bargained for. I couldn't tell her the truth, so I just went along with the lie, even though I knew it sealed my fate forever. How could I stand up in the pulpit and tell folks what I was, then leave your pregnant mother? How could I tell them she was having another man's child? I couldn't do it. I couldn't do it to her, or to you two. I couldn't do it to that baby. And I couldn't do it to . . . well, to everybody who'd looked to me to set an example.

"So I went to Charlie and tried to explain it all to him. But he couldn't accept it. He was getting ready to take Catherine away for a few days to tell her everything. You see, he always had more courage than me."

He began to walk up and down the kitchen. "It'll always haunt me, the way we left it. Watching it slowly dawn on him that we'd never be together. That we'd have to go on pretending to be people we weren't, that we'd have to stand by as men like us were called evil and Lord knows what else. And never say a word. That we'd never be free of it. I stood there and saw it happen—the joy go out of his eyes. I might as well have put that noose around his neck with my own hands."

Henry started to speak, but Seamus held up his hand and shook his head. "We were all out to breakfast the morning it happened. I don't guess you remember, but that's where we were. I'd taken you all out for pancakes. One of the church members walked in, saw me, and came hurrying over. Said I'd better get out to the Barnetts' quick. That something terrible had happened. I didn't really have to ask what. I knew in my bones it was Charlie.

"To be honest, I don't actually remember much of the next few days. I don't know how I got through it. But after it was over, I knew I couldn't live like I'd been living anymore. I couldn't keep a clear thought in my head. I knew I had to do something drastic or I was going to walk down that same dirt road to Bobbin Lake, just like Charlie had done. I was going to die.

"So I joined up with the army to be a chaplain over in the war. I thought I'd try to make another deal with God. 'I'll do this for two years if you'll change what I am.' If nothing else, I figured I might not make it home alive. I'd heard how awful it was over there. But if I died there, it would be a way to end it all honorably, so you and your mother could still be proud of me. Nobody would ever know. But of course my tour ended and I hadn't had as much as a scratch. And I was still like I was. God hadn't kept up his end of the deal. That was when I could feel my faith slipping away from me like sand through a closed fist, and that nearly broke me in two.

"I tried to reenlist without telling Geneva, but the war was winding down then. The thought of going back to Wesleyan scared me so bad I could hardly breathe, so I wrote to Geneva and told her everything. All about me and Charlie. You see, once again I took the coward's way out. I told her I didn't think I could come home. I don't know what I was expecting. Not really.

"When your mother wrote and told me what she'd done, God help me, I was relieved. And I've never forgiven myself for feeling that. She took the decision away from me, you see. She told everybody I was dead and there was no way I could return after that. By the time I got her letter, she'd already had the funeral. To everybody who knew me, I was dead. Dead as I felt inside. As dead as Charlie. And somehow that felt right to me.

"This was the only place I could think of to go, and I took several months getting here. I hiked around Yorkshire, worked on some fishing boats on Mull for a while. But I knew I was heading back to Eynhallow, and once there, I knew I'd never leave. When I finally did get here, I spent a couple weeks just hiking around, sleeping in a tent, and weeping. God, I was a mess. Then one morning I hiked down this tract and saw this very same house that Charlie and I had said we'd buy if we could. And there was a For Sale sign hanging on the wall. Your mother had wired me my share of our money, something I'll always be grateful for. Lord knows she didn't have to do it, and I didn't ask her to. Well, I didn't even think about it, just went down the road to the phone box and rang up the number. Told them I'd pay well over the asking price, and they took my offer that very afternoon. I had the key in my hand the next day.

"The first few months were dark ones for me, literally and figuratively. It was one of the worst winters ever recorded on the island. Gale after gale came up off the sea. The windows rattled for three solid months. I thought I might lose what little sanity I had left. And then one morning, early, I heard a scratching noise at the back door and looked out to see this little collie. She was soaked to the skin, real skinny, just a pup. I wrapped her up and put her by the fire. Gave her some food and started to take care of her. She got stronger really fast and turned into a real pretty little dog. After a while I was talking to her night and day. She went with me every-where, slept next to me in the bed. She pulled me out of myself. I think I would have gone right over the edge if it hadn't been for her. I'll never be without a dog again. Of course she's long gone now, but she was the first in a succession of good dogs that have, in a way, been my family. Since I gave up the family I had.

"I taught myself to weave the second year I was on the island, more out of need for something to do than anything else. That old Hattersley loom was out in the shed, rusty and in terrible shape. I cleaned it up and got some wool in from some of the mills on the mainland. Soon I was dyeing my own. There was something sooth-ing about the work. It was like painting in a way, but with cloth. People tell me now in town that I'm famous. Or at least my work is. But it all kind of happened by accident, so I don't credit it much." He looked over at me. "The fact that you ended up finding the same practice meaningful seems like a link in the chain that bound us together in spite of ourselves. I believe in those kinds of con-nections now." He smiled down at me, the same smile I'd loved for the whole of my life.

He had stopped pacing now and stood at the window staring out past the trees toward the sea. When he spoke, he sounded as though he were thinking out loud. "I wasn't taught to question when I was young. None of us were. We were told what to think, not how to think. I was led to believe I'd been born wrong. Noth-ing I could do about that, except pretend to be other than I was. That was the only way I could be accepted by society, the people I loved, or by God himself. It took me years to let go of that. Took me years to realize that if God made me, then God loved me just like I was. I was not, had never been, an aberration. I still regret leaving you, leaving everything I'd ever known. But it was all I could do at the time. I wouldn't be here if I hadn't."

He sat down wearily, as though he'd just taken off something heavy. "You know, we didn't call it 'gay' when I was young. If it was called anything, it was something clinical or rude. In the church, like I said, it was always an 'abomination.' There was never an attempt to call it anything else. The word 'gay' had always meant happy when I was growing up, so when it became associated with men like me, I always assumed it was intended to be ironic. But apparently it's the accepted term for what I am."

"What *we* are." Henry spoke softly, his voice thick with emotion. He met Seamus's eye with a smile.

"I . . . what?" Seamus looked worriedly over at Henry.

"Don't worry," said Henry, with only a fraction of sarcasm. "It's not inherited. I just think there's a lot more of us out there than people ever were willing to admit, or even notice. I've known since I was little. There was never any question. I'm sorry you weren't lucky enough to have this one for your sister." He lifted his teacup toward me. "She understood who I was and wouldn't let anyone give me any trouble about it. Ever."

"But I can't stand thinking people made you feel bad about yourself. Like they did me. I mean, did you stay at the church after I, well . . . after I left?"

"Oh, yeah, we stayed," said Henry. "Mama was the bereaved widow for the rest of her days. And we were the erstwhile preacher's kids. But people expect preacher's kids to be odd anyway, so we probably got a pass. I mean, I know there were whispers, especially when I'd stay home to watch *Masterpiece Theatre* instead of going to the football games. I just never really cared too much. Things had changed some by that time, and besides, I always knew Wesleyan was just my launching pad. I knew I would leave as soon as I could. Which was, of course, what I did. What Lila and I both did." He looked at me with a wry grin.

Seamus sighed, looking between the two of us. "I hope you don't hold it against your mother for what she did. She was always a proud woman. Too proud for her own good, some would say. But try to put yourself in her shoes. I can't imagine too much that would be as humiliating to a woman as what I did to her. And through no fault of yours, I'm sure she saw my face every time she looked at you." He shook his head. "I never should have married her. But then I never would have had you two." He looked at us and smiled. "And believe it or not, I consider you the biggest accomplishments of my life. My only accomplishment, really."

"I think you might be selling yourself a bit short," said Henry, his anger now mitigated by all he'd just heard. "Yes, we needed you growing up. You leaving that way, us believing we no longer had a father . . . well, it changed us in ways we can never even know. But let's face it, you saved your own life. Sometimes that's the hardest thing anybody can ever do. Sometimes that's the only thing."

HE MADE US toasted cheese sandwiches for lunch, just as he used to do when we were little. We talked together over the next few hours while the view from the kitchen window was continuously remade, the light outside withering and blooming like time-lapse photography. Once the sky darkened to a bruise as a storm blew up behind the mountain and peppered the house with rain, only to be chased away in ten minutes by bright sunlight and winds so strong they seemed visible. The sun was setting by the time we walked down to the sea.

The sight of Ben Mathan stretching his colossal head out into the water was even more stunning than I'd imagined. Waves rose up like skyscrapers before him, crashing across him with a deafening roar, but still he lay there, impassive and strong, almost as if he were sleeping.

"You know, as the legend goes"—Seamus spoke loudly in the face of the wind—"the ancient people of Eynhallow were shapeshifters, merfolk who had magical powers of transfiguration. They wanted protection for this part of the island from the monsters of the sea, so on the night of the summer solstice the oldest member of the tribe transformed himself into a great brown bear. When the sun rose, the bear stood up on his hind legs, looked around, and apparently liked what he saw, so he stretched out into the sea and made himself comfortable. He's been here ever since, guarding the island. He must do a pretty good job. I've never seen a monster on this shore."

The wind nudged us along back the way we'd come, clearing a path for the night that was already creeping up over the mountains. I slipped my hand into Henry's, and he squeezed it tightly. Seamus looked down at us and said, "You know I can never go back."

Henry smiled. "Yes, we know. But would you mind the occasional houseguest?"

Daddy laughed as he threw his arms around us both. "Son, I would absolutely love it," he said.

EPILOGUE

2015

The first time Daddy died, I wore my favorite blue dress to his funeral and threw it in the garbage can as soon as I got home. Then I took my little brother by the hand and led him out to the muscadine arbor, away from all the sad-faced adults swarming over our house. The two of us sat there until dark, watching ladybugs and trying to make sense of what our life was supposed to be now. We had been preacher's kids, always told that God had a plan. But when Henry asked me why Daddy had died, I couldn't think of anything to say.

Doubt entered my life on that long afternoon when I was certain my mother had died. It took root after the death of my father, buried deep in the inarticulate questions that hid in the corners of my childhood, questions that lived inside the secrets and lies that kept me from knowing my mother, that kept me from feeling at home in my soul. Doubt's dark flowers bloomed through the years I protected my brother from the beliefs that would label him wicked. But doubt welcomes questions, and questions are often the doorway to truth.

Truth can be elusive. Rarely is it easy to find. I've had to look for it, sometimes dig for it. There've been days when I've headed down a well-marked road—so sure and so certain—to find that it leads straight to nowhere. It's only when I've turned right around and gone back to square one that I've spied a rarely trodden pathway hidden inside a thicket of trees and known that's the way I must go. Truth, like beauty, reveals itself as you notice it; the more you see, the more you see.

Abigail took the alteration of her history with an equanimity neither Henry nor I saw coming, evidence of the stabilizing power of love. On our return from Eynhallow, we drove down the sand-sprinkled road to Uncle Audie's house with no small amount of reluctance, certain we'd face a scene unsurpassed in the annals of Abby's dramatic career, but were stunned to witness a remarkable change in our sister. Not only had she lost at least fifteen pounds and regained her famous blond hair, but her personality had cooled and straightened like a twisted silk ribbon ironed out smooth for the very first time.

When we told her about Loren Graham, her response was un-expected but still typically her. "Huh. So that's where I got my blond hair. Well, that makes sense to me now. I tell you what, I've never really known Daddy, I was so little when he died . . . well, you know, when he left, I guess. . . . I don't remember much. But he's always been my daddy, and if he's okay with that, then so am I. Besides, I've never seen what the big deal is about people being gay in the first place. I'd like to be able to tell him that to his face." She looked pointedly at Henry when she said this.

We sold Greenwoods not long after the renovations were com-pleted. Henry and I didn't want it, and it seemed that leaving Wesleyan had finally freed Abigail from the expectations and dis-appointments of her past—like so many of us, she is a different person away from her hometown. She and Jackson built a house next to Uncle Audie on the marsh, and they married there last

Christmas in Dot's little Episcopal church. They're expecting a child in the fall.

In what was a considerably generous gesture, especially as no one had told her it was fake, Abby insisted I have the portrait of Charlotte when we cleaned out Mama's house. "It means the most to you, so I want you to have it. Don't say no, now. I've talked to Henry, and it's not his taste—he'd just put it in the gallery and sell it, and I know that's something you'll never do, even though it's worth a ding-dang fortune. I know how you love it, and besides, I think it should stay in the family, don't you? Mama would like that, too, I bet. Lord knows, and thank God, I don't need the money anymore, so it just seems right for you to have it." Charlotte now hangs on my dining-room wall in Maine, a reminder of the chasm that yawns between value and meaning.

We arranged for the new owners to sell us the back part of the garden, the little half acre that is home to the muscadine arbor, and on an unusually warm Thanksgiving Day before they moved in, we all came back to do as Mama wished, trooping out through the meadow and across the creek to scatter her ashes beneath the tangled vine.

While Jackson said a prayer, I saw a muscadine still hanging there among the leaves, fat and warm in the sunshine, and I impulsively reached for it. As my teeth pierced the purple skin, my mouth was flooded with the flavor of summer. I closed my eyes to hold the memory. It was the sweetest thing I'd ever tasted.

We reburied the empty snowman tin along with Mama. I doubt anyone will enter the arbor again. Abigail had a stone engraved and placed it at the entrance, a testament both to our mother and to the past we take with us, along with new understanding and the seeds of forgiveness.

To ever have believed I would stand beside my father as my brother got married to the love of his life would have stretched my imagination till it snapped right in two. But three months ago, on a blue clear morning in May, we all stood together beneath the trees in Daddy's back garden on the Isle of Eynhallow as Henry and Andrew pledged to love and to cherish till death them do part. Abigail and Jackson were there with us, having brought Uncle Audie to see his brother once again.

As for me, I divide my time now between Maine and Eynhallow, though Scotland is where you'll find me most of the time. It's funny, I'd always thought my detachment from home was a permanent thing, something that lived in my soul and could never be rectified by a plane ticket or a change of address, but it seems I've been given a second chance. The kinship I felt to Scotland in those first days I was here has only continued to deepen, and now it feels like the home I never thought I would know. Of course, Daddy tells me that's because it's where my ancestors came from, but more likely it's due to the fact that he's here. Maybe home is more something you carry inside you than the ground on which you stand. All I know is that whenever I look out the ferry windows and see the mountains rising up over the tiny harbor of Eynhallow, I feel like I'm coming back home.

Franklin would be amused to know I'm in one of the pews of a tiny Catholic church most Sundays when I'm on Eynhallow. Our Lady of the Waves is hardly the grand cathedral of my imagination, and it bears no resemblance to St. Patrick's in Wesleyan. It sits at the foot of Kisimul Hill, an unblinking eye of granite that perpetually stares out to sea. A church has sheltered on this spot since the sixth century, and carved into its ancient stone walls are selkies, singing saints and mermaids, the myths and legends that once wore the transient crown of truth only to lose it in the inevitable passage of time. There have been many mornings when, sitting here, I've been struck by the hubris of man, the sheer feebleness of his notion that truth is something to be wrapped up and tied with a bow, that mystery could ever be parsed and explained till it evaporated into something as measly as words.

There are needlepointed kneelers, one for each worshipper, in each of the pews at Our Lady of the Waves. Each is obviously hand-stitched, and in their colorful representations of village life each is highly personal. There are family dogs and barnyard chickens. Shells and ships, moons and stars, flowers and trees, and in my favorite seat in the back, a snowy white owl. These little offerings of beauty—so individual, so exquisitely wrought—are a tangible testimony to the continuation of the ultimate search: another soul reaching out to that hand in the darkness in the unending hope that it will be there. I feel part of that searching community now, finally knowing that certainty, not doubt, is truly the opposite of faith.

Henry always told me I would never be happy till I managed to separate God from religion, and I'd always thought he was wrong. But one rainy morning as I sat in my favorite pew, a thought wove its way through my head like the half-forgotten words of an old song, a lyrical tune that carried with it briefly bright flashes of clarity like a searchlight on dark water. In those slices of light, for a moment I knew that God was infinitely bigger than I had ever imagined, infinitely more mysterious, and infinitely more kind. He was not to be held inside culture or tradition, nor could he ever be fully understood by a finite mind. As easily as it appeared, the thought evanesced like the granular colors of a rainbow, and try as I might, I couldn't call it back at will. But it gifted me with a comfort that has never really left, and from that morning on, God is no longer relegated to the halls of a Baptist church. I'd kept him there far too long. Maybe the wisest thing any of us can do is listen to our own soul's voice while we can still hear it. I've come to see that Henry was right: living your own life with joy is indeed a form of forgiveness.

Two years ago Melanie's mother passed away in her sleep without ever knowing the truth about her husband, and last September I took my old friend to visit my father on the island her own father loved. I left them alone, sitting side by side on the stone wall that looks out over the landscape where both men once wandered free and in love, and I walked down the path to the sea. As I watched them, I once again heard the words of Uncle Audie's sweet friend Dot. "So much hurt in the world, and for so many years. All over who people love."

I walked down to the shore at the foot of Ben Mathan and stood with my face to the sea. With the wind in my hair, I looked across to the big bear stretching itself out into the raucous waves, keeping away all the monsters, and a happiness rose up inside me, a happiness that finally felt like home.

ACKNOWLEDGMENTS

I am in debt to many people for their support and encouragement during the writing of this book:

To my early readers, Allison Adams, Stan Anderson, and Vickie Mabry—you'll never know how much your comments and confidence meant to me.

To my brilliant agent, Kimberly Whalen. You are the agent I always longed for. I'm so happy to have you in my corner. Every writer should be so lucky.

To my kind and insightful editor, Shauna Summers. One simple, perceptive question from you would spark a thousand ideas. Your support of this book was everything. I'll always be grateful.

To my fellow writers, Patti Callahan Henry, Terry Kay, and Daren Wang. Your advice and generosity meant the world to me. Thank you so much.

To all the helpful, talented people at Ballantine who took this book into their hearts, I'm so appreciative. Thank you especially to Lexi Batsides, Maureen Sugden, Kara Welsh, Kim Hovey, Cindy Berman, Ella Latham, and Jennifer Hershey.

Thank you also to the faithful followers of my blog, *From the*

House of Edward. For years, you have been the most interesting, compassionate, and intelligent readers imaginable. I'm happy to call you my friends.

On Scotland's Isle of Skye: I'm very grateful to Roger Holden at Skye Weavers for allowing me to "drive the loom" one drizzly afternoon. To Clare Winskill and Iain Roden at Coruisk House in Elgol for always providing me with such an inspiring place to stay whenever I'm there. To Eva Lambert for igniting my love of knitting all those years ago. And especially to my good friends Eoghain MacKinnon and Frances MacIver for all the good times and wonderful stories.

On the Isle of Harris, thank you to the Harris Tweed Museum and Exhibition at Drinishader, and to the endlessly charming Scarista House, where, one hellaciously stormy day, I really did have the best Victoria sponge cake the world has ever known.

To Jennifer Isbell, for taking such good care of everything at home whenever I'm off gathering ideas. You are a very good friend.

Also, I'm so grateful to Sandee O for being the sister I never had. Old friends are truly the best friends. Thank you for being a constant light in my life.

And, now and forever, to Pat. You always believe I can do it, and you always make me laugh while I'm trying. I love you more than life.

Finally, Albert Einstein said, "The only thing you absolutely have to know is the location of the library." My mother made certain I knew that location early. My memories of our weekly visits to the downtown Atlanta library are luminous. Libraries represent the best, most democratic, part of our society. May they always thrive under the support of a grateful government. I am incredibly fortunate to live within walking distance of the Smyrna Library and wrote a good deal of this book in one of the many nooks and crannies found there. I thank everyone at that wonderful place for never saying, "Oh Lord, here she comes again!"

ABOUT THE AUTHOR

A lifelong southerner, Pamela Terry learned the power of storytelling at a very early age. For the past decade, Terry has been the author of the internationally popular blog *From the House of Edward*, which was named one of the top ten home blogs of the year by the *Telegraph*. She lives in Smyrna, Georgia, with her songwriter husband, Pat, and their three dogs, Apple, Andrew, and George. She travels to the Scottish Highlands as frequently as possible and is currently at work on her second novel.

ABOUT THE TYPE

This book was set in Bembo, a typeface based on an old-style Roman face that was used for Cardinal Pietro Bembo's tract *De Aetna* in 1495. Bembo was cut by Francesco Griffo (1450–1518) in the early sixteenth century for Italian Renaissance printer and publisher Aldus Manutius (1449–1515). The Lanston Monotype Company of Philadelphia brought the well-proportioned letterforms of Bembo to the United States in the 1930s.